RED SPECTRES

RED SPECTRES

Russian Gothic Tales from the Twentieth Century

*Selected, translated from the Russian,
and with an Introduction by*

MUIREANN MAGUIRE

THE OVERLOOK PRESS / ARDIS

NEW YORK, NY

This edition first published in hardcover in the United States in 2013 by
The Overlook Press/Ardis Publishers, Peter Mayer Publishers, Inc.

141 Wooster Street
New York, NY 10012
www.overlookpress.com

For bulk and special sales, please contact sales@overlookny.com,
or write us at the above address.

Translation and introduction copyright © 2012 Muireann Maguire
"The Phantom" by Sigizmund Krzhizhanovsky, copyright © Éditions Verdier, 1991

The epigraph from Alexander Pushkin on page 35 is quoted
by permission of Carla and Dan Mitchell, from Stanley Mitchell's translation of
Eugene Onegin (Penguin Classics, 2008), I.38.ii

Cataloging-in-Publication Data is available from the Library of Congress

Manufactured in the United States of America
1 3 5 7 9 10 8 6 4 2
ISBN: 978-1-4683-0348-3

To Colin, whose idea started me off,
and to Aleksandr Vasil'yevich, for loving Russian Gothic
enough to reinvent it

Contents

*Dates are of composition, which are also those of first publication except in the cases of Chayanov's 'The Venetian Mirror' and Krzhizhanovsky's 'The Phantom', first published in 1923 and 1991 respectively.

Acknowledgements

I am very grateful to the readers who unselfishly gave up their time to read early drafts of my translations. I thank Julie Curtis, Justin Doherty, Lisa Hayden Espenschade, Colin Higgins, Siobhan McNamara, Vanessa Rampton, Joanne Turnbull, and Valery Viugin for their *tshchatel'nost'* and stamina, and Robert Chandler for early encouragement. I would also like to thank Sophie Deisha, granddaughter of Yelena Deisha, for her kind permission to include my translations of 'Gonets' and 'Kurnosaya' in this book, and for checking the biographical details I give on the author. Special thanks are due to my editor Antony Wood for his invaluable contribution at every stage, to Alex Perkins for his enthusiasm, Alexander Darby for advice on poker terminology, and Peter Thonemann for help with Ovid. My fourth-year translation class at Oxford in Trinity 2011 offered inspired suggestions for Bulgakov's turns of phrase. I am also grateful to all the staff of Jesus College Library, Cambridge, for their constant support.

M.M.

Authors

VALERY BRYUSOV (1873–1924), presiding genius of the Russian Symbolist movement and one of the leading literary figures in pre-revolutionary twentieth-century Russia, is the author of the historical novel *The Fiery Angel* (1908–09); he wrote many tales of horror and the supernatural.

MIKHAIL BULGAKOV (1891–1940) is best known for his seminal novel *The Master and Margarita* (first published 1966–67). Other celebrated works are the novels *The White Guard*, *The Heart of a Dog* and the plays *The Days of the Turbins* and *Flight*.

ALEKSANDR CHAYANOV (1888–1937), an agronomist by training and profession, is one of the most important figures in Russian twentieth-century Gothic-fantastic fiction. His story 'Venediktov' exerted a crucial influence over Mikhail Bulgakov and may even have inspired *The Master and Margarita*. He was executed in 1937.

ALEKSANDR GRIN (1880–1932) was a writer, soldier and sailor, well-known for his copious short stories on Symbolist and fantastic themes; he is best known in English for his short novel *Scarlet Sails* (English translation 1967).

SIGIZMUND KRZHIZHANOVSKY (1887–1950), born in Kiev, was a playwright, scriptwriter and author of numerous experimental novels and short stories, unpublished in his lifetime due to their irreconcilability with the ruling Socialist Realist aesthetic. Often compared by modern critics to Borges and Kafka, his work has been emerging from obscurity since its rediscovery in a Moscow archive at the end of the 1970s.

PAVEL PEROV (1886– ?) was a journalist and screenwriter who emigrated from Russia in 1910 and spent most of his life in America, including Hollywood. His books include *Bratstvo Viya* (The Brotherhood of Viy; Riga, 1933), an anti-Bolshevik supernatural horror tale, and the short story collection (published in Berlin, 1924) where the story included here first appeared.

GEORGY PESKOV (1885–1977) is the pseudonym of Yelena Deisha, who emigrated to France following the Revolution and spent most of her life in Paris. Her short stories feature primarily Russian characters, often confronted by supernatural or grotesque events. The two stories included in this book were first published in Russian émigré journals in the 1920s.

Texts Used

Bryusov, *In the Mirror*:
Valery Bryusov, 'V zerkale', from V.R. Bryusov, *Rasskazy i povesti* (Munich: William Fink Verlag, 1970), pp. 96–106; reprint of the short story collection *Zemnaya os'* (1907), pp. 11–191.

Bulgakov, *The Red Crown* and *A Seance*:
Mikhail Bulgakov, 'Krasnaya korona' and 'Spiriticheskiy seans', from *Sobraniye sochineniy v vos'mi tomakh* (St Petersburg: Azbuka Klassika, 2002), vol. II, pp. 42–48 and vol. I, pp. 237–45 respectively.

Chayanov, *The Tale of the Hairdresser's Mannequin*, *Venediktov* and *The Venetian Mirror*:
A.V. Chayanov, 'Istoriya parikmakherskoy kukli, ili Poslednyaya lyubov' moskovskogo arkhitektora M.', 'Venediktov, ili Dostopamyatnyye sobytiya zhizni moey' and 'Venetsianskoye zerkalo, ili Dikovinnyye pokhozhdeniya steklyannogo cheloveka', from A.V. Chayanov, *Moskovskaya gofmaniada* (Moscow: Tonchu, 1996), pp. 49–85, 86–113, 114–37 respectively.

Grin, *The Grey Motor Car*:
A.S. Grin, 'Seryy avtomobil' ', from *Sobraniye sochineniy v pyati tomakh* (Moscow: Khudozhestvennaya literatura), vol. III, 1991: *Rasskazy, stikhotvoreniya, poema*, pp. 417–53.

Krzhizhanovsky, *The Phantom*:
Sigizmund Krzhizhanovsky, 'Fantom', from *Sobraniye sochineniy v pyati tomakh*, edited by Vadim Perel'muter (St Petersburg: Symposium, 2001–2010), vol. II (2001), pp. 543–68.

Perov, *Professor Knop's Experiment*:
Pavel Perov, 'Opyt professora Knopa', from *Amerikanskiye novelly* (Berlin: 1924, publisher unknown), pp. 50–72.

Peskov, *The Messenger* and *The Woman With No Nose*:
Georgiy Peskov [pseudonym of Yelena Deisha], 'Gonets' and 'Kurnosaya', from *Pamyati tvoyey* (Paris: Sovremennyye zapiski', 1930), pp. 27–36 and pp. 61–69 respectively.

Introduction

Russian Gothic is as old as Russian prose: almost every major writer of Russia's Golden Age experimented with supernatural fiction. Tales such as Pushkin's enigmatic 'The Queen of Spades' (1834), Gogol's 'The Overcoat' (1842), Turgenev's 'Klara Milich' (1883) and Chekhov's 'The Black Monk' (1894) enriched European literature with uniquely Slavic visions of ghosts and incubi, doppelgängers and delusions. Russia's capital St Petersburg was reimagined by successive generations until its reality became confused with its uncanny doubles. Pushkin and Gogol sent vengeful phantoms stalking mortals through its neoclassical streets; Dostoyevsky's novels filled its tenements with spectres of mental illness; in Andrey Bely's novel *Petersburg* (1913–14) the city is terrorized by its own past; in Vladimir Nabokov's short story 'The Visit to the Museum' (1939) Petersburg is a dystopian dreamscape, reached through a portal in a haunted museum. In the early twentieth century, Ivan Bunin, Yevgeny Zamyatin and Mikhail Bulgakov used supernatural imagery and settings to convey the internal decay of imperial Russia and the chaotic Communist society that replaced it. Yet the Revolution of 1917 allegedly imposed a full stop to this rich tradition of Gothic fantasy; in 1934 the official adoption of Socialist Realism as Russia's literary programme effectively excluded any other kind of fiction from publication for the next half-century. In that year the Soviet novelist and bureaucrat Konstantin Fedin announced that fantastic literature, including Gothic, had been "shut in its coffin".[1] Such official disavowals, however, overlooked the lingering persistence of Gothic literature within the gates.[2]

Bulgakov, two of whose early stories appear in this collection, continued writing supernatural fiction long after deliberate censorship had stifled his career: he entrusted his last and greatest novel, *The Master and Margarita* (1940), to his wife for safekeeping. (It finally appeared in print in 1966–67.) Aleksandr

Chayanov and Sigizmund Krzhizhanovsky, Bulgakov's close contemporaries, were less fortunate. Chayanov, an agronomist by training, published five Gothic-fantastic short stories in limited print runs between 1921 and 1928: although they appeared under the pseudonym 'Botanist X', they possibly helped to fuel the public hounding that culminated in his execution for treason in 1937. Krzhizhanovsky, like Bulgakov, moved from Kiev to Moscow at the beginning of the 1920s: although he scraped a living over the next two decades producing encyclopedia entries, reviews and occasional screenplays, almost none of his five novels and over one hundred short stories were published in his life-time. They gathered dust in a government archive until their rediscovery in 1979. Valery Bryusov, one of the greatest poets and critics of Russian Symbolism, supported the Bolshevik takeover but died in 1924. Two of the other writers included in this book, Pavel Perov and Georgy Peskov (pseudonym of the female writer Yelena Deisha), chose life in emigration over precarious survival in Soviet Russia. Perov worked as a journalist in America and Germany; Peskov settled in Paris, gaining a modest reputation as an author among the émigré community. Aleksandr Grin, whose proletarian origins helped keep him in print during the early Soviet years, nevertheless died in poverty in 1932. The eleven stories presented here by these seven writers, all but two of which[3] appear in English translation for the first time, use Gothic themes to convey the turbulence, terror and dissonance – the uncanny ambiance – of Soviet Russia in the transitional decade of the 1920s.

What exactly is Gothic fiction? Gothic began in the 1790s with the English Gothic novel, German Romantic horror, and the French *roman noir*. It was no coincidence that the Gothic appeared at this historical moment. Behind and beyond their frequently overblown plots, the subtexts of Gothic fiction explored social faultlines radiating from the French Revolution, and questioned the basic structures – legal and moral – of modern civic society. In the 'shock' Gothic of 'Monk' Lewis, in the decorous spec-trality of Ann Radcliffe's bestsellers, and in the American Gothic of Hawthorne, Poe and Brockden Brown, the same characteristi-cally Gothic obsessions recur: death, insanity, deformity, decay, and most insistently of all, retributive justice, the repossession of the present by the past. Entropy and terror are the key motive forces of Gothic plot.[4] As the nineteenth century merged with the twentieth, Gothic became a tool for exploring the dark underside of the machine age. Fear of modernity, fear of deviance, fear of our own bodies: Bram Stoker's *Dracula* (1897) reveals as much about aberrant humanity as it does about vampires. New research into the mechanisms of human physiology and new directions in technology – including ubiquitous electrification and the arrival of motorized vehicles – fostered a sense of scientific invulnerability, along with an underlying unease.

'If the dominant national story was about progress, and a part of this set of values was faith in science and technology to improve everyone's life, then the Gothic can expose anxiety about what the scientist might create, and what threats might be posed by machines, if they escape our control.'[5] This passage on American literature applies equally well to Russian Gothic. In 1920s Russia, where pre-revolutionary, internationally trained scientific cadres fused awkwardly with a brand-new, semi-educated, overambitious Bolshevik bureaucracy, science rapidly acquired utopian overtones. Senior figures in government and the academy promoted scientific aspirations toward hormonal rejuvenation, eugenics, space travel, immortality, and even the resurrection of the dead (on his death in 1924 Lenin's corpse was embalmed in the hope – at least partially sincere – that resurrection technology was imminent). Pavel Perov captures this aura of scientific arrogance – and its defeat – in 'Professor Knop's Experiment', while Aleksandr Grin's 'The Grey Motor Car' is an ironic retort to the raucous Futurist technophilia of Marinetti and Mayakovsky. Grin's automobile-hating hero is part Luddite, part mystic; unlike early Soviet poets of industrialization, who hymned the ideal fusion of man and mechanism, Grin's narrator sees machines as invidious entities, actively undermining human values.

Besides its due share of cultural dissonance, Russia by the mid-1920s had endured two revolutions (1905 and 1917) and a shattering civil war (1917–22). The nascent Soviet state struggled to sustain its damaged economy, inculcate loyalty and dedication in its surviving citizens, and contain or liquidate dissent. It did so by reintroducing a tentative, short-term capitalism (Lenin's New Economic Policy, 1921–28); through massive propaganda and re-education campaigns; and by building a formidable secret police force, the Cheka (later the NKVD), which reported or 'disappeared' intractable individuals. In this chaotic, often sordid atmosphere, intellectuals felt increasingly threatened; like the former middle classes, now stripped of their privileges, they suffered hardship and isolation. Writers and artists frequently resorted to Gothic imagery to express their experiences: the poet Zinaida Gippius explicitly likened post-revolutionary St Petersburg to a corpse rotting in a grave, while Aleksandr Blok used images of death, reanimated corpses and vampires in his efforts to conceptualize the chaos of the early Soviet period. In the present collection, Peskov's stories 'The Messenger' and 'The Woman With No Nose' describe characters who have failed to integrate into this interim society. In 'The Messenger' an elderly married couple, impoverished aristocrats, are completely marginalized by the new society: they use a planchette to talk to old friends who have 'passed over' and in the hope of receiving news about their son, serving with the Whites in the Crimea. When a real spirit messenger arrives, they refuse to trust him – just as doubting Thomas failed to believe in Christ. 'The Woman With No Nose' is a first-person account of typhoid delirium by a clerk who attempts to flee south with the retreating White Army while protecting now-meaningless documents. His hallucinations of a grotesque wedding ceremony with a disfigured bride – the noseless woman of the title – combine surreally with the real-life nightmare of securing a seat on a train packed with refugees. In Krzhizhanovsky's 'The Phantom', the young doctor, forced to assume responsibility for the unnatural child he accidentally delivers, may be a metaphor for all the naïve pre-revolutionary intellectuals whose political ambivalence unintentionally paved the way for the 1917 Revolution and its consequences. The child's Oedipal intent to kill his 'father' in order to beget offspring foreshadows Stalin's mass executions of intellectuals and specialists in order to safeguard the survival of the Soviet regime. In Gothic logic, as in history, innocence is never an excuse.

The stories in this collection, however, transcend the specificities of the Soviet era. They also explore such characteristically Gothic problems as mortality and the nature of the human soul (Chayanov's 'Venediktov', Perov's 'Professor Knop's Experiment', Peskov's 'The Messenger'); dread of and fascination with technology (Chayanov's 'The Tale of the Hairdresser's Mannequin', Grin's 'The Grey Motor Car', Krzhizhanovsky's 'The Phantom'); doubles and psychological disintegration (Bryusov's 'In the Mirror', Chayanov's 'The Venetian Mirror', Peskov's 'The Woman With No Nose', Bulgakov's 'The Red Crown', Grin's 'The Grey Motor Car'), besides the traditional Gothic repertoire of ghosts, monsters, obsession and retribution. These eternal questions can be traced through more than one of the tales.

The materiality of the soul, for example, is a theme treated – in very different ways – by Chayanov and Pavel Perov. Perov's 'Professor Knop's Experiment' is a Faustian parable about an arrogant scientist defeated by the noumenal forces he challenges. (Contrast the American writer Edmond Moore Hamilton's 'The Man Who Evolved' (1936), another science-fiction cautionary tale.) Professor Knop thinks he has proven that the human soul is a product of electrical activity: with this knowledge, human life can be indefinitely prolonged by switching the electrical life-force to a new host when the body dies – even to a new species. But Knop's scheme backfires disastrously. Briefly poised on the pinnacle of scientific hubris, he is abruptly 'hurled backwards into the dark ages, when nature's terrifying secrets loomed fatefully over mankind' – a typically Gothic comeuppance. In Chayanov's 'Venediktov', set in late-eighteenth-century Moscow, a student called Bulgakov discovers the materiality of his soul the hard way, when it comes into someone else's possession. The mysterious Venediktov – part Faust, part picaro – wins seven human souls, in the form of solid gold triangles inscribed with cabbalistic sigils, in a card game with demons. One of the souls belongs to the woman Bulgakov loves; another belongs to a sinister officer called Seidlitz, who is possibly part demon himself. Chayanov's plot is deliberately enigmatic and baroque, garnished with a wealth of period detail, from popular culture to military campaigns. 'Venediktov' continues the rich tradition of Russian demon literature inaugurated by Pushkin and Lermontov; it played a unique role in literary history by influencing *The Master and Margarita*, which developed Chayanov's themes of gambling, theatricality, and demons abroad – besides sharing the same Moscow setting. Mikhail Bulgakov, who discovered 'Venediktov' in the mid-1920s, was struck by the coincidence of sharing a name with Chayanov's hero. Although the two men never met, Bulgakov admitted his debt to Chayanov's inspired fantasies.[6]

Mannequins and automatons are another enduring theme in Gothic fiction (like Olympia, the clockwork fiancée in Hoffmann's 'The Sandman'), richly represented here. 'The Tale of the Hairdresser's Mannequin', Chayanov's first and most contemporary story, traces the bizarre infatuation experienced by Vladimir, a middle-aged Moscow architect at the height of his career. A lifelong philanderer, Vladimir's jaded senses are aroused by two eerily lifelike mannequins, modelled on a pair of beautiful Siamese twins, who are now touring Europe as circus artistes. Vladimir's tortuous quest to track down the twins and his scandalous passion for one of them ends in a series of dramatic scenes in Venice, where Thomas Mann had set another tragedy of sunset infatuation, *Death in Venice*, ten years previously. In 'The Grey Motor Car', Aleksandr Grin's machine-hating hero believes (with tragic consequences) that the woman he loves is actually an automaton pretending to be a real human. For Grin's hero, modern civilization is a labyrinth of Gothic pitfalls: the motor car in particular is a 'metallic monster, with a six-sided, projecting snout, like a galosh on wheels', poised to fell unsuspecting pedestrians. Krzhizhanovsky's 'The Phantom' describes the life cycle of a unique type of mannequin: the preserved corpse of a stillborn child, used in teaching medical students obstetric method. The word 'phantom', according to the Oxford English Dictionary, bears the additional meaning of 'a model of the body or of a body part or organ [...] used to demonstrate the progression of the fetus through the birth canal'. In this chilling tale, a wooden gynaecological model gives 'birth' to the tiny phantom, which attains liminal maturity – half man, half apparition – during the famine and privation of the Civil War. After starting an affair with a dressmaker's mannequin, the phantom sets out, like Frankenstein's monster, to trace the medical student who inadvertently gave it life and then abandoned it, the ambiguously named Twoman-Sklifsky. Twoman-Sklifsky, quite unwittingly, becomes the monster's father, victim – and double.

   The double in supernatural fiction has received special attention ever since Sigmund Freud singled it out in his essay 'The Uncanny' (1919) as a 'thing of terror', the self transformed into its own worst rival.[7] Valery Bryusov's 'In the Mirror' and Chayanov's response 'The Venetian Mirror' both use mirrors to explore the theme of the double. The narrator of 'In the Mirror' is a woman obsessed with her collection of mirrors, or rather, with the infinite range of alternative selves and worlds they contain. Eventually, one of these selves escapes from the mirror, forcing the narrator to take its place. After a long battle of wills, the narrator regains her own life; but she continues to doubt that 'she' – the implied author – is the original self and not another reflection. 'In the Mirror' can be read on at least three levels: literally, as a haunting; secondly, as a parable of schizophrenia; and thirdly, as a fable of *fin de siècle* feminine sexuality. The heroine's self-obsession stems from her extreme passivity. Through stray references to her husband and children, we gather that her entire life is a composite of stereotypical feminine roles: society belle, theatregoer, mother, wife. Dutifully reflecting external assumptions, her inner self is almost annihilated. Her sexuality is certainly unfulfilled: one of her rival's first acts is to entertain lovers in her boudoir. Even the revenge the heroine finally achieves – reversing their positions and sending the mirror away – is a mere reflection, a mirror image of her rival's plans for her. She calls her reflection 'commanding', yet she cannot take command of her own life: only by abnegating conscious choice can she live the life she secretly craves. Chayanov's 'The Venetian Mirror' re-enacts this scenario from a male perspective: Aleksey, a wealthy, jaded art collector, is hypnotized and dominated by his reflection in an antique mirror. Forced into the reflection's place, he helplessly watches his double and rival sexually assault his wife Kate. He acts to free himself only when her life is in danger. Aleksey's struggle to subdue his mirror-double plays out in a sinister looking-glass version of Moscow, with Kate as the ultimate trophy. The Russian word meaning 'to reflect', *otrazit'*, is a lexical cousin of *porazit'*, to strike a blow or to vanquish. Every reflection is thus a loss, a defeat. The most remarkable aspect of both stories is that self-expression can only be achieved by violence against the self: a gloomy conclusion given that the Soviet state had been forged in the fire of a bloody civil war.

While 'In the Mirror' and 'The Grey Motor Car' culminate in the incoherence of mental breakdown, two other stories in this collection explicitly track psychological collapse: Peskov's 'The Woman With No Nose' and Bulgakov's 'The Red Crown'. The latter follows a White Army officer driven mad with guilt over his failure to prevent his brother's death in action. He is haunted by the sound of artillery fire and by a recurring vision of his brother's bloody head, which appears to be wearing a red crown of gore. This theme of unatoned guilt, which had its roots in Bulgakov's personal self-indictment, re-emerges in two later major works, both dealing with the Civil War: the novel *The White Guard* (1924), where the heroine dreams of her brother's imminent death, and the play *Flight* (1927), where a cruel White Army commander is haunted in exile by the ghost of an orderly he executed. Its ultimate expression is the Pontius Pilate theme in *The Master and Margarita*. The other two stories in this collection by Bulgakov and Peskov also share common themes: spiritualism and an unhappy love triangle. Most ghost stories about spiritualism end with a macabre warning against meddling with the occult. Although structurally the most traditional ghost story in the collection, 'The Messenger' avoids this resolution. Peskov's elderly heroine actually gains emotional security from her otherworldly contacts. 'A Seance' treats the same topic very differently. Bulgakov's acerbic sketch wittily portrays social comedy – an unfaithful wife deceiving her husband with a fraudulent medium – against the background of the New Economic Policy, ubiquitous poverty and rationed cigarettes. The spiritualists are blatantly anti-Communist, like their 'spirits': manifestations of Socrates and Napoleon which predict (by tapping a table-leg) the downfall of the Bolshevik Party within three months. Bulgakov's satirical pen spares neither the shallow bourgeoisie nor their enemies, the 'savages' repossessing Russia. A police agent lounges on the staircase in a ludicrously macho uniform; gossiping servant girls, spraying sunflower husks all over the tiled lobby of the apartment building, offer no moral or intellectual alternative to the self-interested spiritualists upstairs. This opposition between the educated but isolated middle classes and the greedily aspirant proletariat, staged in stairwells and doorways, would be revisited by Bulgakov in *Heart of a Dog* and in his other short fiction of the early 1920s. *The Master and Margarita* is foreshadowed in the epigraph from Gounod's *Faust* and the medium's brief invocation of the Devil just before the dénouement. Ksyushka the maid, the 'idiot girl' whose loose tongue lands her master and mistress in trouble, is a forerunner of Annushka, the equally ignorant servant who spills the fatal sunflower oil in Bulgakov's last great novel. The irony of 'A Seance' lies in the unexpected form taken by the apparition that warns them off future meddling.

The supreme irony of Soviet efforts to expunge the Gothic from Russia's cultural legacy is that such attempts merely guaranteed its resurrection. Gothic fiction is founded upon 'the disturbing return of pasts upon presents'.[8] To dismiss the Gothic – to dismiss horror, violence, pain or wrongdoing – is to incur its return in the shape of haunting memories and literary phantoms. Many of the authors featured here, denied print in their lifetimes and unjustly condemned by Soviet critics, have posthumously received the literary honours they merit. Some, like Bulgakov, have even attained cult status in Russia and abroad, while others, including Krzhizhanovsky, are reaching new audiences in translation.[9] Russia herself, however, is still living down her Soviet ghosts.

RED SPECTRES

Russian Gothic Tales from the Twentieth Century

VALERY BRYUSOV

In the Mirror

From the archive of a psychiatrist

I fell in love with mirrors when I was still very young. As an infant, I wept and trembled, peeping into their translucent, truth-telling depths. In childhood my favourite game was to walk through the house or garden holding a mirror in front of me and gazing into its chasm, every step carrying me over the brink, catching my breath from terror and vertigo. As a young girl, I started to deck my room with mirrors large and small, some truthful and some distorting, some clear and some clouded. I formed the habit of spending entire hours and days in between these intersecting worlds, each of which mingled with the others, shimmering, vanishing and reappearing. My sole passion became to yield my body to these soundless depths, these echo-less perspectives, these separate universes, which interpenetrate our own and which exist, defying conscious thought, in the same time and place as this world. This inside-out reality, separated from ours by the smooth surface of glass, somehow inaccessible to touch, drew me and lured me to itself, like a precipice, like a mystery.

Even the shade that always appeared before me whenever I approached a mirror, queerly doubling my being, attracted me. I tried to guess how this other woman might differ from me, how my right hand could become her left, and how all the fingers on that hand could be reversed, although one of them wore my wedding ring. My thoughts became tangled when I tried to understand and solve this riddle. In this world, where everything can be touched, where voices can be heard, I lived, the real me: in that reflected world, which can only be contemplated, she lived, the shade. She was almost the same as me, and not me at all; she repeated all my gestures, and not one of them was the same as my own. She, the other, knew what I could not fathom; she possessed a secret hidden forever from my reason.

I noticed, however, that every mirror has its own separate and unique world. Try putting two mirrors in the same place, side by side, and two different worlds will appear. And in these different worlds, confronting me, different shades appeared, all resembling me, but never identical with each other. In my little hand-mirror lived a naive, bright-eyed young girl, who reminded me of my own early youth. In my round boudoir glass lurked a woman steeped in every kind of sensuality; she was shameless, liberated, beautiful, bold. In the square mirror set in my wardrobe door there flourished a strict, powerful, chilly figure, with an inflexible stare. I knew still other doubles – in my pier-glass, in the three panels of my gilded folding mirror, in my oak-framed pendant, in the little glass I wore around my neck, and in many, many more of the mirrors I kept. I gave all these beings hidden in my mirrors both the chance to live and a purpose in living. The strange conditions of their world forced them to wear the appearance of whoever stood before the glass, but inside this borrowed exterior, they kept their individuality.

There were mirror worlds that I loved; and there were some that I hated. I loved to project myself into some for hours on end, losing myself in their enticing spaces. Others I avoided. Secretly, I did not love all my doubles. I knew that all of them were hostile towards me, if only because they were forced to don my hated appearance. But I pitied several of these mirror women, forgave them their hatred, and treated them almost as friends. There were others for whom I had contempt; I liked to laugh at their helpless fury, I taunted them with my independence and tortured them with my power over them. On the other hand, there were some I feared, who were too powerful, and who dared in their turn to laugh at me, who tried to command me. I hurried to dispose of the mirrors where these women lived, I did not look into those mirrors, I hid them, gave them away, even smashed them. But each time I broke a mirror I sobbed helplessly for whole days afterwards, realizing that I had destroyed a whole universe. And the reproachful faces of a perished world gazed at me reprovingly from the shards.

The mirror that was to prove fateful for me I bought one autumn, at some sale or other. It was a large cheval-glass, swinging on hinges. The unusual clarity of its reflections impressed me. The ghostly reality within was transformed by the slightest tilt of the glass, yet it was extremely lifelike and distinct. When I studied the cheval-glass at the auction, the woman who reflected me stared into my eyes with a kind of arrogant challenge. I did not want to submit to her, to betray that she frightened me; I purchased the glass and ordered it to be placed in my boudoir. Once I was alone in my room, I immediately approached the new mirror and fixed my eyes on my rival. But she did the same: standing opposite each other, we began to pierce each other with our stares, like two snakes. I was reflected in the pupils of her eyes and she in mine. My heart stopped beating and my head spun from this fixed glare. But by an effort of will, I finally tore my gaze away from those strange eyes and kicked the mirror so that it swung to and fro, compassionately rocking the phantom of my rival. I left the room.

Our struggle began from that moment. On the evening of the first day we met, I lacked the courage to go near my new glass; I went to the theatre with my husband, laughed too loudly, and pretended to be cheerful. The following day, in the clear light of a September morning, I boldly entered my boudoir alone and deliberately sat down directly opposite the mirror. In the same instant she, the other, also entered by the same door, came towards me, crossed the room, and sat down facing me. Our eyes met. I read hatred for me in her eyes; she read the same in mine. Our second duel had begun, a duel fought with the eyes alone. Two unremitting stares, commanding, threatening, hypnotizing. Each of us was trying to control her rival's will, to break her resistance, to force her to submit to the other's desires. What a terrible sight we must have been, two women, sitting unmoving opposite each other, linked by the magical influence of their stares, almost fainting from the mental strain ... Suddenly I was called away. The spell was broken. I rose and went out.

After this, our duels became a daily affair. I understood that this adventuress had deliberately invaded my house in order to destroy me and seize my place in the world.

Yet I lacked the strength to refuse our struggle. Some secret rapture lay in this rivalry. In the very possibility of defeat there lurked a kind of sweet seduction. Sometimes for whole days I forced myself not to approach the cheval-glass, occupying myself with tasks or amusements – but at the bottom of my soul the memory of my rival always lurked, waiting patiently and confidently for me to return. I would come, and she would appear before me, more exultant than before, to sink her victorious gaze into me and pin me to my place before her. My heart would stop beating and, helplessly furious, I would submit to the power of her gaze. Sometimes, when away from her, I considered fleeing my home, travelling to another town and hiding there from my enemy; but I would immediately realize that this was impossible. It would change nothing; I would still return here, to this room, to my mirror, submitting to the pull of her hateful will. Sometimes I wanted to strike the glass, smash it to fragments, and destroy this unknown world which threatened mine; and sometimes, in a frenzy, I even flung myself on the mirror with some heavy thing in my hand, but my rival's scornful sneer would restrain me. Victory attained at that price would have proved her superiority and my defeat. And our struggle went on and on; it had to end in victory for one of us.

I soon felt, however, that my rival was stronger than me. Each time we met, more and more power over me was concentrated in her stare. Little by little, I lost the ability to let a day go by without visiting her. She ordered me to spend several hours a day seated before her. She ruled my will, as a mesmerist controls the will of a sleepwalker. She commanded my life, as a ruler commands his slaves. I began to do everything she demanded; I became an automaton, obeying her silent commands. I knew that she was leading me to my ruin deliberately, carefully, but ineluctably, and even then I did not resist. I had guessed her secret plan: to hurl me into the mirror world, and herself escape into our world. But I no longer had the strength to interfere with her plans. My husband, my family, seeing that I was spending whole hours, days and nights in front of the mirror, thought that I had lost my wits and wished to send me for treatment. I did not dare to be open with them; I was forbidden to tell them all the terrible truth, all the horror, to which I was doomed.

The day of my defeat was a day in December, before the holidays. I remember every detail of it clearly and distinctly; nothing is confused in my recollections. As usual, I went into my boudoir early, at the very beginning of the winter twilight. I placed a soft, backless armchair before the mirror, sat down, and yielded myself to her. She came at my call without delaying, also drew up a chair, also sat down, and sank her gaze into me. Dark forebodings troubled my soul, but I had no power to lower my eyes and was forced to submit to my rival's insolent gaze. Hours went by; shadows clustered. Neither of us lighted the lamp. The glass gleamed faintly in the darkness. Her features were barely visible, but her self-assured eyes gazed with all their former strength. I felt neither malice nor dread, as on other days, but only the unappeasable sorrow and bitterness of knowing that I was in another's power. Time swam by, and I floated with it in infinitude, in a black expanse of powerlessness and lack of volition.

Suddenly, she – the reflection – rose from her chair. I trembled all over from the insult. But some unconquerable exterior pressure forced me to stand also. The woman in the mirror took a step forward. So did I. The woman in the mirror stretched out her hands. So did I. Constantly staring straight at me with her hypnotic and commanding eyes, she continued moving forwards, and I came to meet her. And strangely, despite all the horror of my position, despite all my hatred for my rival, somewhere in the depths of my soul there fluttered a bitter comfort, a secret joy at entering, at last, this mysterious world, into which I had been gazing since childhood and which had remained closed to me until now. Momentarily, I almost forgot who was calling whom: whether she was drawn to me or I to her, whether she coveted my place or whether I had dreamt up this entire struggle in order to take hers.

But when, as I stepped forward, my hands touched hers through the glass, I grew numb with revulsion. She masterfully seized me by both hands and wrenched me towards her. My arms plunged into the mirror as if into fiery, freezing water. The cold of the glass sank agonizingly into my body, as if every atom of my being was turning inside out. An instant later I was face to face with my rival, I saw her eyes directly before my own; I melted into her in an unnatural kiss. Everything was extinguished in deadly, unimaginable suffering – and, when I recovered from my faint, I saw before me my boudoir as I looked out from the mirror. My rival was standing in front of me and laughing. And I – oh, the cruelty of it! – I, who was dying from torture and humiliation, I had to laugh as well, repeating each of her grimaces, in exultant, joyful laughter. And before I could even grasp my position, my rival abruptly turned, made for the door, and disappeared from my sight. I was plunged without warning into numbness, into non-being.

From that moment, my life as a reflection began. A strange, half-conscious, but secretly pleasurable life. There were many of us in that mirror: dark souls, slumbering minds. Although we could not speak to each other, we sensed one another's nearness, we loved each other. We saw nothing, heard dimly, and our existence resembled the exhaustion of asphyxiation. Only when a being from the world of people approached the mirror could we, suddenly assuming his appearance, look into that world, distinguish voices, breathe with full lungs. I think the dead may exist like this – in unclear consciousness of their own 'I', dimly recalling their past and tormented with longing to be embodied again, to see, to hear, to speak, if only for a moment . . . Each of us concealing, nursing and cherishing hopes of freedom, of finding a new body, of escaping into the world of constancy and stability.

At first I felt utterly miserable in my new circumstances. I understood nothing, and could do nothing. Submissively and unthinkingly, I assumed my rival's image when she drew close to the mirror and began teasing me. And she did this quite often. It gave her great pleasure to parade her liveliness, her physicality, in front of me. She sat down, forcing me to sit too; she stood up, rejoicing when she saw me stand also; she waved her hands and danced, forcing me to repeat all of her movements; she roared with laughter to make me laugh too. She shrieked insults in my face, and I could not reply to her. She threatened me with her fist and sneered at the feeble, forced counter-gesture I made. And then suddenly, with one blow, she swung the mirror around on its axis and at a stroke flung me into utter void.

However, little by little, her insults and humiliations roused my consciousness within me. I realized that my rival was now living my life, wearing my clothes, posing as my husband's wife, taking my place in society. Hatred and the desire for vengeance began growing in my soul, like two fiery flowers. I started cursing myself bitterly for the weakness or culpable curiosity that had allowed me to be vanquished. I became convinced that this adventuress would never have triumphed over me if I had not aided her schemes myself. And now, accustomed somewhat to the conditions of my new existence, I decided to start the same struggle with her that she had waged against me. If she, a mere shade, had succeeded in taking the place of a real woman, then surely I, a human being, only temporarily reduced to a shade, would be stronger than a ghost?

I began in a very small way. At first I pretended that the gibes of my rival were tormenting me more insufferably than ever. I deliberately afforded her all the pleasures of victory. I played on her secret instinct for torture by shamming exhaustion and despair. She fell for this lure. She relished playing with me. She exhausted her fancy by thinking up new torments. She invented thousands of cunning ways to remind me that I was only a reflection, that I had no life of my own. She would play the piano in front of me, torturing me with the deafness of my world. She would sit before the mirror and swallow my favourite liqueurs, mouthful by mouthful, forcing me to mime drinking them too. Finally, she would bring men that I hated into my boudoir and allow them to kiss her body in front of my eyes, letting them think that they were kissing me. And afterwards, when left alone with me, she guffawed triumphantly and gloatingly. But this guffaw no longer stung me; I found pleasure in its bitterness: I was waiting for my revenge!

Unnoticed by her, as she continued to insult me, I trained my rival to look me in the eye; I gradually mastered her with my gaze. Soon, by my own will, I could force her to raise or lower her eyelids, or to make some facial movement. I had already begun to rejoice, although I concealed my feelings under a mask of pain. My willpower was increasing, and I was bold enough to order my enemy: today you will do such and such, today you will go to such and such a place, tomorrow you will come to me at such and such a time. And she obeyed me! I trapped her soul in a web of my wishes, I wove a firm thread, with which I directed her will; I exulted secretly, counting my victories. When once, as she was laughing, she spied the victorious smile on my lips which I was unable to hide, it was already too late. She fled raging from the room, but as I fell into the sleep of my non-existence, I knew that she would return, that she would submit to me! And the ecstasy of victory hovered over my involuntary helplessness, piercing the gloom of my deathlike trance with its rainbow-coloured fan.

She did return! She came to me in rage and terror, shouted at me, threatened me. But I gave her orders, and she was obliged to fulfil them. A game of cat-and-mouse began. At any moment I could hurl her back into the depths of the glass and myself venture once more into the real world of sounds and solid things. She knew that this was my intention, and her awareness doubled her suffering. But I took my time. It was pleasant to linger in non-being a little longer. It was sweet to savour my power. At last (and surely this was strange), pity for my rival, for my enemy, for my torturer, woke within me. There was, after all, something of me in her; I dreaded ripping her out of reality and transforming her again into a ghost. I wanted for courage and hesitated; I procrastinated from day to day; I myself did not know what I desired and what I feared.

Then suddenly, on a bright spring day, men carrying boards and axes came into my boudoir. I was not alert at the time, I was lying in a sensuous trance, but even without seeing, I understood that they were there. The men began busying themselves around the mirror which contained my universe. And one after another, the shades dwelling there with me woke and donned their ghostly flesh as reflections. A dreadful fear shook my drowsy spirit. Anticipating the horror to come, anticipating my final extinction, I mustered all my strength of will. What effort it cost me to resist the languor of half-being! Living people battle in this way against a nightmare, bursting free of its suffocating bonds into reality.

I concentrated all my forces on summoning her, my rival: 'Come here!' I hypnotized her, I magnetized her with all the power of my half-sleeping will. There was so little time. The mirror was already swaying. They were already preparing to box it up in a wooden coffin and carry it away – where, I did not know. Almost with a death-rattle, I called her again and again: 'Come!' And suddenly I sensed the return of life. She, my enemy, had opened the door, and pale, half-dead, was approaching me, on my summons, with dragging steps, as one walks to the scaffold. My eyes met hers; I transfixed her gaze with my own, and I knew then instantly that I had conquered.

Straightaway I compelled her to send the men out of the room. She submitted without even attempting to resist. We were alone again. I could not delay any longer. I pitilessly ordered her to come closer. Her lips parted with a groan of agony, her eyes widened as if seeing a ghost, but she came – swaying, tottering – she came. I also walked towards her, my lips twisted in triumph, my eyes wide with joy. I staggered with the drunkenness of ecstasy. Our hands touched once more, our lips again drew close, and we plunged one into another, scorched by the inexpressibly painful return of flesh. An instant later I was standing before the mirror, my lungs filled with air, and with a joyful and victorious shriek I collapsed on the spot, in front of the cheval-glass, felled by exhaustion.

My husband and the servants ran to my side. I was barely able to ask for my earlier orders to be fulfilled, that they should take the mirror out of the house directly. Then I fainted. They put me to bed and called the doctor. After all I had endured, I suffered a nervous fever. My relatives had already long considered me unwell, even abnormal. In the first flush of victory, I abandoned my guard and told them everything that had happened. My tale only confirmed their suspicions. I was transferred to a psychiatric clinic, where I still am. My entire being, I concede, is still deeply shaken. But I do not wish to remain here. I long to return to the joys of life, to all the innumerable pleasures that a living person can enjoy. I was deprived of them for too long.

I have no doubts about my triumph, none whatsoever! I know that I am – myself. And all the same, when I begin to think about that other, trapped in my mirror, I begin to be seized by a strange hesitation: what if the real 'I' is *there*? Then I myself, the I who thinks this, the I who writes this, is a shade, a ghost, a reflection. The memories, the thoughts and the feelings of her, the other me, the real one, have only been poured into me. And in reality 'I' have been abandoned in non-being in the depths of a mirror: I suffer, I perish, I am dying. I know, I am almost sure, that this is untrue. But in order to banish the last clouds of doubt, I must once again, one last time, see that mirror. I must look into it one more time, in order to be convinced that the usurper is there, my enemy, who acted my part for several months. I will see her, and all the conflict in my soul will disappear, and I shall once more be carefree, gay and happy. Where is that mirror, where can I find it? I must look into it one last time, I must!

1903

ALEKSANDR CHAYANOV

The Tale of the Hairdresser's Mannequin
or, The Last Love Affair of a Moscow Architect

A Romantic Tale written by Botanist X[1]

*The author dedicates this modest work to the memory of the
great master, Ernst Theodor Amadeus Hoffmann*

I Prologue

> A malady, whose explanation
> Is overdue ...
> **ALEXANDER PUSHKIN**

M., a Moscow architect who had designed one of the city's most
popular cafés, was better known in city society for his eventful
private life, as full as Casanova's memoirs. Yet one day, as he was
passing a café on Tverskoy Boulevard, he suddenly felt his age.

The café, which had figured in one of Yuon's paintings;[2]
the evening crowd of *flâneurs*; the autumn-dyed boulevards of
Moscow unrolling like yellow ribbons; all this ordinary gaiety
and good cheer was abruptly quenched in his soul. The city's
late-summer dishevelment, the motor cars on Strastnaya Square,
the hooting of trams, the groups of prostitutes, and the little boys
selling flowers – all of it left him unmoved.

All those thoughts which had so recently disturbed his heart
now struck him as banal, wearisomely repeating themselves
a hundredfold. Even that evening's assignation, which he had
spent so many months contriving and which was supposed to
inaugurate a new chapter in the annals of his life, now appeared
needless and tedious. Only the autumn leaves, as they slipped
from the trees to lie under the feet of the evening passers-by,
succeeded in penetrating his soul with their mournful pallor. He

stood momentarily undecided, unthinkingly bought an evening paper, then turned and walked briskly back to Tverskaya Street, where he made his way to Stepanov and Krutov the florists' and ordered an enormous bouquet of crimson roses, to be sent to the lady whose seduction that evening was to have woven new laurels into the wreath of the Moscow Casanova.

He had no wish to return home; he did not want to see the mahogany chairs again or the Elizabethan divan, evocative of so many names and so many amorous conquests, now superfluous. He had no wish to see the Gobelins, nor the erotic drawings by the now-insane artist Vrubel which he had once purchased so delightedly, nor his china, nor his Novgorod icons; in a word, he wished to see none of those objects which had once gladdened and quickened his existence.

Vladimir – for that was his name – suddenly craved to plunge his being into the simmering cauldron of the great city's life. He walked down Petrovka and, at his usual gait, not allowing himself to reconsider, he walked into a small, arty café, nodded to a young lady he knew, and ordered black coffee with cheesecake.

All around, at tables and in the aisles, thronged dozens of his acquaintances in evening wear, in silk dresses, velvet coats and plebeian pea-jackets. They smiled at him but, perhaps for the first time ever, he remained aloof. Listening abstractedly to the violin music mingling with the clatter of crockery, he was borne off on the stream of his own thoughts. The people fluttering around him might have been made of cardboard; they oppressed his brain with a hopeless weariness. When the elegant compère took the stage and called, with difficulty, for silence, announcing a contest for lady poets, Vladimir could restrain himself no longer and he slipped from the brightly lit café into the darkness of the Moscow streets.

The city with its nightlife, its night-time passers-by, its half-shaded windows, the lights of gambling dens, and the hoof-beats – plainly audible in the nocturnal silence – of a late cab, suffocated Vladimir with its ubiquity, its unrelenting familiarity. He cast a bored glance over the familiar nocturnal silhouettes of the capital's streets and decided to venture on the ultimate cure for the melancholy that was crushing him. He made his way to Trubnaya Square; in one of the side-streets there he found a Chinese opium den with which he was familiar.

But only a few minutes later he rushed out again, even more fiercely impelled by misery.

'Cabby, take me to Kazan Station!' Vladimir shouted, leaping into the cab.

Just after the second warning bell rang, he rushed up to the ticket office. The 12.10 night train bore him to Kolomna. Vladimir hoped to gather his thoughts in the depths of provincial Russia.

2 Kolomna

> And since that time, no events worthy of note have taken place there.
> *Historical chronicle of Kolomna*

> Kolomna is famous for its *pastila*, a kind of fruit fudge.
> *A contemporary guidebook*

Kolomna, once a famous fortress defending the shore of the Oka from assaults by the steppe Tatars, and later an important centre of the bread trade, now led the sleepy life of a quiet provincial town. The age-old silence of the central redoubt was broken only by the droning of horns from the nearby factories. A tipsy craftsman's harmonica occasionally roused the half-slumbering streets. But for all that, it was a fine little town.

The night train rumbled off across the steppe, leaving Vladimir and a couple of worried-looking commercial travellers on the dark platform.

The clumsy cab-driver knocked and rang for a long time at the door of Ivan Shvarev's Grand Hotel before the sleepy porter unlocked the doors and led the visitor into a 'luxury' room with a green velvet couch and a bed behind a wooden partition. The floor attendant informed him that there was no food to be had until morning except beer and ham. A few minutes later, having placed the promised supper on the table, he made himself scarce.

Silence fell – an infinite silence. Two candles flickered on the table, playing on the glass of the tumbler, on the yellow bottle of local beer, and illuminating the white sauce-boat filled with horseradish and mustard, served – according to local custom – with ham.

Vladimir silently paced to and fro on the carpet, and the freshness of the provincial night gradually clarified his mind.

Alone with his thoughts, he perceived with terrifying clarity that he was old; that everything which had filled his life for so many years was used up; that he had had a surfeit of living. He craved simple words, provincial naivety, muslin curtains and geraniums. In the wardrobe where he hung his coat he found a book, torn and forgotten by one of his predecessors. It was Lazhechnikov's *The Ice House*, a narrative which perfectly suited Vladimir's thirst for provincial impressions.[3] He carved off a large slice of ham, poured himself some beer, and began devouring page after page, washing down the adventures of Peter's commanders with Kalinkin brew.

Day had broken and the cocks had long been crowing when he put out the candles and lay down to sleep.

3   Romantic Encounters

> At Galliani's or Collioni's
> When in Tver, order yourself
> Macaroni with parmesan
> And a frittata too ...
> ALEXANDER PUSHKIN

At eleven o'clock Vladimir woke and looked around him in amazement. A coachman's droshky was rumbling along the road, off in the background a bass baritone was cursing someone called Vanka, richly and obscenely, and the autumn sun was leaching through the heavy lowered blinds.

Recalling his circumstances with difficulty and feeling more oppressed than ever by his strange inner emptiness, Vladimir rose reluctantly, called the floor attendant, ordered him to fetch some soap and a toothbrush and to procure a towel from somewhere, and at the same time to bring a samovar and a loaf with some caviar. He began dressing.

Gradually the novelty of his position started to intrigue him. An hour later – sitting over a cup of tea, nibbling the hot loaf and reading the handbill he had been given, which announced that on that very evening in the town park Mr A. Chekhov's comedy *The Bear* would be performed by amateur actors in aid of the fire brigade fund for the acquisition of a motorized hydrant, and that Madame N. I. would sing – he was already feeling purged, to some degree, of his Moscow *ennui*.

He found the town square to be a little dirtier than desirable, whereas the fire station tower he judged to be built in an authentic Nicholas I style. But the two high school girls in white stockings and kid half-boots were delightfully fresh and entertaining. After sitting for half an hour at the lemonade stand in the pavilion of the town park, which was completely cloaked in dust, but which gave a splendid panorama of the river, Vladimir had learned all the town gossip from the buxom lady who dispensed lemonade. Acting on her practical suggestion, he went off to inspect the town.

He walked through the Pyatnitskiye Gates, from which Prince Grigory Volkhonsky once denounced the hetman Sagaydachny; he visited the Church of the Resurrection; he was already beginning to yawn, but he recovered remarkably on noticing the slender nuns of the Brusenetsky Convent. Soon, however, his aimless *flânerie* was interrupted by a youthful stranger in yellow ankle-boots, an orange dress clinging tightly to her slim waist, and a green hat with a feather. Weighed down with shopping, warding off the sun's rays with a red parasol, she dropped an elongated parcel and struggled to lift it without dropping the others. Vladimir hurried to her aid and, after accepting her thanks and a decisive refusal of his offer to accompany her further, he followed her at a respectful distance all the way to a little wooden house with a terrace, twined with ivy, windows hung with muslin drapes, and charming geraniums in pots on the wooden benches beneath the windows.

From the shopkeeper opposite he learned that her name was Yevgeniya Nikolayevna Klirikova, that she was married to a veterinary surgeon, and that she played the guitar and sang Ukrainian songs.

The clock struck three. It was time to return to the hotel for the meal he had ordered: sturgeon soup and goose with cabbage.

Thoughts of the sentimental romance he had begun with the veterinarian's wife preoccupied Vladimir as he made his way through the town's already well-known streets.

Suddenly he stopped as if nailed to the ground. The familiar sensation of the imminence of a grand passion shook his entire being. In front of him was the 'Grand Moscow Hair Salon of Master Tyutin', and through the dusky pane of its large window a red-haired wax mannequin was observing him.

4 The Wax Mannequin

> Those born under the sign of Pisces must
> beware of a red-headed woman.
>
> *A horoscope*

It was an extraordinary wax mannequin.

Thick, snake-like locks of reddish, almost bronze-coloured hair framed a pale face tinted pale green opal, with flaming cheeks and scarlet lips, dominated by enormous black eyes. In spite of the somewhat crude craftsmanship, the mannequin radiated the impression of a portrait drawn from life. It was quite clear that this wax sculpture had had a living original, an astonishing, miraculous original.

All of Vladimir's yearning for the ultimate feminine, of which all the women he had known were simply distant approximations, was outlined in that face. Kolomna, Madame Klirikova, the nuns of the Brusenetsky Convent and the sturgeon broth at the hotel, all were forgotten in a single instant.

Akim Ipatovich Tyutin, an already elderly craftsman who had once worked on the Arbat under Rulier, where he had mastered the coiffeur's complex art, enthusiastically agreed to sell his advertising mannequin for the five hundred roubles he was offered for the cheaply acquired thing. He also related everything he knew about the origins of the wax sculpture. A month and a half before, a large panopticon called 'The Worldwide Panorama' had arrived in Kolomna, where, besides an officer expiring on a battlefield, Cleopatra the Lion's Bride and the famous murderer Jack the Ripper, a pair of famous Siamese twin sisters had been displayed: Tyutin could not recall their family name.

The mannequin that had caught Vladimir's eye was one of these sisters, and this was how it had come to stand in the window of the 'Grand Moscow Hair Salon'.

Joseph Chantrain, a lean-limbed Belgian, the owner of the panopticon, had boarded at Tyutin's. The panopticon business, at first prosperous, was declining. Chantrain, having reaped plentiful profits, had failed to move on in time from Kolomna. He was delayed by some sort of romantic entanglement and became mired in debt. Interest in the panopticon dwindled to nothing, casual viewers paid only pennies, and finally the unfortunate Belgian was forced to liquidate his business by selling several of his figures.

Cleopatra was purchased for a healthy sum to decorate the living room of a recently wealthy ship-owner, Mr K., while Tyutin, going halves with his son-in-law, who kept a hairdressing salon in Serpukhov, acquired both twins in exchange for settling Chantrain's debts. They separated the sisters with a fretsaw and placed them in the windows of their establishments.

According to Akim Ipatovich, Chantrain had left Kolomna for Moscow with all his remaining worldly goods.

On the evening of that same day, having made the best of the inevitable goose with lingonberry sauce, Vladimir cautiously boxed up the wax reproduction of the woman who had impressed him so deeply, wedging it on all sides with rolled-up newspapers and pages torn from his unfinished copy of Mr Lazhechnikov's *The Ice House*.

Just before the train left, Madame Klirikova's orange dress and red sunshade sparkled on the platform among the throng of strollers and cottage dwellers. Vladimir recalled his sweet sentimental Kolomna romance and blew her a kiss as the train pulled away, making a disagreeable impression on the local cooperative's lecturer in accountancy, Sakharov, who had more right to consider Madame Klirikova a close friend than did the Moscow architect.

5 The Search Begins

> At that very moment Amenophis
> was sailing to Cyprus.
>   MADAME DE FONTAINE

It cost Vladimir M., refreshed in spirit and revived in body, no little time and effort to search out Chantrain.

His manservant, Grigory, managed to travel to Serpukhov twice and purchase the second red-haired mannequin from Tyutin's enterprising son-in-law Korolkov for the sum of one and a half thousand roubles. The Serpukhov hairdresser, forewarned by Tyutin, thought that his father-in-law had sold too cheaply and demanded a 'real' price, never suspecting, of course, that M. would have paid five or six thousand roubles for the wax mannequin that he desperately sought. The head from Serpukhov, somewhat damaged by Korolkov, who had fitted earrings in its ears, was even more beautiful than the first. But it had less of that feminine essence which had so impressed Vladimir in Kolomna.

The search for Chantrain, for which he hired several agents, made slow progress.

The register listed him as having left Kolomna, the police had a bill for him from the Moscow merchant Shablykin, and at the Trade Union of Artists of the Variety Theatre and Circus, Vladimir was shown two counterfoils from a receipt book, showing that Chantrain had paid his membership fees scrupulously for two years; he was also told that three years before, Chantrain had worked as a sword-swallower for the ringmaster Nikitin. More than that no one was able to tell him.

Meanwhile, an irresistible emotion was growing in Vladimir's soul. He shut himself up in his room, where the two wax busts now stood close to the pot-bellied Alexandrine closet against the background of ancient French wallpaper. M.'s hand, directed by his passion, sketched over and over again the features of the face that had captivated him. His search continued.

He had already begun to lose hope when he had the ingenious notion of advertising in the newspapers.

Within three days he had paid five visitors a hundred roubles each to show him where Chantrain was to be found. On the fifth day the river-boat *Glinka* brought him to Korcheva, where the white tents of Chantrain's panopticon were shining on the high bank of the Volga.

6 The 'Worldwide Panorama' Panopticon

> 'I'm no madam, and I'll let you have it.'
> *Provincial conversation*

The elderly lady selling tickets explained that the owner was not to be found in the panopticon, and for a rouble she sold Vladimir an orange ticket conferring right of entry to the 'Physiological Hall', where 'ladies were allowed separately between 2 and 3 pm daily'.

To kill time while he waited, Vladimir occupied himself in examining the figures on display. Although he thought he had sampled every experience in the world, he had never chanced to enter a panopticon, and he looked at the crude figures with the curiosity always aroused by novelty.

He was struck by 'Julia Pastrana, born in 1842, who lived all her days covered in hair like a beast', the 'Seated Venus,' and a long row of wax figures of pale eminences, beginning with Jack the Ripper and finishing with Bismarck and President Félix Faure. He dropped a small coin into a slot and thus forced a mournful suicide to see in a mirror the glowing image of his unfaithful fiancée.

A sharp young lad informed him that the 'Siege of Verdun' was damaged, but that the 'Parisienne's Toilette' and the 'Crocodile Hunt' were working. Sacrificing another small coin and turning the handle of the stereo-cinematograph, Vladimir, to his shame, observed within himself a certain interest in each of these nonsensical displays. In order to crush this interest, he returned to the ticket-seller to enquire when Mr Joseph Chantrain would return.

The elderly lady, hearing her employer's name from a stranger, grew more and more embarrassed and told him uncertainly that

Mr Chantrain had left for an unknown destination without saying when he would return. It was plain from her tone that she was lying, and that the Belgian, unnerved by the newspaper notices about him (and having, no doubt, numerous grounds to fear Madame Nemesis), was simply hiding. However, it was clearly impossible to extract the truth from this slow-witted old lady.

He was forced to resort to devious methods, enquiring of the locals where the mannequins' owner lived, bursting into the house where the latter lodged, and once again coming face to face with Madame Sukhozadova, the ticket-seller for the panopticon.

Pelageya Ivanovna was the widow of Mr Sukhozadov, a Korcheva businessman, and she lived in a very modest house on Kalyazinskaya Street, bequeathed to her by her late husband. She supported herself by making preserves, for which purpose she maintained a long-standing subscription to the *Russian Gazette*, as in her view the paper used by this publication was the best of its kind for sealing jam-jars.

Vladimir M. sat in the spacious room with its icon of the Virgin by a Palekh craftsman, decorated with wreaths of paper flowers. Rugs lay on the cleanly mopped, painted floor, and the bed was covered by a patchwork blanket. He inhaled the scent of the rosemary and jasmine houseplants ranged on the windowsills as he determinedly persuaded Pelageya Ivanovna that he certainly wasn't Shablykin, nor was he any other merchant or an enemy of Monsieur Joseph; he was simply an artist wishing to purchase the marvellous statue of 'Mary Stuart, the Unhappy Queen of Scotland, upon the Scaffold' which embellished his panopticon.

After two hours of persuasion and the exchange of several documents bearing the signature of the president of the national bank, Pelageya Ivanovna finally agreed, with a sigh, to 'try' to pass Mr Joseph a letter from Mr Artist.

That evening Chantrain called at the room in the squalid hotel where M. was staying, which stank of cabbage soup and beer and where billiard balls rattled constantly, accompanied by the crude jokes of the players.

The Belgian was unable to tell him anything relevant, apart from the address of the factory in Heidelberg where he had bought a set of their latest mannequins. For fifty roubles he sold a receipt from the firm of Papengut and Son, Heidelberg, to the effect that three hundred marks was the price paid for the model of the twins.

Later that evening, on the poop-deck of the *Mussorgsky*, Vladimir treated himself and the writer Sh., whom he happened to meet, to champagne and felt happier than he had ever been in his life. He had found a lead.

7   Departure

> For the sweet memory of days long-past
> I can find no lament or tears.
> ALEXANDER PUSHKIN

On the twelfth of October, on the platform of the Alexandrovsky Station, a small group of friends privy to the secret of the Moscow Casanova's new infatuation saw Vladimir off on the Northern Express.

His manservant Grigory had brought, besides his toilet cases, bags and two wheeled suitcases, a carefully packed box containing the two waxen beauties. A few minutes before the train left, a panting boy from Noyev the florist handed over a bouquet wrapped in paper and a note, with an urgent request not to unseal the latter until the train had departed.

In verse and prose, his friends wished Vladimir success in pouring hot blood into those wax veins; night was already settling over Moscow as the train pulled slowly away, leaving behind Khodynka, Presnya, Dorogomilova and Fili ...

After walking down the carpeted corridor of the international coach to his compartment, Vladimir opened the mysterious parcel. Dried roses spilled out on the cushions of his couch – the same roses which he had sent to the only woman who had offered herself to him and been rejected, on that memorable evening when the mysterious impulse had sent him to Kolomna.

He smiled, chose one of the flowers, and tossed the others out of the window. He took his seat and gazed into the ever-receding distance. When the train reached Mozhaysk, he strolled up and down the platform twice, ordered a glass of coffee in his berth, and then lay down to sleep.

8 The Secret Becomes a Little Clearer

> A secret is like a lock to which the key has been lost.
> EDGAR ALLAN POE

The managing director of the firm of Papengut and Son, Heidelberg turned out to be a portly German of about forty-five, whose manner was extremely pompous and condescending. Vladimir was forced to listen to a host of maxims about the significance of wax; about Leonardo da Vinci's *Flora*, which was in the Kaiser Friedrich Museum in Berlin and represented on the watermark of the Papengut firm; about the educational value of panopticons (so undervalued by the governments of Europe); and only after much more in this vein was he told that, to judge by the transaction receipt, Joseph Chantrain had been sold damaged goods, which had not been itemized in the bill; and that to establish any further details he would have to produce the actual sculpture. This concluded the interview; the next morning a fast-moving motor taxi, rumbling over the gravel avenue, brought Vladimir with his precious box up to the factory gates of Papengut and Son of Heidelberg.

Released from their wrappings, the bronze locks of the red-headed Gorgons – or Medusae – shone in the sun, and their searching gaze once again pierced the Moscow architect's soul to its depths.

Silence reigned around them. It was as if the director was himself astounded by the products of his own factory. He rang a bell and ordered the servant who responded to call Mr Pings, the head of the assembly department.

'Are these the same ones, Mr Pings?' the director asked the lean American who entered.

'The very same, boss, no doubt about it,' Pings replied, opening the order book, which the director passed to Vladimir.

'These are the Henrickson sisters, twins from Rotterdam, eighteen years old, who were displayed in a host of circuses in the Old and New Worlds. In Paris at the Cirque de Paris; in London at the Piccadilly Music Hall; in Heidelberg they modelled for the sculptor Van Hoote.'

The director let Vladimir copy this record into his jotter and added, shutting the book:

'Thanks to this sculpture, we lost one of our best craftsmen. When we heard about this marvel and when their manager, who was then in Heidelberg, offered our firm exclusive copyright for two thousand marks, we, appreciating the extraordinariness of the phenomenon, agreed to pay the named sum and sent our best craftsman – Van Hoote – to make the initial sketch. However, the unfortunate Dutchman, lacking moderation of temperament, abandoned himself to an unnatural passion for one of the Henrickson sisters, and after finishing the sculpture, he hanged himself.'

As Vladimir came downstairs from the offices of Papengut and Son his head was whirling.

9 In Search of the Red-Headed Aphrodite

> My heart beat faster.
> NIKOLAY KARAMZIN

Neither the meagre directions from the offices of Papengut and Son, Heidelberg nor any other source yielded Vladimir more precise information about the Henrickson Sisters or their subsequent fate.

It was known that after Van Hoote's tragic death they had hastily quitted Heidelberg, that they had made two appearances in Schultz's Circus in Mainz, and that was all ... later the thread was lost, and it seemed more than likely that the sisters had left Germany or changed their stage names.

Notices placed in the world's most widely distributed newspapers produced no results, despite the size of the rewards offered for any information on the twin sisters' whereabouts.

Three international clippings bureaux dissected thousands of newspapers and theatrical notices in twenty-seven of the world's most important languages, tearing out any news about theatrical spectacles, but they failed to come up with a single line on the subject of the Henrickson Sisters.

It was true that the name Henrickson was common in circus notices, but generally as the stage name of tiger-tamers; not once did the patient scissors of the clippings ladies encounter a mention of the mysterious sisters. The clippings from old newspapers contained no small amount of material, but it all amounted to the same sort of thing. Vladimir was able to trace the entire course of the sisters' career. Their name first appeared on the 15th of May 19— on the billing of a *café chantant* in the small Belgian resort of Spa, hidden in the hills of the Ardennes, and famous for its health-giving dullness, its waters, its games of *petits chevaux* and its 'Spa liqueur'.

Later, the sisters appeared in Liège and Namur; after this they were 'discovered' by the talented entrepreneur Gauchecorps, and the name of the Henrickson Sisters had prominent billing on the programmes of the Piccadilly Music Hall, Parisian circuses and in variety theatres in the largest cities of the Old and New Worlds; they even appeared on the stage of the Solomonsky Circus in Moscow, but after their performance in Mainz they disappeared without a trace. No comparable performers had appeared on the circus arena in the intervening three years, and many people suggested that the sisters, as a result of some unfortunate coincidence of circumstances, had stopped working with respectable impresarios and become obliged to perform in the sort of third-class circuses and panopticons that didn't advertise with posters or in the papers.

Disappointed with his search, Vladimir handed over the rest of the work to a firm called 'Achievement', which ran a Parisian office for 'Inquiries of Any Type'. He took to searching all the cities of Europe, big and small, at random, trusting in his luck and hoping to find some trace of the vanished sisters.

He became a constant visitor to circuses and panopticons he would never have even glanced inside before. He watched for hours as different acts succeeded each other on the sandy floors of arenas: a Negress skimpily dressed in green silk, who accompanied her rope-dance with screeches; a trick-cyclist executing loops; a lady rider who leaped with crazy *salto-mortales* over galloping horses; the foolish mime artists and the quick-witted clowns; the wonderful Pichel and the eye-catching Montégrioux. He learned to tell a gifted acrobat from a talentless one; he began to understand the perfection of the sustained circus style and the subtle compositional art of circus programmes. He grew fond of the age-old circus traditions and disliked any signs of modernism in the big top.

He made the acquaintance of outstanding artistes of the arena, and circus managers; he met many people who had actually seen the Henrickson Sisters, who confirmed their beauty and the accuracy of the wax busts, which always accompanied M. on his travels. However, none of them could add even one new detail to the facts that he had already collected.

On just one occasion, in Antwerp, he was dazzled by the smile of a mysterious stranger.

Her horse's white rump had just flashed past the blinding brilliance of the electric lamps, and Mademoiselle Montégrioux was taking a bow and bestowing farewell kisses to left and right, when a red-haired girl, swamped in green frills, ran out onto the arena and began to ripple her way through the complex 'Serpent-Woman' routine. She contorted her body like a huge flower on a turquoise carpet, flung down like a stain on the red sand of the arena.

Vladimir's heart beat faster, so great was the resemblance between the performer and the wax figures; but a thorough examination through his opera glasses established that the features were different. Most tellingly, her eyes were blue.

'Pretty, very pretty,' Vladimir's neighbour, an elderly colonel, commented aloud, 'but all the same, a long way off Kitty Henrickson!'

It is hardly necessary to relate how eagerly Vladimir began to ask the colonel which Kitty Henrickson he meant, or how wildly happy he felt to meet an admirer of his sisters.

Almost all night long they sat in front of the wax mannequins in a comfortable room at the Hotel Bible, and Vladimir listened in ecstasy to the colonel's long tales about the mysterious Kitty and the cheerful Berthe Henrickson, such intelligent and cultured girls; and in spite of their disfigurement, such different individuals and so fond of one another. The colonel, who had not seen them for four years, judged them to be either dead or surgically separated, beginning a new life on money earned from their deformity.

They parted before dawn, and for all of that happy night Vladimir never closed his eyes.

10 Misfortune

> What a delight to flee in a speeding carriage
> From the lunacies of the North to Goldoni's homeland ...
> M. KUZMIN

Six months went by. Vladimir had made no progress in his search. His heavy spending had depleted his resources, and his friends warned him by letter to abandon his mad obsession and return to Moscow, where he would find many novelties and many new people.

He had grown thinner and older; once again, as he strolled through the alleys of the Prater Park, he felt his former Moscow sorrow; he gazed sadly around and, with characteristic decisiveness, forcibly put aside his passion and decided to take a month's rest in Venice before returning home. He would look at Giorgione, Titian, Palma il Vecchio, portraits by Moretto and ceilings by Tiepolo, feed the pigeons on St Mark's Square, and recall the far-off days of his first love, discovered in the torrid glow of the Venetian sun.

11 A Meeting in Venice

> You are the reader, not the writer, of your life;
> You have no notion how the tale will end.
> M. KUZMIN

After a delay in the snows near Pontebba, the Vienna express did not reach the rice fields of the Marcito, watered by the turbid stream of the Po, before sunset. Only after midnight did it arrive at the platform of Venice station.

The two American steam engines were puffing heavily, their great metal bodies shuddering and exhaling steam. Travellers bustled around, collecting their cases; porters moved about briskly and calmly. Hotel agents yelled the names of their establishments: 'Palace Hotel!' 'Majestic!' 'Albi!' 'Savoy Hotel!' . . .

Vladimir was determined to stay in the same hotel where, twenty years before, he had brought Valentina directly from Yuletide Moscow. She had been wrapped in a winter fur that still seemed to be powdered with snowflakes from Petrovsky Park, where they had gone skating before their train left. No matter how hard he tried, he could not remember the name of their hotel until a livery and a peaked cap with the inscription 'Hotel Livorno' flashed in front of his eyes. No doubt remained: it had been the Hotel Livorno, and the room was No. 24.

A moment later, a gondola was carrying him over the black waters of the canals of that great city of masks, ghostly mirrors, silent doges, Goldoni's heroes, Gozzi's characters, and the great Venetian painters.

It was a gloomy night: his small room seemed all the more cosy for a downy quilt, a pitcher of water, an enormous bed, an ancient Venetian mirror and a cup of hot chocolate before he climbed between the soft sheets. Despite the flurry of suddenly revived memories, tiredness claimed its due, and after barely managing to swallow the hot drink, Vladimir closed his exhausted eyes. It was already late when he woke . . . Somewhere doves were cooing; the plashing of water in the canal, the cries of gondoliers, and the shouts of street traders reached his ears. Brilliant glints of sunshine soaked through the closed blinds and swam with pleasant languor across the floor, filling the whole room with a sunny haze. Vladimir stretched blissfully, disentangled the blanket, placed his feet on the carpet, and quickly walked to the window and raised the blinds.

A scorching Venetian midday confronted him, and he almost exclaimed with astonishment. On the opposite side of the canal was an enormous booth, flaunting a huge gold-painted sign: 'The American Panopticon! All new! A miracle of nature! All new! An astonishing phenomenon! The Henrickson Sisters!'

12   The Henrickson Sisters

> At this point the whole theatre was lit up
> by chandeliers, and the audience clapped
> to show their appreciation.
>
> KARAMZIN

As Vladimir approached the colourfully painted entrance of the American Panopticon, he could no longer entertain any doubts. On a huge white placard the heads of two strikingly beautiful women had been drawn in bright colours; their features were well known to him.

A lively crowd was surging around the ticket office. Women in black lace mantles, soldiers in pale blue dress uniforms, soldiers in black, Bersaglieri, little boys, two Russian tourists (evidently schoolteachers from Yelabuga, visiting the panopticon in search of strong sensations), two or three workers with extremely long scarves wrapped around their necks, a German family, and other typical characters from the Venetian crowd.

On a wide platform two Scaramouches were beating a drum, and a red-cheeked Columbine was making eyes at a dashing officer.

The performance was in full swing when Vladimir entered the overcrowded auditorium. A Chinese magician, who had just produced twelve plates of hot macaroni and several bottles of Dolce Spumante from an empty drum, now filled two glass dishes with water, lashed them together with a rope and, with a wide backswing, launched them whirling around himself in circles, accompanying their whistling flight with a guttural cry.

Vladimir felt his heart beat faster; that familiar sensation of passionate turmoil, similar to what he had experienced in Kolomna with his first glimpse of the wax mannequin, suffused his entire being.

The Henrickson Sisters were named in the programme

directly after the Chinaman Ti Fan-tai. In a state of voluptuous inertia, tainted with secret dread, Vladimir waited for the end of the Chinaman's ingenious performance.

The Chinaman, catching the shining dishes one after another on the ends of thin bamboo canes, set them spinning rapidly, controlling their trembling flight with a dozen or so canes. The steady whirling of the bowls, underscored by rumbling chords from the crude orchestra, compelled Vladimir to shut his eyes to stave off vertigo.

A burst of applause recalled him to himself. The Chinaman finished and left the stage, pressing both hands to his breast.

Silent lackeys collected his belongings and placed on the stage an Egyptian-style double throne; then they blocked it from view with screens painted with ibises, sphinxes and columns covered in hieroglyphics. Behind the screens steps were heard, and a small Arab boy emerged from the side in an enormous white turban and turquoise harem pants; meaningfully, he put his finger to his lips. 'Ssssh ... ssssh,' was heard on all sides, and little by little, silence descended. The notes of stringed instruments issued from behind the screens, and the Arab boy swiftly drew back the panels.

Vladimir, digging his hands into the armrests of his seat, felt his pulse speed up and a cold sweat break out on his forehead. Before his eyes appeared two almost nude bodies, barely clothed by the breastplates and belts of Egyptian dancing girls. Familiar serpentine coils of bronze hair fell low over the luxuriant curves of their pale-green opal bodies: Berthe's black eyes melted his soul, and her red mouth was wreathed with a sensual smile.

He did not see what the sisters actually performed; he no longer even knew where he was; all the fantasies of his wildest imagination, his most daring speculations, were being exceeded by the reality.

Those thick snakes of reddish, almost bronze-coloured hair framed a pale face with a greenish cast, a burning flush and scarlet lips; the entire composition was unified by the black eyes; the lines of the shoulders, hips and belly flowed together like the curves of Botticelli's wonderful Venus. All Vladimir's dreams of the ultimate feminine, to which every woman he had previously known was merely a distant approximation, seemed fulfilled in that body.

The little Arab boy pushed the screens together. The sisters disappeared. The crowd protested furiously.

Vladimir rose and stared in surprise at the shouting people.

'Why are all these ugly fools here? Get out of here! Clear off!' he wanted to shout, but he restrained himself and, almost staggering, made his way to the exit.

13   The Red-Headed Aphrodite

> On the couch lay a corset, proof of the slenderness of her waist, a cap with rose-coloured ribbons, and a tortoiseshell comb.
>
> KARAMZIN

On the evening of the same day Stanislav Podgursky, the panopticon's owner, an Austrian Pole originally from Zakopane, introduced Vladimir to the Henrickson Sisters.

The Dutch ladies spoke very correct German. They behaved graciously and were extremely modestly clothed in a white spotted dress. On the walls of their room hung a faded photograph of a family group and a masterfully executed oil portrait in the style of Anders Zorn. A copper coffee-pot gleamed dully on the table.

At first the conversation dragged. Vladimir preferred to gaze at them rather than explain his story. However, one had to find something to say. Soon Berthe's husky contralto drew him into animated chatter about famous circus personalities.

Berthe was the original of the wax reproduction that had struck Vladimir so forcefully in Kolomna: she was a little thinner than her sister, who was a typical German beauty. Her face was possibly less beautiful than Kitty's calm, classical features. But some piquancy, some wordless secret enriched her entire being. It was as though everything she said barely interested her; her conversation was inauthentic, an act undertaken only as a courtesy to her interlocutor.

Her assumed liveliness was cold, and her large eyes often

misted over with a dull, leaden sheen. It seemed that somewhere inside her, beyond the gaze of any interlocutor, she pursued a different life, engrossing and profound. However, none of this prevented her from being an entertaining conversationalist, and the beauty spot on her neck told louder than any words what a fine woman good-hearted Kitty's sister was.

Vladimir, at first embarrassed by the twins' unnatural closeness, soon ceased to notice it as he regaled them with the story of his search. The sisters were surprised by his intense interest in their lives. They parted in the friendliest manner. As he left, Vladimir learned that the portrait on the wall, after Zorn, depicted the sculptor Van Hoote.

14   Summer Lightning

> Beneath a purple canopy
> A bed all golden gleams.
> ALEXANDER PUSHKIN

All night long Vladimir was oppressed by nightmares. He suffocated in the serpentine embrace of bronze-coloured braids. Damp water-nymph hands encircled his burning neck, and harsh, drunken kisses sank into his body, leaving traces like the bites of vampire fangs.

In the morning he brought the sisters a bouquet of magnolias and found them smiling and talking gaily over their morning coffee. They asked him to stay longer. In the evening he took them for a gondola ride along the Grand Canal. The next day he visited them again, to Podgursky's visible disquiet.

Berthe's husky voice and her childish little songs enslaved him wholly and forever. They were the only reality that existed for him: everything else dissolved into a haze. He rifled antiquaries' stalls in order to decorate that green-tinted body with necklaces and to plait precious cinquecento jewels into those bronze braids.

The unnatural link between the sisters, and Kitty's necessarily constant presence, at first embarrassed him. But as soon as his experienced heart sensed how the wild passion smouldering in his beloved's soul had kindled, he forgot about Kitty. The storms of his desire seemed to subdue both sisters. And only once, when he forgot himself and kissed Berthe's bared knee, did his eyes meet Kitty's horrified gaze. But that was only for an instant. Soon the entire world was drowned in a heaving ocean of passion.

15 Disaster

> Her eager tongue contended with my kisses;
> Her wanton thigh beneath my thigh she thrust ...
>
> OVID

....
....
....
....

16 Kitty's Notes

> A broken mirror means death.
>
> *Omen*

September 1st. Venice
Berthe is dozing.

I will use these moments to tell the monstrous tale of our life. I never thought I should become a writer, but the events overtaking me are so strange, the breath of Death surrounds us on every side, and the fateful culmination must be nearing. May these pages serve as the testament of poor Kitty Van Hoote, one of the unhappy Henrickson Sisters of the circus ring.

My sister Berthe and I were born twins conjoined at the hip, to a prosperous merchant family, the Van Hootes, in Rotterdam.

My mother's labour was very difficult and our father, wishing to conceal our freakishness and planning subsequently to separate us surgically, sent us away to a cousin of our mother.

But the surgeons refused to operate, claiming that it would risk killing one of us. Our mother did not recover from our birth, and soon afterwards, she died. Our father, not wishing to become a figure of fun in the eyes of his clients and his stockbroker friends, had us educated very thoroughly, never once, however, visiting to see how we were.

He soon married a second time and died from a chance outbreak of plague, carried with a cargo of spices from the island of Java by one of his company's steamers. His widow, who bore a son after her husband's death, knew nothing, or almost nothing, of our existence. Our father's solicitor sent our aunt a small sum of money, which had been bequeathed towards our education. However, within a few years even this meagre source of support was exhausted. We were already preparing to learn the horrors of poverty when the owner of a travelling circus invited us to join the performers in his troupe, and use our deformity to earn our daily bread. After a momentary hesitation caused by our aunt's tearful dissuasion, we, then mere thirteen-year-old girls, agreed. Within a week we were appearing under the name 'The Henrickson Sisters' on the boards of a *café chantant* in Spa.

I shall not describe our life in the circus, monotonous and wearisomely dull as it was, especially for us, confined by our deformity to a life behind closed doors.

However, we didn't grumble. We were always able, despite our nomadic life, to construct a warm and snug family haven in our rooms, to find a few devoted friends. I still remember the colonel in Antwerp who was so tender to me and who anticipated our needs so attentively.

We had never known a father's care, but he often seemed like a father to me. I have heard that even afterwards he referred to us in the warmest terms. Where is he now, that kind old Colonel Wautar? Sometimes we were driven in a carriage around the towns that our troupe was visiting. On rare occasions we went to the theatre, concealing ourselves in the depths of our box after the curtain had risen and leaving before the performance was over.

We were earning a great deal and hoped, once we had saved a few tens of thousands of francs, to leave the ring forever and live out our lives quietly, far from other people. Then suddenly, while we were on tour in Heidelberg, tragedy overshadowed us for the first time. Our ringmaster persuaded us to offer, for a very large sum, the right to reproduce the image of 'the phenomenal Henrickson Sisters' to a Heidelberg firm that made wax mannequins ... I have forgotten what it was called.

Two days later we were introduced to a young sculptor, who began making wax models of us with great skill and delicacy.

To our misfortune, Berthe took a great shine to him, and my sister's sweet songs ultimately drove the young man out of his mind. The artist's unnatural passion for the beautiful freak blazed like a bonfire on St John's Eve. The feverish glitter in my sister's eyes, her heightened pulse, revealed her as a new creature, who was a stranger to me. A deep gloom clouded the artist's eyes.

The storm grew closer.

The tragedy was played out ...

Berthe is stirring. I must stop.

September 3rd. Venice

I will go on. The tragic outcome turned out to be closer and more terrible than we could have guessed.

One evening, when the atmosphere of passion surrounding us had grown so dense that I felt almost ready to seize the axe belonging to Germain, the circus carpenter, to sever the fateful link between my sister and myself, and fling myself out of a window – the artist, whom we knew as plain Mr Prosper, told us his full name, Prosper Van Hoote.

I could not restrain a shriek. Two questions were sufficient to remove any doubts. At our feet lay our father's son, our own younger brother. Like a madman he leaped to his feet and, his head in his hands, rushed out through the door.

The following morning we learned that he had hanged himself.

My sister succumbed to a nervous fever. After her recovery, we were contractually obliged to appear twice more on stage in some little German town. Then we left first for Ghent and then for Bruges, relying on our accumulated savings to live a few years of peaceful, cloistered existence.

The melancholy ringing of the bells of Bruges, the silence of the almost deserted streets, and the black swans on the dark green water of the canals provided a healing balm for us.

For the first few months, we spent whole days by our window. I re-read books, and Berthe looked with crazed eyes at the slowly floating swans, repeating hundreds of times a quatrain that Prosper had once written:

> A black swan sails on a green wave,
> > And the fronds of magnolia sway.
> I remember we used to meet, you and I,
> > But when I cannot say.

Thus a year or two went by, unnoticed ... Berthe's eyes began to smile again, she took up sewing and more than once placed her slender fingers on the strings of her lute. In the third year our savings began to run out, and the time came for us to consider 'work'. We wrote a letter to a certain old friend. Within a week a man in a round hat came to see us. He turned out to be the impresario Podgursky, who was preparing a tour of the ports of the Mediterranean Sea. Berthe was intrigued. We signed a very favourable contract. With the Panopticon we went to Heliopolis and Alexandria, visited Algiers, passed two months in Barcelona, and wintered in Palermo, until our fateful destiny brought us to Venice.

September 10th. Venice

I will continue. On the third morning of our Venetian tour, while she was combing her luxurious bronze tresses, Berthe dropped and smashed a round looking-glass ... We gazed at each other in horror. Of all unfortunate omens, this was the surest. And on the evening of that day Podgursky brought to see us an architect from Moscow, Voldemar M., who had already long sought to make our acquaintance.

Pale, with a short Assyrian beard, he gave the impression of being a man who had sold his soul to the devil, and his voice, like that of all German-speaking Russians, was melodious and somehow reminded me of the sweet Malaga wine we had drunk in Barcelona.

How clearly I remember that accursed evening and night, when Berthe's heart beat with a new rhythm, just as in those well-remembered Heidelberg days.

It was as though Prosper's spirit had been reborn in this Northern man, as if the secret power of our late unfortunate brother over Berthe's soul had been granted by someone to this pale man with feline manners. My words and my warnings were in vain, vain were my sleepless nights and the shared tears that soaked our single pillow, as vain as Berthe's oaths, sworn at sunrise.

Passion blazed, its fierce torrent swept everything away, and even I, chained by our deformity to my sister, was somehow strangely transported by its waves. His words, his smiles, his touches, like molten metal, branded the stigmata of passion on our souls. And then once, as I sank my teeth into the pillow in a maddened frenzy, Berthe gave herself to him.

He fled from us in the dark of the night. My sister spent three days struck dumb as a stone. Then she recovered herself. She chased him away. She summoned him to us again. He, as pale as death, lay for hours at her feet, then fled and disappeared for days. Months of frenzy and madness wore on ... We sensed that a new life had kindled under Berthe's heart. The circus had left long ago. Voldemar paid Podgursky a huge fee for us to break our contract.

September 21st. Venice
Berthe has spent a second night in delirium. The doctors fear a difficult labour. They talk about operating to separate us. Voldemar is pacing about like a madman. Berthe, when she is herself, sends him away. At night, delirious, she calls for Prosper.

September 23rd
Today I woke and screamed. Berthe wasn't beside me. My

right arm was completely free. The doctors say that Berthe had a little girl and that she is in a different ward.

September 29th

They finally told me everything. For the last week Berthe has no longer been among the living. When her labour began, they separated us. They feared that the septic infection which had begun would be fatal for me too. Dear God! Give me the strength to survive this.

September 30th. Venice

I am still so weak. Today they showed me my tiny pink niece. They say that when her pains began, Berthe sent Voldemar away and ordered him to leave the city.

I understood her outburst and asked the doctors, if Voldemar should return, to tell him that we had all died – Berthe, myself, and little Jeannette. When I recover, we will go far, far away, and no-one will ever tell Jeannette about the strange shadows surrounding her birth.

17 Madness

> Agronomic help for the population was perhaps more necessary in Italy than in in any other country.
>
> A. CHUPROV

Vladimir M., in fulfilment of Berthe's deathbed command, practically tottering with exhaustion, his eyes burning insanely, found his way to the station and got into the first train to depart, which bore him away to some unknown destination.

This train seemed to him unusual. There were no foreigners on it. Stocky, sturdy tillers of the soil laughed and chatted loudly about superphosphates and Randall's disc harrows, complained about their agronomist, referred respectfully to men called Bizzozero, Luzzatti and Poggio, and swore loudly, spitting on the floor, about a breed of horned cattle, which they called the *bergamasco*.

The train stopped in Piacenza, the agricultural centre of the Italian north. This was an unknown Italy: the stuff of the real nation, which no foreigner ever sees. Italians like to dream of a 'third Rome'. If the first was the Rome of antiquity and the second the Rome of the Popes, the third Rome will be a Rome of cooperative farms, perfected agriculture and the nationalized industry of Italian democracy.[4]

However, Vladimir M. had nothing to do with any of this, and he wandered gloomily through Piacenza and through the agricultural show, looking at fat, overfed bulls, running his eyes over the colourful farm placards and listening absently to the fiery speeches made by a priest about the advantages of English drainage for the eternally green Marcito.

Tiring of the dull, monotonous spectacle of agricultural labour and peasant culture, Vladimir moved on to Pavia and found nearby a small Carthusian monastery where liquor was distilled. The luxurious baroque chapels, the light and slender colonnades of the monastery courts and the sweet-smelling rose gardens offered him a chance to gather his thoughts.

Rationality returned to his vague gaze, and four days later he found within himself the strength to return to Venice. He listened passively to the news of the deaths of the sisters and of his daughter. Immediately he grew hunched and aged; he left for the station, lacking the strength to remain in the city which had entombed his happiness.

When a black gondola bore him down the narrow canals, twilight was falling. The lively nightlife of Venice was already seething and ringing.

18 In Moscow Once Again

> At the end of May 1694, Madame de Sévigné made her last journey to Grignan.
> *Plutarch for Young Ladies*

The express train slowly made its way to the Moscow platforms. It passed the Gates of Triumph and the carriages with rubber wheels on Tverskoy Boulevard. Vladimir M. returned to his old apartment in an alley between the Arbat and Prechistenkaya.

Vladimir looked sadly at the mahogany chairs, at the Elizabethan divan, evocative of so many names and so many amorous conquests, now superfluous, at the Gobelins and the erotic drawings by the now-insane artist Vrubel, at the china and the Novgorod icons once purchased so delightedly; in a word, at all those objects which had once gladdened and quickened his existence.

His wealth, once considerable, was now reduced to bare essentials. He had to sell the erotic drawings, some of the furniture, the marvellous Novgorod Flora and Laura with their red-on-blue glazing, and the impressive footed cabinets.

Vladimir felt like a mannequin himself, a marionette dangled on a string by an unknown hand. His friends no longer recognized him. He led a private and solitary life. However, he did accept commissions, and this last stage of his creativity afforded Moscow several whimsical and unusual buildings.

19 Aphrodite's Ghost

> More than the living, you are carnal,
> You are voluptuous, brilliant shade!
> YEVGENY BARATYNSKY

More than a year went by. One day Vladimir was strolling along the paths of the Alexander Gardens. His indifferent gaze followed the springtime courting couples and the gymnasium students cramming for their examinations. He raised his head and stared at the crenellated line of the Kremlin walls lit by the setting sun, and he suddenly felt, with his entire being, the nearness of death.

With painful keenness he wished to breathe in, one last time, the warm rays of the Venetian sun, to hear the plash of oars on the night-time water of the canal. He mentally reckoned up his still-unpaid debts and, with a wave of his hand, decided to travel to Venice.

When the Vienna express, delayed as usual, descended on to

the Italian plain, entering the Marcito and the rice fields watered by the turbid stream of the Po, it was already evening, and only after midnight did they arrive at the platform of Venice station.

The two American locomotives were puffing heavily, their great metallic bodies shuddering; travellers bustled around, porters calmly dragged cases and valises to and fro. Hotel agents yelled the names of their establishments: 'Palace Hotel!' 'Majestic!' 'Albi!' 'Savoy Hotel!' Everything was hideously unchanged.

Vladimir stayed in room 24 of the Hotel Livorno.

It was already late when he woke ... Somewhere doves were cooing; the plashing of water in the canal, the cries of gondoliers, and the shouts of street traders reached his ears. It was all, terribly, just as before. Fate's sarcastic smile shone through everything.

Vladimir stepped onto the carpet and slowly went to the window, raised the blinds with a jerk, and shivered with horror. Before him, on the opposite bank of the canal, where the Panopticon had once stood, he saw the large window of a luxurious hairdressing salon. Staring at him, through the green glass of this window, were the wax busts of the Henrickson Sisters, forgotten during his flight from Venice.

The ill-omened mannequins glared into his devastated soul with their black eyes, the shadowy green opal of their bodies, and the red, almost bronze-coloured snakes of their hair.

Vladimir collapsed to the floor and, pressing his forehead against the marble sill, burst into tears.

20   *Sic transit gloria mundi*

In M.'s Moscow apartment thick layers of dust settled on the mahogany chair, the Elizabethan divan, the pot-bellied Alexandrine closets, and two volumes of Palladio lying forgotten on the divan.

An elderly rat finally gnawed into a drawer of the writing-table and began on a packet of letters. The narrow silk ribbon parted, and the letters, written in a woman's elegant hand, spilled across

the drawer. The rat took fright and fled.
    There is my tale, dear readers.

Barvikha, on the Moscow River.
August 1918

ALEKSANDR CHAYANOV

Venediktov
or, The Memorable Events of my Life

A Romantic Tale, as told by Botanist X

To a dream reborn

Chapter 1

Of late, Plutarch has become my favourite and indeed my only reading. I must admit that the deeds of the Attic heroes are a trifle monotonous, and the descriptions of innumerable battles have often wearied me. Nevertheless, a reader may find much unfading charm in those pages devoted to the noble Titus Flamininus, the passionate Alcibiades, the raging Pyrrhus, King of Epirus, and to a host of their peers. In contemplating the lives of the great, one cannot help reflecting on one's own existence, now guttering drearily like a candle, the best years long past. As one strolls of an evening along the sloping banks of the Moscow River, watching the cloud-shadows creep across the Lutskoye meadows while the Barvikha cattle rise lazily to their feet, as one observes the boughs of the apple trees bending under the weight of their fruit, one recalls the sweet fragrance of spring flowers on those same branches this past May.[1] At such times one feels keenly how everything flows along the pathways of life. One begins to surmise that not only great battles or the teachings of philosophers are meaningful, and that every insect alive under the sun has its own significance. Before God, our own lives are no less worthy of remembrance than the Battle of Salamis or the deeds of Julius Caesar.

After pondering thus for many years in my rural retreat, I have finally decided to follow the Boeotian's example[2] by telling the life story of an ordinary man, a Russian. Lacking information about anyone else's life and having no libraries at my disposal, I have chosen – perhaps immodestly – to describe the memorable events of my own life, hoping that many of them will not be without interest for my readers.

I was born in the days of Catherine the Great in our nation's original capital, Moscow, in the parish of the Church of the Annunciation in Sadovniki. I have no memory of my father, a Colonel of the Guards who accompanied Count Chernyshev in his famous raid on Berlin.[3] Widowed young, my mother raised me in great poverty, somewhere in the Tolmachi district. We spent our summers in Kuskovo or with our distant relatives, the Shubendorfs. One of these, Ivan Karlovich, managed a stud farm on Prince Golitsyn's estate of Vlakhernskaya near Moscow, also known as Kuzminki, which, however, the old prince himself liked to call plain 'The Mill'.[4]

After years of valiant effort (and not without help from friends and comrades of my late Papa), my mother succeeded in securing me a place at Moscow University's preparatory school for noble youth, a memory I bless to this day. Oh, my friends! How can I convey to you the emotion I felt then and still feel for Anton Antonovich, our father and benefactor? Lamiral taught me the rules of etiquette and of dancing, while the celebrated Sandunov directed our children's theatre.[5]

In 1804, decked out in a new blue uniform with a crimson collar and cuffs and gold buttons, I accepted the ceremonial sword from the hands of the Dean, proof that I was worthy to join the University. I will pass over my first year of student life. Shevyrev's wonderful history of the University has celebrated the brainchild of Shuvalov, Melissino and Kheraskov, and it is not for me to repeat his words. I note only that I had been working for half a year under Professor Bauze, studying the ancient Russian Slavs, when my life entered the phase of those remarkable events which would divert it forever from its former course.

In May 1805 I was returning from Kolomenskoye Park with Konstantin Kalaydovich, listening with half an ear to his inspired talk of the ancient town of the Kholops and the meaning of the Tmutarakan Stone.[6] I was paying rather more attention to the larks singing in the high, limpid spring sky. After entering the city and parting with my companion, I sank abruptly into an unusual oppression of soul. My spiritual freedom and mental clarity seemed to vanish irretrievably; a heavy hand might have been pressing on my brain, splintering the bony shield of my skull. I spent entire days prone on my couch, ordering Theognostus to brew me more and more punch. All my former interest in Slavic antiquities was snuffed out in my soul. Not once that entire summer did I call on Ferapont, the bibliophile, whom I had been in the habit of visiting regularly.

As I walked the streets of Moscow, visiting theatres and pastry-shops, I could sense, at large in the city, a palpable presence of terrible power. This feeling grew weaker and stronger by turns, until it reached an intensity that made cold sweat break out on my brow and my fingers tremble: I fancied someone was watching me, poised to seize my arm. This presentiment poisoned my life, strengthening day by day, until on the night of September 16th, it was terribly fulfilled, drawing me into a sequence of extraordinary events.

It was a Friday. I had spent the afternoon at my friend Tregubov's; after tightly shutting his doors and windows, he had shown me his copy of the *New Cyropaedia* and spoken mysteriously about the good deeds of the Moscow Martinists.[7] On my way home I felt the familiar intolerable oppression, intensifying to a physical burden as I was passing the Maddox Theatre.[8] Lamps illuminated the bulk of the theatre building; I fancied that the solution to the mystery tormenting me was concealed inside. A moment later I was walking through the masquerade rotunda leading to the auditorium.

Chapter 2

The performance had already begun when I stepped into the semi-darkness of the silent stalls. Chandeliers lit up the trembling shadows of al-Rashid's palace. Kolosova, obeying the thunder of the strings, sailed out, twirling in a dark crimson cape.[9] Kolosova was the queen of the stage, and I could have applauded her endlessly.

However, all the fairytale visions of the Caliph's palace, and even Kolosova herself, melted away as I sank into the seat I was shown to in the second row. In the darkness of the silent hall I sensed even more sharply and tormentingly that mighty, overpowering presence which had dominated my soul for many months. Unexpectedly yet clearly, I recalled how, when I was a boy, my Aunt Arina had showed me an insect trapped in a spider's web in a window-sash, too afraid to move as the spider crept ever closer.

'Bravo! Bravo!' Kolosova was making her exit, and the pirates' chorus was recounting the charms of the captive Greek maidens to the ruler of the True Believers. I slid deeper into my seat, focused my opera-glass on the stage, and tried to conquer my depression. In the narrow circle of my lens, amidst a shoal of female arms and naked shoulders, I glimpsed a pretty face gazing anxiously out into the darkness of the auditorium. My first sight of the beauty spot on her neck and the coral necklace, lifting on her bosom with every gentle breath, would remain with me all my life. In her searching gaze I read pained submission and inner anguish. I knew somehow that she and I were both subject to the same terrible power, oppressive and inexorable. A moment later I lost her amid the action on stage and, short-sighted as I was, could not immediately find her without my opera-glass. Meanwhile, the stage filled with new throngs of black and white slave girls, and the complex pirouettes of the corps de ballet replaced the line of pas de deux.

Suddenly a piercingly sonorous voice sank deep into my soul. I recognized *her* voice, and once more her enchanting face, framed by pale curls, floated into the lens of my opera-glass. Her voice, deep and overflowing with sorrow, seemed to be pleading for mercy: but it addressed not the Caliph of the True Believers, but the ruler of both our souls. I distinctly sensed his diabolical will and infernal breathing close by in the darkness, somewhere to my right. The curtain fell. The act had ended. My searching gaze slid over undulating waves of blue and black tailcoats, fluttering fans and sparkling lorgnettes, silk bodices and Brabant lace capes; and then it halted. I could not possibly be mistaken. It was he!

I cannot now find words to describe my agitation at this fateful encounter. He was taller than average; he wore a grey, slightly old-fashioned frock-coat. His hair was greying; his lacklustre gaze was still bent upon the stage. He was seated a few paces to my right, leaning one elbow on the arm-rest of his seat and fidgeting absently with his lorgnette. There were no tongues of fire circling him, no stink of sulphur; everything about him seemed quite ordinary and normal, but this diabolical ordinariness was saturated with meaning and power.

Slowly and wearily, he tore his gaze away from the stage and went out into the corridor. Like a shadow, like an Augsburg automaton,[10] I followed him, not daring to come too close yet lacking the strength to walk away from him. He never noticed me as he roamed distractedly through the corridors. When the audience, obeying the clamour of unseen bells, started pouring back into the theatre, he stopped, swept the emptying foyer with a blank stare, and started down the theatre's internal staircase.

I followed him along an unfamiliar corridor, wanly lit by occasional candles. The dark, dismal corridors, the internal staircases leading upwards, the walls steeped in Maddox's secrets, all recalled to me the Minotaur's labyrinth. A patch of bright light unexpectedly shone out. A door opened, and a woman hidden in the folds of a heavy cloak walked in the flood of light towards us. She leant wordlessly and distractedly on the arm that he offered and, with a rustle of skirts, swiftly passed me and disappeared up the winding staircase.

I recognized her. Now I even knew her name, for the playbill had announced that the role of the first slave girl would be sung by Nastasya Fyodorovna K.

Chapter 3

The spectral quality of the Moscow streets by night refreshed me a little. I left the theatre just in time to see a black carriage, which I fancied to be of gigantic size, bearing Nastasya Fyodor-ovna away. It disappeared around the corner of the Church of the Saviour, driving off along Petrovka.[11]

I love the Moscow streets by night, gentle reader; I love to wander through them in solitude, without any goal in mind. The dozing houses might be made of cardboard. Neither the noise of my steps nor the bark of a wakeful guard dog disturbs the calm peace of the gardens and courtyards. The few lighted windows seem to me to be full of peaceful life, of maidenly reveries, of solitary nocturnal thoughts. As one observes how the little churches dream their dreams, unexpected sights often loom up in the empty streets: now the gloomy colonnades of the Apraksin Palace, now the towering bulk of Pashkov House, or the stony shadows of Catherine's great eagles.

However, on this night my troubled soul was in no state to make such peaceful observations. Thoughts of diabolical encoun-ters persecuted me relentlessly. I was unable to think clearly. My ideas could not circulate: I simply plunged, as if into a pool of stagnant water, into endless mulling over the stranger.

An abrupt collision brought me to a halt. I was so distracted that, in the dank mist, my shoulder had bumped against a tall officer, who muttered an indistinct curse. In the Moscow fog he seemed to me to be of monstrous proportions. His old-fashioned uniform lent him a queer resemblance to the heroes of the Seven Years' War.

'Oh, so it's you!' the colossus said, measuring me with a pene-trating look; then he stepped into a brightly lit house, slamming the door behind him.

I stood in a sort of stupor, staring without understanding at the steamed-up windows gleaming in the dark night. I finally grasped that I was standing outside the Shablykinsky Inn, and I walked off through the murky streets. Once again I fell into distraction; my thoughts floundered, like flies trapped in treacle, and all my senses dwindled to infinitesimal proportions. Only one sense grew keener, gaining supernatural acuity: through the foul Moscow fog I sensed clearly that somewhere in the streets, the vast black carriage was bearing the stranger now closer to me, now farther away. In an effort to banish this insistent fancy,

I shook my head decisively and filled my breast with night air. On my left I descried the black silhouette of a willow tree. Before me, the lanterns of the Kamer-Kollezhsky Wall shone faintly in the gloom. Beyond that, the little houses of Marino Grove stretched in sleepy rows.[12] Fog wove itself around me; it was long after midnight.

I was already pondering the most direct route home. I was thinking of waking Theognostus and ordering him to boil some raspberry juice and warm up some punch when I felt the approach of a fresh attack. Amid the gloomy streets, I again sensed the black carriage drawing nearer. I wanted to flee, but my feet seemed rooted in the ground, and I stood unmoving. I could sense the terrible carriage approaching, turning down one street after another. The roadway trembled as it neared me. A cold sweat dampened my brow. My strength deserted me, and I should have fallen had I not leaned against the trunk of the willow.

After several torturous moments, the monstrous coach appeared on my right. By the trembling blue glimmer of the waning moon it drove down the avenue, rocking on its springs. On the box sat a driver in a tall top-hat, his eyes wide-open and glassy.

As the carriage drew level with me, its doors suddenly opened. A woman in white, clutching something in her hands, tumbled out of the moving vehicle and, tripping over her dress, fell to the ground. The carriage drove a little further, turned sharply and stopped. Its frame tilted unnaturally to one side.

Out stepped the stranger, and went quickly over to the woman. Nastenka – for she it was – leapt to her feet, cried, 'Your power over me is ended!' and ran to the pond. Lacking the strength to run all the way, she lifted the object she was carrying over her head and threw it with all her might into the water. Then she collapsed. The thing she had flung was swallowed by the dark, viscous pond water.

The stranger came closer. Nastenka's sobs filled my soul with horror. I would have rushed to her aid, but I was unable to take a single step. Once more I sensed myself completely under his sway; as though spellbound, I remained beside the willow.

'You there!' I heard his forceful voice cry out, and my legs began to move towards him.

I don't remember how we lifted my Nastenka from the ground or how we laid her in the carriage, how I sat down beside her, how the carriage moved off. I only remember that as we drove away through the foggy night, for a long time I watched the hunched figure of the stranger standing by the brink of the pond, persistently bending and searching, hunting for something.

Chapter 4

Marya Prokofyevna threw up her hands when I carried Nastenka into her little house on the bank of the Neglinka stream, just beside the Church of St Anastasya of Sirmium.

This good woman, may Heaven bless her, fussed around us. We laid Nastenka on the couch, under a Karelian birch clock. Marya Prokofyevna sent me off to put on the samovar, while she herself loosened Nastenka's stays. For a long time we struggled to bring her to her senses. Poor Nastenka was weeping and muttering nonsense in her sleep.

Day was breaking. As the third cockerel crowed, my own darling recovered her senses, smiled at us and fell into a peaceful slumber. Through the muslin curtains and rosemary planted by the windows, the morning sunshine blushed pink. Marya Prokofyevna quenched the candle we no longer needed. Nastenka's bosom rose and fell with her even breathing, a gold curl spilled onto the delicate cloth of her pillow. The morning silence lent the ticking of the clock a special significance and calm. From the Church of the Saviour bells rang for morning prayers.

Regretfully, I rose from my chair and started searching for my hat, preparing to set off. But Marya Prokofyevna refused to let me go and implored me to drink a cup of morning coffee with her. The good lady treated me like an old acquaintance, although we had never met before. I shall never forget that day; I remember everything about it, even the rugs on the lacquered floor, the clavichord with music by Mozart open upon it, the china and silver services in the cabinet … But more than anything else I remember the deep couch with its mahogany back, over which the sun's morning rays floated languidly and calmly; and the rows of silhouette portraits in quaint frames over the couch, delicately sketched in Indian ink on mother-of-pearl.

Marya Prokofyevna was pouring me a third cup from the round-bellied copper coffee-pot and was urging me to tell, for the fifth time, how I had rescued Nastenka, when the door creaked. Nastenka herself came out of the bedroom to see us, in a pink dressing-gown, all prettily flushed from overhearing my tale.

Chapter 5

It was already almost evening as I walked down Petrovka on my way to the Arbat.[13] I bore a light blue, medium-sized envelope, inscribed in Nastenka's hand: 'To be placed in the hands of Pyotr Petrovich Venediktov, the Madrid Inn, on the Arbat'.

The envelope smelled pungently of violets, and my soul was full of a strange sensation of jealousy. I had no right to be jealous.

I walked on absent-mindedly; at the Petrovka Gates I was almost knocked off my feet by the carriages filled with visiting notables on their way to the English Club. The club's monumental white colonnade, framed by golden autumn leaves, awaited the visitors. The autumnal boulevards, bright and cheerful as ribbons, emphasized the blueness of the heavens. Scraps of clouds floated above Moscow. Autumn's gold was falling on a new Muscovite Danaë,[14] ambling slowly along the avenue in front of me in expectation of some gentleman friend. She wore a blue bodice, and her slender hand clutched a spray of wilting Michaelmas daisies.

Venediktov was sitting in room 38 on a stained, green, worn-out divan, smoking a long-stemmed pipe. He had on a colourful Bukhara robe, gaping over his hairy chest. Various things were flung untidily around the room. Open trunks and suitcases bespoke his imminent departure. An iron casket stood on the table.

'Oh, it's you?' Venediktov greeted me frostily and disapprovingly. Silently, full of apprehension, I handed him the letter. He took it unwillingly, glanced at the handwriting, and shuddered.

'How can this be?'

He rose, ran his hands over his damp brow, held the envelope up to the light, and opened it. He began to read with the greatest agitation.

Assuming my work to be done, I thought it best to slip out unnoticed, leaving him in the middle of the room with the fateful letter in his hand. The filthy, half-lit staircase to the furnished rooms stank of sour cabbage, and some pock-marked, freckled little boy was shining a hussar's jackboots with spit. Walking out into the street, I breathed freely.

Oh gentlemen, how unbearably difficult it is to deliver to someone else a sealed letter from the woman you love with all your heart!

Treading in puddles, uncertain where to bend my steps, I sensed again the pressure of the stranger's will upon my soul. I was painfully aware that he was ordering me to return. I wrapped my cloak around me, determined to resist his will and continue on my way. My spirit was like a weeping willow, bent by the blasts of an oncoming storm, branches twisting with every gust.

My soul weakened and melted without trace into that other, demonic will, murky as the waters of the Styx.

Silently I opened the door of room 38; I stood by the lintel like a naughty schoolboy. Venediktov was radiant; the entire room had been transformed. The luggage prepared for his departure was tossed under the couch. On the table champagne sparkled in Bohemian goblets; Limburg cheese and oysters were jumbled up with fruits from Moscow hothouses.

'How can I thank you enough, Bulgakov!' Pyotr Petrovich cried, handing me a glass. 'The Angel Gabriel himself could not have brought me more joyful tidings than you did! Oh! If only you could understand any of it, Bulgakov. Her soul is now free, the chains are cast off, she loves me!'

The undrunk wine sparkled in the bottles. Venediktov was already far from sober. He seated me at the table and, drunkenly affectionate and insistent, urged me to share his victuals.

The sparkling nectar of Champagne had loosened his tongue, and he spilled out the tale of his unhappy love to me. He grew steadily tipsier, repeating every minute: 'Oh, if only you understood, Bulgakov!' At last, working himself up to a frenzy, he struck the table with his great fist (on which an iron ring sparkled) so hard that the candles flickered and a glass rolled on to the floor and loudly shattered. He shouted, 'I am an emperor! You are a worm before me, Bulgakov! Weep, I tell you!' I felt my soul fill with grief. A hard lump formed in my throat, and tears poured from my eyes. 'Laugh, you slave soul!' he went on, guffawing wildly, and a flood of sunny, excruciating joy swept away my sorrow. Everything, it seemed, resounded with gladness – from the peaches scattered across the table to the shards of the broken goblet and the candlesticks with their flickering tapers set out on the crumpled wine-stained tablecloth.

'My power is limitless, Bulgakov, and so is my sorrow: the greater the power, the greater the suffering.' And with tears in his eyes, he related how human souls bowed down before him, how they submitted to the whims of his will. How he had fallen in love with Nastenka and desired her to love him – not from mere obedience, but of her own free will. Not by his command, but by the impulse of her own soul. How he had dreaded renouncing his power over her, terrified of losing her forever. How on the night just past he had given up his power over Nastenka's soul and how the Almighty had rewarded him with her freely given love, heralded by the blue envelope I had delivered.

His mind grew confused: he paced the room as if delirious, waving his hands, making little sense. The shadow or, more accurately, the many shadows cast by his striding form swayed on the walls. The moon's cold light poured through the uncurtained windows, mingling with the flickering yellowish glow of the wax tapers in the candelabra. The muffled sound of the bells of the Kremlin's Spasskaya Tower pealing midnight reached us.

'You don't understand a thing, Bulgakov!' My terrible companion stopped abruptly in front of me. 'Do you know what lies inside this iron box?' he asked, in a spasm of drunken frankness. 'Your soul is inside it, Bulgakov!'

Chapter 6

It was about two o'clock in the morning. Venediktov filled his own goblet and, after drinking it off, continued his tale.

'And so, you'll understand, when I walked out of the darkness into that room, tears welled up in my eyes from the acrid tobacco smoke mingled with an odour like sulphur. Thick plumes of smoke swirled in the air, and small lamps glittered: instead of candles there were lampions spewing red and blue tongues of flame, like spirit-burners. On an enormous circular table, draped with black cloth, some golden triangles sparkled, jumbled up with cards. Thirty or so gentlemen, elegantly dressed in red and black redingotes and black top-hats, all with the same haemorrhoidal faces as my companion, were playing piquet in utter silence, broken only by oaths. The red-headed fellow, the one I'd saved from a furious crowd of clergymen on a street corner in Whitechapel, shook hands with the nearest gentlemen and seated himself at the table, completely forgetting my presence.

'Left to my own devices, I made an effort to get my bearings. The room, which I had originally thought to be vaulted, as far as one could see through the wreaths of evil-smelling haze, might have had no ceiling at all or a transparent one, as a myriad of stars glittered all around, obscured by trails of smoke. In the right-hand corner towered an enormous sculpture; I recognized it as a ceremonial image of Asmodeus[15] in the form of a goat. Just as Brighton's book describes him. I simply can't convey all the foulness and lewdness of the savage pose in which he was shown. From head to foot the sculpture was smeared with excrement, smouldering with blue flames, and constantly renewed throngs of visitors, with the most heartfelt spasms, were emptying their bowels in honour of the god of demons. The noisome steam rising from this Black Mass half-hid the decrepit Hierophant standing on the monster's head, his stomach bulging, waving a pair of torches. In the sulphurous haze, the round, cloth-covered tables loomed up as brighter patches, where gentlemen were devoting themselves to cards or gluttony ... I realized I was present at a sabbath of male witches.

'"Ha, Schlüssen!" A shabby old man tugged my hand. Passing me his cards, he asked me to finish his game for him while he absented himself, promising to split the winnings evenly. I sat down without thinking and picked up the cards: the blood rushed to my head and throbbed in my temples when I looked at them.

'All earthly pornography paled in comparison to the images trembling in my hands. Swollen hips; bosoms taut as balloons; nude stomachs; my eyes blurred with blood, and to my horror I felt that these images were alive, breathing and stirring under my fingers. The red-headed fellow prodded me in the side. It was my turn. The banker showed me the jack of spades – a repulsive Negro, convulsed by lustful shudders; I covered him with the queen of trumps. The two cards, clinging together, rolled head over heels passionately, and the banker tossed me a few gleaming triangles. The blood throbbed in my temples like hammer-blows. But, terrified of giving myself away, I continued playing. I was dealt a lucky hand; the frenzied orgies of the live cards, intertwining their bodies in homage to Priapus, worked in my favour.

'When the shabby gentleman returned, a considerable heap of metal lay before me on the table. Clearly pleasantly surprised, he thrust a heap of triangles into my hands and slapped me on the back. With a cry of "Ha, Schlüssen!" he plunged back into the game. Tearing myself away from the diabolical cards, I stared blearily around the room with bloodshot eyes. I could no longer doubt that I was in the London demons' club. I had to find a way to escape. The red-haired gentleman I had met in Whitechapel was unlikely to help me. He was losing heavily, and the hair in his sideburns was furiously curling and uncurling, as if on springs. Fortunately, I spotted two plump, pot-bellied chaps in red redingotes, amber breeches and black top-hats who were quarrelling about something and bidding farewell to their neighbours, evidently heading for the exit. Unobserved, I followed them. They walked up to the solid brick wall and, without slowing down, melted into it. I threw myself towards it, thrusting my right shoulder forwards, expecting to strike cold stone. I had hardly touched its surface when I found myself in the hurly-burly of the evening throng in Piccadilly.'

Venediktov paused, wiped his damp brow with a handkerchief,

drained his glass at a gulp and went on:

'When I returned to my hotel and laid the seven triangles I had won on the table, for a long time I could not puzzle out what they signified. They were made of thick slabs of gold and what seemed to be platinum, engraved with pentacles and symbols from the Aiq-Beker,[16] badly worn and evidently much used. They had probably absorbed the infernal flame of Asmodeus's Black Mass.

'Puzzled, I picked one of them up and, as I stared at it, drifted into a trance. Gradually, steadily, new sensations took hold of me. I felt a flood of new emotions and my suddenly sharpened gaze somehow passed through physical objects, reaching infinitely far into the distance. Through a sort of bluish haze – yet neither through a haze nor a wall; I don't know how to explain how my new sense acted – I saw a girl tossing and turning on her bed. In her restless sleep she had flung off her blanket; she lay before me in lovely nudity. I was overcome by agitation. Her face was hidden from me, and my whole being longed passionately to see it. As if obeying my desire, she turned reluctantly towards me. How beautiful her face was! How lovely her naked breast! I wished her to open her eyes, and they opened. The girl awakened. Horrified, she sat up in bed. I wished her to stand, and she stood, after a painful struggle. Her shift slid to her feet, and an instant later she stood before me like Aphrodite, risen from the foam. Then she came to her senses, pulled on her shift, and sank down in horror before the icon niche, where a lamp was burning. The Saviour's face looked sternly into my soul, and my vision grew dark.

'I flung the triangle down and for a long time stared straight ahead at nothing. Perhaps a couple of hours went by ... The logs were smouldering in the fireplace. Little by little, I regained my senses and placed another triangle on the palm of my hand. I almost dropped it from shock ... The walls dissolved, and I saw Jeannette Leclerc, an actress from the Palace Theatre, whom I was vainly pursuing. She was reclining on a sofa, and a Scots Guards officer was on his knees beside her. The disorder of their dress and their tender attitudes left no doubts about the romantic nature of their encounter. Jeannette, quivering all over with languid pleasure, reached out for him with bare arms and parted lips. With all the force of my will I ordered her to draw back. But

I had no power over her, and she wrapped her naked arms around the colonel's greying head. Rage overcame me. I ordered him to stand. Obediently, he rose from his knees, shaking off Jeannette's embrace. I realized that I controlled his soul. Jeannette, with a shamelessness I had never seen before in a woman, pressed her body against his; and I, overflowing with fury, aware that I controlled every muscle in the Scotsman's body, seized her throat with his hands and frenziedly throttled her, until her whole body was seized with convulsions.

'The vision showed me Jeannette's death, and by an effort of will I flung the Scotsman's head against the corner of the stove.

'The vision disappeared; the triangle dissolved into dust, leaving a burning sensation. I threw myself on the divan and lapsed into heavy slumber.

'I hardly need to describe my limitless horror when the next morning I went to Jeannette's house, meaning to tell her about my dreadful dream, and found it surrounded by a crowd, Jeannette strangled, and the Scotsman I had seen the night before lying in the corner of her room with a broken skull. Part of my life ended there. I understood that I had won human souls from the demons of London.'

Chapter 7

Venediktov lost the thread of his tale. He grew more and more intoxicated. With his vision of the past torturing his brain, he sank deep into his chair and, inhaling deeply, smoked his long-stemmed pipe. Pale as death, he told me how he had controlled the soul and body of a young lady, just married to Lord Crewe, a member of the House of Lords, and how he had crushed her life as the heavy foot of a passer-by crushes a meadow flower; how he could not see, even through the haze, the possessor of the soul that was marked with the Pentacle of Aldebaran.

Pyotr Petrovich opened his box and showed me the four remaining triangles, telling me that the fifth was the talisman of

Nastenka's soul – he had failed to find it in the pond at Marino Grove where she had cast it.

Now completely intoxicated, Venediktov struck the platinum plating of the mysterious soul with his fist, ordering it with curses to appear before him. Then he grew calmer and eagerly agreed to play a game of piquet with my soul as the stake; I won it from him quickly, without difficulty. With a shaking hand, I took the diabolical triangle. The candles burnt down and went out. By the glow of the soot-blackened lamp, I watched as Venediktov let his heavy head fall on the table.

As I ran down Dead Street[17] past the Church of the Dormition in Mogiltsy, the Spasskaya Tower was chiming three.

Chapter 8

My heart was thumping and my eyes were burning as I splashed through the autumn puddles. I walked on, wholly overcome by my extraordinary adventures.

Night-time Moscow swallowed me up. I cannot recall where I went. A harlot called after me, pulling up her skirts and inviting me into the gutter ... night watchmen hailed me twice. I came to my senses when I glimpsed a light shining in front of me. Staring around me, I saw the brightly lit posting station for the light Kursk mail. There was nowhere else to shelter from the drizzle and collect my thoughts as I waited for sunrise. I entered, brushing off raindrops. The rain poured down with redoubled force. The large room of the posting station was dimly lit by two lanterns.

On my right, at a little table, a few clients were huddled together over a couple of half-bottles; the landlord, an aged fellow from Yaroslavl, was dozing behind the bar; on my left there sat a single guest, all alone at a large table. At the sight of him I gave an involuntary shudder. It was the strange officer I had stumbled into the night before. He was seated, writing something. The dimly flickering candle-stub lit up his old-fashioned travelling uniform

and his high jackboots; I was reminded again of the heroes of the
Seven Years' War. An extraordinary tension could be felt in the
room: the other drinkers, seemingly worldly men, had hushed,
like small birds watching the approach of a hawk. They did not
touch a drop from their glasses, staring gloomily at the officer, as
he wrote with a badly sharpened, squeaking quill on a half-sheet
of paper. Tossing the pen aside and folding his message in four,
the stranger rose and, spurs ringing, made his way to the exit.

'Make the horses ready, Petrukhin, I'm off in an hour,' he told
the landlord. Then he walked out into the now furious torrent of
rain drumming into the puddles.

'Damned cut-throat!' a shabby man, easy to place as an
archival registrar, muttered through gritted teeth.

'Meeting the likes of him leads to no good,' his companion
agreed, raising his half-bottle. 'Hey, landlord, who was that
swell?'

'Seidlitz,' the sedate Yaroslavl landlord answered, a peculiar
mix of fear and respectful caution in his tone.

'And what sort of fellow is he?'

'No-one knows! There are all sorts of stories. A couple of years
ago he was stationed in Novotroitsky and he threw Berlinsky the
card-sharper out of the window. They say Berlinsky died!'

The surname struck a chord, and the shabby man, hunching
himself up even more, told a tale he had heard once in Petersburg, about a certain Seidlitz who should never be mentioned
after sundown, who came into God's world in an unnatural way.
In those days, he told us, a fellow called Mesmer was at large
in Paris, winding people around his little finger: whatever he
told them to do, they'd do it; whatever he told them to be, they'd
imagine they were. If he said: 'Your Excellency, turn into a wolf!'
his Excellency would be crawling on all fours and howling. If he
told a countess she was a chicken, she'd start clucking. This way,
so they say, he made a German colonel of the hussars imagine
he was seven months pregnant. The man's stomach swelled up,
and then this Mesmer fellow died on the spot from the strain.
No-one could break the spell on the hussar, and a couple of
months later he died, and the Prussian king's court physician cut
out of his stomach a child that was green and slimy all over, with

a huge head ...

The tale was cut short by the squeak of the door and the jingle of spurs. Seidlitz returned and threw the stationmaster a leather bag and a letter sealed with five sealing-wax stamps. 'Send that to the commander in the morning,' he ordered sharply, and made for the door again. Everyone fell silent. A pall of nocturnal dread descended upon us. We had all seen clearly that, despite the drenching rain, Seidlitz's cloak was untouched by a single drop of water. Soon after, I paid and left.

Chapter 9

A morning nap refreshed me substantially. When I awoke, the sun's rays were filtering through my lowered blinds. Round sunbeams filled the room with a peaceful half-light, now playing on a glazed Chinaman, now on the engraved handles of the pistols given to my father by General Pyotr Rumyantsev-Zadunaysky,[18] which I hung over the couch that served as my bed.

I felt completely free from the spiritual burden that had oppressed me for the last several months, but for some reason I didn't even remember the triangle I had won. That was how insignificant my own fate appeared to me. My soul had been purged: I felt neither joy nor sorrow. I seemed to have no desires. Only the thought of Nastenka shone brightly in my soul.

But what did I mean to her? Moreover, what would become of me without her?

When I entered the little blue house, everything in it was glowing with happiness. Marya Prokofyevna, with rolled-up sleeves, was baking a turnover to celebrate. Rosemary and euca-lyptus gave off a pleasant, cheerful fragrance. A little white cat in a new blue ribbon was arching its spine especially high from gladness. The strings of the clavichord seemed ready to ring out Mozart's melodies all by themselves. In front of the mirror, Nastenka was arranging her curls and settling the pleats in the lace mantle of her rustling white dress. Miserably tormented by jealousy, I heard that Venediktov was expected within the hour, at two o'clock; that Father Vasily from the Paraskeva Good Friday Church would come in person for the betrothal, and that I was a very original, good-natured and fortunate fellow.

The clock struck two. Uncle Nikolay Polikarpovich arrived with his wife, who wore a taffeta dress, then came two or three young girls with broad ribbons on their heads, friends of Nastenka's from the theatre. We tasted the turnover. At three o'clock Father Vasily arrived. Joy became overshadowed by anxiety. We ate a little, talked about Bonaparte, and had more food. Father Vasily left, saying he would come back at five o'clock. The atmosphere became oppressive and fearful. I repressed a wicked sensation of joy, and eventually offered to call on Venediktov and find out what the matter was. I caught a grateful, hopeful glance from Nastenka. Almost at a run, I hurried down Petrovka.

When I reached Arbat Square, I immediately noticed the alarmed faces of the passers-by; everyone looked troubled. I found the Madrid's furnished rooms surrounded by a crowd of common folk; the police inspector's familiar carriage stood nearby. For a long time the waiters and the police refused to admit me, but when I gave my name and said that I wanted Pyotr Petrovich Venediktov, someone grasped me smartly by the elbows and I was shoved without any particular politeness into room 38. I entered and froze in my tracks.

Everything in the room had been turned upside down and showed the signs of a desperate struggle. In the middle of the floor, among shattered chairs and the rumpled rug, lay Pyotr Petrovich with his skull broken. Staff-Captain Zagorelsky was questioning the portly landlady, now pale with horror.

Chapter 10

I was already in sight of the little blue house with its mezzanine when timidity finally and utterly overcame me. I could not take another step. Let Nastenka sleep tonight in ignorance before exchanging worry for the darkness of despair!

I made my way home. When I looked in the mirror, a wasted face stared back at me from the Karelian birch frame. My sunken, heavy-lidded eyes were lined with dreadful blue shadows. I could not force myself to touch any supper, and after drinking two swallows of hot punch I told Theognostus to make up my bed on the couch and to stuff two pipes as full as he could with Capstan tobacco.

Although it was the middle of the night, I could not collect my thoughts sufficiently to undress and go to sleep. I stared dully, understanding nothing, at the dwindling flame of my candle.

A knock at the window – I had forgotten to draw the blinds – interrupted my troubled thoughts. An archangel's trumpet could not have roused me faster; I rushed to the window and, through the steamed-up glass, saw Nastenka standing in the moonlight – wrapped in a thick shawl, her hair loose. 'Save me: the murderer is chasing me!'

I asked no more questions: a moment later, forgetting modesty (oh, my friends! what could I not have forgotten in that moment!), I quickly dressed Nastenka, who stood before me in just a chemise, in my own clothes. As we were climbing over the fence into the priest's wife's garden, my hand convulsively squeezed my father's pistol: someone was knocking heavily and insistently on the door of my house. Half an hour later we were at the familiar inn in Sadovniki, and by dawn my childhood friend Terenty Kokurin (we were nursed together as infants) was galloping us in his troika to the town of Kirzhach,[19] without stopping to change horses, without even our documents, to the home of my dear mother's sister, Pelageya Minishna.

Chapter 11

'... And that's the whole story, Pelageya Minishna. I know no more myself.' I finished my tale and looked at the old lady. My good old aunt sighed and set about taking care of us, without asking any questions. Only every so often she looked closely now at Nastenka, now at me.

We sewed Nastenka a simple little dress from English flannel, which suited her wonderfully well. Even my aunt's hoop-skirted dress (from the reign of Elizabeth Petrovna[20] and the glorious days of Catherine) suited Nastenka.

For the first few days my own darling sat in a corner of the couch without stirring, like a caged animal, and stared at us fearfully. I remember distinctly and with joyful sorrow those days when my aunt, after finishing her housework, would sit with us and knit stockings, needles flashing rapidly. Nastenka would gaze into the garden, where the last yellow leaves were falling, and, in a reverie, would stroke the little white cat. Sitting at her feet, I would read Kotzebue's plays, Mr Karamzin's account of his travels, and the great Derzhavin's touching verses.[21] Oh, my friends, how long ago it was! After a week I went to Moscow, to find Nastenka's little house burned to the ground and Marya Prokofyevna vanished, no-one knew where. About a month went by while I struggled to obtain an overseas passport. In those days passports were just as difficult to come by as they are today. So only by the end of October did we cross the Prussian border. We hastened through Berlin, still bearing traces of the life of Frederick the Great, Cologne with its towers and the grey waves of the Rhine, and Paris, where the precepts of the incorruptible Robespierre were already being obscured by gold, women, wine and the thunder of military glory.

Nastenka remained indifferent to everything we saw. Even I began to lapse into doleful brooding. The little bead pouch, in which my dying mother had passed on to me my father's fortune, which she had carefully preserved, grew lighter by the day. The future troubled me. Nastenka and I were now bound inextricably together, but our position was a false one. She did not even want to think about marriage. When she went to bed, she took care to lock her door. When I tried to ask her questions about her life, she answered unwillingly, mostly about her childhood and the theatrical school. Some fateful secret seemed to overshadow her; and tragedy would have to cross our path once more before our happiness was secure – at the price of fresh blood.

On the 29th of April 1806 we were strolling in the woods in the vicinity of Fontainebleau, where French kings have hunted for centuries, and where François I planned the frescoes for his castle. Ivy-twined beech trunks and thorny bushes choked our path. Just as I was growing concerned that we had lost our way, we suddenly heard the clang of clashing swords. Raising my head, I saw that Nastenka had turned deathly pale as she stared through the thicket into a meadow. Following her gaze, I saw a group of men on the green grass in brightly coloured cavalry uniforms, carefully observing two others, who were engaged in a fierce duel. To my horror, I recognized Seidlitz as one of the duellists. At the same moment he saw Nastenka and stepped backward. Like a dart of lightning, his opponent's sword flashed and pierced his breast. He cried out and fell face down in the grass. The seconds ran towards him. 'C'est fini!' exclaimed an elderly officer, raising the lifeless Seidlitz's hand.

'Take me away from here,' I heard Nastenka whisper.

That evening she told me, her tale interrupted by sobs, that on the night that would prove so fateful for him, a drunken Venediktov had received in his room the diabolical soul that refused to submit to him; he then lost Nastenka to Seidlitz at cards and perished attempting to wrest his IOU back from the Prussian by force.

'Now I am free,' she finished her tale, reaching out to me with both arms. And that night she did not lock her bedroom door.

Chapter 12

I don't know what more to write ... The history of these memorable events, which changed my life, is long since over. Nor am I even the main character in the tale. It pleased God to make me a witness to the death of a man who overstepped the portion allowed to humanity, and to place his precious legacy in my hands.

Nastenka and I were married that very year, after our return to Moscow, in the Church of the Saviour. Our life went by serenely, and even when the French invaded, our little house in the Gruziny district was spared by both fire and robbers.[22] Nastenka gave up the stage and devoted herself to keeping house. Our marriage was not blessed with children, and now I visit Nastenka's grave in the Donskoy Monastery in heavy solitude.

That is the whole tale of my life. By way of conclusion, I will just mention that five years after the French invasion, when we were rifling our trunks for formal costumes to attend the unveiling ceremony for the monument to Minin and Pozharsky[23] – for which Nastenka and I had tickets – we found my old student uniform. From one of the pockets fell the golden triangle of my soul. For a long time we didn't know what to do with it; we looked at it mistrustfully, until I lost it to Nastenka at Old Maid. Nastenka took the triangle with a shiver, slipped it onto the same chain as the cross she wore around her neck, and – strange to say – since that moment I have never known grief or sorrow. Even now I am spared them, as I wander on the Moscow Hills, leaning on my cane and knowing that my Nastenka keeps my soul safe in her little coffin in the Donskoy Monastery.

1922

ALEKSANDR CHAYANOV

The Venetian Mirror
or, The Extraordinary Adventures of the Glass Man

A romantic tale by Botanist X

The author dedicates this book to Olga Emmanuilovna Chayanova[1]

Chapter 1

In which the reader becomes acquainted with the general state of affairs, and meets the heroes of our tale

Afterwards, Aleksey never could explain his mirror experiences to his friends using the ordinary ideas and images of our world. What's more, his badly shaken mind retained almost no recollection of the days just before his terrifying adventure in the mirror.

His last clear-cut, even exaggeratedly sharp memory was of that fateful day when he found, in the cellars of a Venetian antiquary, the object he had long been seeking. He recalled, down to the smallest details, how Signor Bambacci, after exhausting his vocabulary of praise in five European languages, had wearily picked out the pearls of his collection.

The sweltering Venetian sunlight, infused with scents of honey and salt water, was speckling the hips of Baroque cupids, playing on the glass pendants of the Florentine tables and casting reflections of the waves in the Canale Gracio onto the antiquary's ceiling. However, just as with the offerings of other antiquaries in Europe, none of the treasures of Signor Bambacci's shop stirred Aleksey. The six months he had already wasted on the outer trappings of his new life had not come close to resolving his self-imposed quest. In the eight rooms of his new house on the banks of the Yauza River in Moscow, he had amassed *objets d'art* from five centuries. But his collection, based on the bright spectrum of Expressionist colours, had not become an integrated whole, despite all his efforts. It lacked one detail, a detail which by its sharp and piquant impact would surpass every other element in the mix, just as a drop of elixir surpasses and unifies all the ingredients of a complex cocktail. His attempt to employ a wooden Negro idol from the shores of Benadir for this purpose had already proved fruitless, as had his original plan to focus the entire compositional framework around the *Little Venus* of Palma il Vecchio.

Aleksey was noticeably losing his sang-froid. He felt that his failure to perfect his house on the Yauza was a bad omen for his future life with its mistress, she whose red tresses promised finally to resolve his restless, complicated and generally troubled existence. With unconcealed irritation, Aleksey waved away a brightly coloured wedding chest of ancient Tuscan workmanship proffered by the baffled and exhausted antiquarian. He decided to resort to his ultimate expedient, which had more than once rescued him from the well-known collector's ennui.

Ten minutes later, Bambacci, grumbling, rattling his keys and lighting the way with a gloomy lantern, descended with him down dank stone steps into cellars piled from wall to wall with ancient rubbish. This was the mother-lode from which the old Venetian extracted the precious jewels of his antiquarian stock.

Aleksey hoped that the old storekeeper's gaze, dulled by years of haggling, might have missed some treasure amidst the multifarious furnishings from old palazzi and monasteries, bought in lots and heaped up in the bottomless cellars beneath the Canale Gracio. However, in the wavering light of Bambacci's lantern, the stacks of old, dusty chairs, the wooden church fittings and the pale, armless antique statues resembled one of the gloomy antechambers of Dante's Hell, a crumbling cemetery for countless generations. Aleksey was overcome by a sensation of grinding despair. He was about to dismiss everything with a wave of his hand and depart directly for the station and the next Moscow train when he abruptly stopped in astonishment.

On the right side of the dark room, near an enormous painting and behind the wreckage of some Louis XVI chairs, he had sensed a powerful and dominating presence. Aleksey paused. His heart beat faster. He felt as though his steps had been directed here, as though a powerful, snake-like gaze was fastened on him by whatever waited in the gloom. He took a few paces into the darkness. By the flickering light of Bambacci's lantern, two frenzied eyes bored into his.

After an instant – which seemed an eternity to Aleksey – he realized that, behind some fragments of mahogany, a mirror stood in front of him, covered in cobwebs and layered with dust.

From that moment Aleksey had ceased to be conscious of his own actions.

By making a great effort, he later recalled confused images of how he brought his discovery back to the front door of his house on the Yauza. For some reason, he clearly recalled how the fat neck of his butler, Grigory, had reddened with effort as, groaning, he heaved the box containing the Venetian mirror out of the car. He even remembered, as though in a dream, the fateful moment when he was confusedly explaining his adventures to Kate. As he began loosening the packaging around his Venetian discovery, she faced him in a white spring dress lit up by the sun. When the last layers of yellow cloth had fallen to the floor, the mirror's black surface reflected Kate in curving lines, along with his pots of cacti and the church domes rising uphill towards the sunset sky. Everything within the little house had been miraculously transformed, as if invisible streams of liquid glass were flooding the rooms, dissolving every object and rendering it translucent. The mirror's surface appeared to radiate a subtle, centuries-stored venom, which suffused the air, the furniture, the paintings, the flowers, the walls.

Aleksey's head spun, and his chest was heaving. Before his eyes, in the lead-coloured gloom of the mirror, his own image flickered beside Kate's, gradually merging into one. As he stared into the glass, he did not recognize his lover's serene features in her reflection. Nor did he recognize her real face when he tore his gaze from the mirror. Pushing aside the heavy furniture, unthinkingly touching her hands and hips, he sensed that Kate's entire being had been transmuted. Her body, always cool and calm, now seemed to burn like molten metal.

Bewitched by the strange mirror, Aleksey felt as though he had also changed into someone else. All those parts of his being which, over the years, he had learned to suppress, reasserted themselves with unexpected violence and strength.

Feeling his lover's trembling, desiring body in his arms, Aleksey pressed her to his breast in a surge of passion and was about to kiss her greedy lips. He dimly recalled later that Kate hid her face in his shoulder and, slipping from his embrace, disappeared.

A moment afterwards – and this moment would be seared on his memory for the rest of his life – he found himself standing before the darkened surface of the Venetian mirror.

The glass reflected him as though upon a moving film of oil, breaking his outline into intersecting Cubist planes. Aleksey stared tensely into the distorted features of his own face, registering all the coarseness of his passion. In some strange way, that coarseness pleased and delighted him.

Some dreadful force was pulling him closer and closer to the mirror's yellowed, lacklustre surface. Suddenly he shuddered, and a cold sweat broke out all over his body; just as in the cellars under the Canale Gracio, he saw two utterly alien, frenzied eyes fixed upon him. At the same instant he felt a sharp jerk. His mirror double had seized his right hand and forcefully tugged it under the surface of the mirror, triggering circles of ripples as if across a pool of mercury.

For an instant their bodies fused, struggling. Then Aleksey saw his reflection spring free and start to dance, leaping high, in the centre of the room, while he was forced to copy each movement within the gradually settling interior of the Venetian mirror.

Chapter 2

*In which the glass man appears on the scene; a depiction of his
wicked deeds, as witnessed by Aleksey while immured in the mirror*

The restless mirror man, who until a moment ago had reflected
Aleksey in the mirror world, gambolled with irrepressible joy
over the wide Persian rug, bought in Shiraz, trampling it under
his heels and kicking his legs high. A moment later he stopped.
Turning to the mirror, he broke into a wild guffaw, poking out
his tongue and flourishing his fists.

Reaching an extraordinary depth of despair, Aleksey realized
that his own features were repeating the grimaces of his diabolical
double, while his arms and legs were, somehow, in spite of all his
resistance, numbly mimicking the gestures of the double's body.
Drunk with his power, the glass man stepped up almost flush
against the mirror. Ironically bending into the most improbable
positions, he compelled Aleksey to twist his body into movements
recalling the poses of Jacques Callot's most fantastic caricatures.

Bending his arms and legs in these demonic and involuntary
gymnastics, Aleksey was crushed by the vile lasciviousness and
vulgarity of his monstrous double. He even felt a trace of satisfaction that his consciousness remained the same as before; not a
single one of his thoughts was forced to echo the thoughts of the
glass man.

Furiously resisting, he was also soon slightly cheered by realizing that the glass man could not force him to follow all of his
frenzied movements. Sometimes, by a desperate effort of will,
Aleksey restrained his hands from reproducing some disgusting
gesture of his double's. This enraged the double and forced him
to retreat from the mirror in fear.

This tense combat, waged through the silent glass membrane,
was suddenly broken off.

Kate entered the room.

Her red tresses were tied back with strings of pearls, and a
light-green, completely transparent oriental fabric traced the

opaline contours of her body.

Shaken to the very bottom of his soul, Aleksey wanted to sink to his knees, but his hands unexpectedly and tormentingly began to clap, repeating the actions of the delighted glass man, who had also noticed Kate's arrival and had turned towards her.

Aleksey thought he felt the bones of his neck crunch as, compelled by an unknown force, his head turned toward the depths of the mirror world. At the same time, he felt in his arms the slippery glass body of his lover's double.

Kate was hidden from his eyes. Turned inwards to the glass world by the will of the glass man, Aleksey could only gauge what was happening to her from the movements of the glass being standing before him. The mirror woman, whose slippery glass hips he was compelled to embrace, smiled a crooked, ironical smile. Then her face expressed fear and surprise, as the real Kate must have done. Aleksey would dimly remember how, a moment later, under the compulsion of another's will, he roughly seized the struggling glass body that filled him with disgust. With unsuspected strength, he turned it to face the surface of the mirror.

In the same instant he – enslaved, humiliated, without any will of his own – watched how his own living, beloved girl struggled in the arms of his diabolical double and how the glass hands squeezed her in their dead embrace, cruel fingers leaving bruises on her opaline body.

Then everything dissolved into the glass ether and merged in Aleksey's memory into a feverish dream.

Days passed: the heavy, lead-coloured days of Aleksey's mirror existence.

Afterwards, he could not recall without a shudder of horror that transparent, speechless ether in which pale beings swam, now and then repeating the gestures of their flesh-and-blood originals; and the still more dreadful semi-existence when the surface of the mirror caught no images for the glass doubles to reflect.

Aleksey was astonished by the joys and sorrows, pitiably minor in worldly terms, which constituted life for those ghostly beings: their constant resistance to their 'masters' and their desire to control the latter and force them to reflect *their* actions and thoughts. Shuddering, he encountered in the flickering twilight of the mirror world the reflections of people long dead, people who had once been great and who now dragged out a dwindling mirror existence, only rarely peeping through the glass membrane into the flesh-and-blood world, terrifying their descendants and frightening girls divining fortunes in their looking-glasses. Feeling all the horror his gradually fading emotions could muster, Aleksey grew convinced that his double was steadily strengthening his control over his earthly destiny. With ever-greater ill-will and mockery, the double would wink at him in the evenings, putting down his razor and ducking his cheeks and chin to look at himself in the mirror before going into Kate's bedroom.

Unable to voice his grief, Aleksey watched his lover's sad fate. Taken by force, she submitted; as a young birch collapses under the blows of an axe, she gave way to the mirror man's will, believing him to be Aleksey, not realizing what had happened, not even trying to think, passive and helpless.

There were nocturnal orgies which Aleksey was forced to enact within the mirror, grasping Kate's glass double in his arms. Kate gave herself obediently to the shameful game, like a doll, joyless, impassive, unresisting.

Aleksey fancied that Kate's apathy offered him some kind of moral satisfaction within the closed circle of his misery. With still greater satisfaction he noticed that the shameless passion of the glass woman, thrown into his arms by the laws of the mirror world, and the simmering fury of her dark glass soul, were limited by the real Kate's movements, so that she could not change even by one millimetre the languid motions of her glass body.

However, even this insignificant moral comfort soon came to an end. To his own horror, Aleksey one day felt an alteration in his own consciousness, as though the glass ether surrounding him had begun to seep through the pores of his body and the bony roof of his skull, turning the essence of his humanity into glassy nothingness. When, obedient to his diabolical double, he performed some frenzied mime, he realized, with piercing horror, that a kind of moral dam he had not known existed was washing away, and that soon the glass waves would engulf and dissolve his soul.

A desperate sensation of hopelessness and utmost despair possessed him, made still more painful by watching the suffering of his earthly beloved. Pale, exhausted, with hollowed but still beautiful eyes, her lips vulgarly daubed with colour, Kate swayed, barely able to stay upright, like a sleepwalker. She was fading away with every passing day.

But Aleksey was powerless to help her. His consciousness was foundering under waves of glass.

He finally lost all memory of his former existence; only rarely was the hellish murk of his being brightened by a flicker of consciousness. In one of these moments Aleksey was shaken to the core, despite his numbed feelings. He saw the glittering teeth of the glass man sink into Kate's shoulder; trails of blood covering her breast; glass fingers digging into her throat; and utter horror and despair in the eyes of his lover. He watched her tear free, rush through the room and hurl herself against the locked door of her studio. After a moment's desperate struggle the door burst from its tiny hinges and Kate fell at the foot of the Venetian mirror.

Aleksey saw the glass man catch his lover by the hair, pull her to him, raise her and fling her in fury to the floor, then prepare to fall once again upon his victim. Circles of fire blazed in Aleksey's eyes. With all the strength of his remaining will he threw himself towards the frenziedly struggling bodies ...

He heard glass shatter as he tumbled to the floor of his real room amid the splinters of the Venetian mirror.

An instant later, he saw Kate's horrified eyes as she stared at the two Alekseys: his double fled in brute terror. It did not even occur to Aleksey to pursue him; he flung himself at the side of his sobbing, long-suffering lover and, pressing her head to his breast, began to stroke her hair and cover her weeping eyes with kisses.

When she grew a little calmer and her body no longer shook with convulsive sobbing, he carefully lifted her in his arms and carried her into the bedroom. As he passed her oval looking-glass, he accidentally glanced into it and almost dropped his precious burden in horror. In the mirror reflection, Kate's lifeless body hung in the air, supported by nothing. Nothing in the glass ether reflected Aleksey, and he realized that his reflection was racing in panic somewhere through the Moscow streets.

Chapter 3

Being relatively peaceful, thus affording a pause not only for the author and the heroes of his tale, but also for the reader

A week had passed since the day Aleksey regained his flesh-and-blood existence. Kate was sleeping. Her hair lay tumbled across a cambric pillow; her eyebrows quivered as she dreamed. Aleksey had put aside his yellow-covered French novel, and for more than an hour he had been watching her gentle breathing, and pondering.

He was attempting to reckon the destruction his life had suffered from the stormy episode of the Venetian mirror, and also to decide the essential question: could this damage be undone? The cactuses, tortoiseshell pieces and erotic German engravings which the double had scattered through the rooms had been thrown out immediately. The outward appearance of his former way of life was being gradually restored, yet Aleksey still seemed to smell something rotten, and a foul sense of defilement filled his soul as he walked through the rooms that had once delighted him. The loss of his mirror reflection and his reluctance to constantly remind Kate of what had happened obliged him to dispose of all the mirrors in the house, and the harmonious décor that had been arranged around the bottomless depths of facing mirrors was irrevocably destroyed.

However, Aleksey was confident that everything in the physical world could be made right. He was also sure that the glassy numbness of his mind, which recurred from time to time, transforming him into a wordless mannequin, would disappear. Hot baths and the leisured peacefulness of his life were already beginning to wash away the poison of the mirror world.

He was much more concerned about Kate. She had seemed genuinely delighted by his return; she was profoundly astonished by his account of his glass existence; she shuddered with horror at the memory of her own sufferings, and she dreamed of a long holiday somewhere remote. However, Aleksey's calm caresses, his tender, meek kisses no longer seemed to content her. It was a mystery to him how volcanic passion, once awoken, could not be satisfied by mortal love or caresses, and this troubled him immeasurably.

His worry grew to extreme proportions when he dimly began to suspect that his glass double had not dissolved like a puff of smoke, like a monster from a children's fairy tale, but was still living somewhere nearby, watching over his prey. The struggle between the two of them was still far from finished.

The previous day, in the evening crowds on Kuznetsky Bridge, among the top-hats and the nodding egret feathers of the ladies' bonnets, he had seemed to catch a momentary glimpse of familiar features. In the figure of a passer-by hurrying rapidly down Petrovka he thought he had recognized the bony limbs of the mirror man. This suspicion of an encounter was bolstered by the constant gossip of Moscow friends about adventures that Aleksey had certainly never had in gambling houses and other Moscow dens of ill-fame.

Thus in the darkness of the night, as the pendulum slowly struck the hours, seated beside a sleeping Kate, Aleksey could almost physically sense his enemy wandering through the streets of Moscow, climbing long flights of stairs from floor to floor.

Kate shuddered, frowned, and woke, sitting up on the divan. His smile froze on his lips when he saw her peaceful, half-asleep eyes suddenly open wide with wild horror. Flinging her arms out before her, she collapsed with an inhuman scream. Aleksey turned in the direction where she had pointed. Beyond the misted glass doors on the balcony, before a background of twisted black trees in the garden, he met the unbending gaze of those eyes which had first transfixed him in the cellars beneath the Canale Gracio.

Chapter 4

Which recounts Aleksey's struggle against his mirror double, and which obliges the reader to travel from one corner of the city of Moscow to another and back again

Aleksey fired a final random shot into the reeds beside the humpbacked willow where he thought he had seen the shadow he was pursuing. Then he paused in exhaustion, nervously squeezing the handle of his Colt. Eddies of wind rustled the autumnal leaves on the twisted willow branches on the river bank; fragments of cloud skated feverishly through the sky, throwing moonlit shadows on the overgrown garden.

Aleksey was shaken. Mentally evaluating his much-reduced moral strength atom by atom, he realized how far he had already surrendered to despair.

Late in the evening, while a pale, anaemic Kate, withdrawn deep inside herself, was pouring tea in the round dining room, he apathetically discussed with her plans for the struggle and defence against their elusive enemy; he strove harder to catch his lover's eye, worriedly trying to fathom her secret thoughts, than he did to heed her languid replies.

The blinds were fully drawn across the windows; the hearth, half-covered by a screen, supplied warmth and peaceful comfort. But a worrying extra meaning pervaded everything, even the flickering flame of the smouldering logs, the rustle of the wind in the garden as it filtered through the window-blinds, the casual clink of tea-cups, the quiet conversation, and the random barks of the guard dogs roaming the garden.

Kate languidly rejected all Aleksey's cunning plans to trick the glass man into a trap, along with all other ways of organizing their defence; in an exhausted voice, she asked to spend the entire winter in the countryside outside Moscow, where Aleksey would doubtless recover from his shock and where he would be able to consider himself safe from his terrible pursuer. Studying her face, Aleksey noticed that it had become dark and embittered;

that darkness was inflicted on her soul by the gaze of the other, against whom he was powerless to fight and by whom he had been driven to the final border of despair.

Gradually, his consciousness seemed to physically contract. The room, the smouldering hearth, and the Empire lines of the furniture sank into a misty gloom. His brain was overcome by an attack of glassy numbness, and soon everything seemed to swim in motionless motion. In his semiconscious state, he saw Kate rise and go out, but he was unable to follow her.

He imagined that his entire house had sunk to the bottom of the mirror realm and that there, beyond its walls, where a glass storm was raging, dozens of his doubles, all as completely identical as a shoal of fish in a still pool, were circling in expectation of their prey. He could feel how only the thin membrane of the walls and curtains separated him from an all-engulfing glass nightmare, and how those same walls of his house were gradually dissolving in the mirror ether, just as sugar dissolves in a glass of hot tea.

He gazed at the smouldering coals of the fire, and their blue, upwards-arching tongues of flame grew and filled the entire space, blocking the whole room from his gaze, wherever he looked ...

Through this enchanted radiance, he saw the door open. Neither entirely awake nor entirely dreaming, he descried the respectfully inclined figure of his butler Grigory.

With difficulty, Aleksey persuaded himself that the flickering outline of the figure trembling in the murk was real. But the figure immediately dissolved into the surrounding air when Aleksey noticed a silver tray in its hands, and on the tray, the only solid object in a world of quivering shapes, the firm, fixed rectangle of a light-blue envelope. With endlessly elongated fingers he picked up the blue envelope, which he fancied was made of glass. Suddenly, words written in backwards mirror script flared up and blazed through its parchment; at the same moment, an ocean of glass ether seemed to gush into the room through the collapsing walls.

Losing his last lifeline, Aleksey cried out; and the nightmare, swirling around him, melted away.

Before him stood a very frightened Grigory, who really did

hold a tray bearing a large light-blue envelope.

After sending Grigory away and opening the envelope, Aleksey found a sheet of his own writing-paper, covered in his own handwriting, which was somehow written backwards, mirror-style. In the note, the diabolical glass being jeered at everything Aleksey held sacred, called him a murderer, and suggested that they resolve their struggle by meeting at six o'clock in the morning the following day under the walls of the Simonov Monastery, in order to decide in a fair duel which of them deserved to live under the sun.

Aleksey did not try to sleep that night. Grigory went to the door of his study at two and at four in the morning, and each time saw his master bent over his desk, sorting out papers in the glimmer from the flickering candelabra.

Aleksey had regained all the acute clarity of conscious thought. The decisive nature of the moment was clear to him; he put all his affairs in order and wrote three letters setting out the terms of his will. As soon as it began to grow light, he threw on a dark-blue coat, placed a new cartridge in his pistol, put out the candles, whose smoke sank in slow spirals, and with a final glance at the spot where he had dreamed and planned so much, he pressed a barely noticeable panel on one of the book-cases. The case soundlessly moved away from the wall and revealed a secret passage under the garden, leading to the Yauza.

Within half an hour, Aleksey was standing at the foot of the willows by the brink of Liza's Pond.[2] A patch of fog covered the surface of the water and the bend of the road; the trees' twisted black limbs, already stripped by autumn, showed black against the light-grey mist of morning. The rising sun sparkled on drops of dew. A splendid Indian summer's day was dawning in Moscow.

For twenty minutes, Aleksey anxiously paced backwards and forwards along the muddy bank. People began to appear. A rag merchant, rummaging with his staff in a pile of rubbish, stared curiously at Aleksey. Carts carrying cabbages rumbled by, and two women in brightly-coloured dresses and pea-jackets passed chattering loudly, pulling their shawls more tightly around them against the morning's freshness and glancing mistrustfully at Aleksey.

It was clear that he had wasted his time.

Aleksey glanced around, and was suddenly possessed by a dreadful suspicion. He realized that he had fallen, with unpardonable stupidity, into an elementary trap. He ran for the gate.

And when the cabman's foaming horse brought him to the house on the Yauza, he saw that it was surrounded by an agitated crowd. Moments later, the rough hands of the police shoved him into his study, which he had left two hours before. Behind his desk he saw a man he had met somewhere before, the police inspector Ivantsov.

Chapter 5

The final chapter, providing an end to our tale as well as not a few proofs that beyond the Moscow River there exist more things than respectable pedants will admit

Aleksey immediately realized what had really happened when he was accused of the forcible abduction of his wife Kate and of murdering the old man Grigory for trying to prevent it.

For three days he tried to prove the unprovable. For three days, shut up in his study, he endured humiliating medical assessments and unflattering cross-examinations. Only the evidence of a cab-driver, Khorkhordin, and a rag-merchant (found by advertising in the newspapers) established his alibi, which was supported by undeniable differences in dress and by the unanimous assertion of all witnesses that the murderer was left-handed, which matched the nature of the fatal blow.

After that, Aleksey was left in peace in his deserted house on the Yauza.

For entire days and nights he wept in Kate's abandoned room, lacking the will even to think through what had happened. His troubled soul was distressed by everything that had belonged to Kate. He burst into tears when he found the red pencil she had used to outline her lips. Dumbly and uncomprehendingly, he stared at her grey slippers, discarded in the middle of the room; with horror, he tried to guess the last lines she might have read in the book she failed to finish on that fateful night.

Only after two more days had passed did he begin to doubt the inevitability of her death, which had seemed so obvious to him at first. Aleksey gradually collected his thoughts and memories and began to re-establish the events leading up to her kidnapping more calmly. As often happens, the new shock wiped away the traces of the old one; he completely freed himself from the attacks of glassy numbness, and gradually recovered his former spirits.

Examining Kate's room for the hundredth time one day – still just as she had left it on that dreadful morning – he noticed between the edge of the mattress and the bed-board some coppers, a toothbrush and a card folded in two, evidently thrust down there during the struggle and overlooked by the police. The card was an advertisement for the chiromancer and fortune-teller Eleanor de Ramanesco, who lived somewhere on the Kanava in the alleys off Pyatnitskaya Street.

This was very little to go on, but nonetheless, it was a lead. A surge of unexpected good cheer filled Aleksey's spirit; he even imagined that the ornately printed black letters of the card radiated some sort of energizing fluid.

He set to quartering the Kanava bank between Pyatnitskaya Street and Kadashevsky Street until he found the place indicated by the typically cryptic Moscow address. The city's Indian summer had reached its peak. A water-cart plied the middle of the dried-up Kanava, decanting buckets of water into a green barrel. Two little boys were splashing in the cloudy water, and a crowd of small children had flocked around an ice-cream seller. Cobwebs floated on the light breeze, and puffs of white cloud hung unmoving in the translucent autumn sky.

On the property of the burgher Perkhushkin, behind some trees and an ochre-coloured two-storey house, he found a neglected garden, choked with acacias and lilies. Beyond this stood a monumental, gloomy stone building with tiny windows, built long before the Sevastopol campaign. Aleksey rang and knocked for a long time, unable to decide whether to enter by

the half-open door. At last he gathered his courage, stepped over
the wooden threshold lined with thick felt, and started up the
sagging, right-slanting staircase towards the inner rooms.

A strange odour of lamp-oil, incense and old books, such as
may be found in archbishops' palaces and episcopal museums,
confounded his senses. He entered the first chamber, evidently
the fortune-teller's parlour. An involuntarily ironic smile flickered on his lips at the sight of the naive decor, obviously intended
by the mistress to impress her clients. Pentacles and astral triangles were daubed wildly on the walls, there were zodiacal symbols
and strange tripod-shaped pieces of furniture, Egyptian-style
censers and Empire sofas resembling the one on which Madame
de Récamier reclines in David's painting. In the light of a clear
autumn day, all these things looked like cheap theatrical props,
purchased randomly in Smolensky Market.

Aleksey coughed and waited, listening. In the oppressive
silence he could hear only the sound of some liquid dripping,
drop by drop, in a distant room. Evidently the mistress, not
expecting visitors, had gone out to visit a neighbour and might
return to the abandoned house at any moment. Aleksey almost
seated himself on one of the 'magical' chairs to wait, but recalling
his essentially investigative intentions, he moved on decisively
into the depths of the inner rooms.

The next chamber impressed him by its still more pronoun-
cedly magical decoration. Ancient retorts and stills, various
astrolabes and great heaps of ancient books, bound in greyish-
yellow pigskin with black Latin letters on their spines, disturbed
Aleksey strangely, all the more so as these objects did not
resemble a museum collection but looked well-used, lying as
though someone had only just put them down. It suddenly struck
Aleksey that all these objects were not decorative, but kept their
genuine, original, serious purpose, and his head began to spin.

He took up a fat volume with the word *Occulto* on its spine,
but before he could undo the clasp on the binding, the book flew
open, wrenched itself out of his hands and hurtled around the
room like a spinning top, scattering pages and knocking over
everything it touched. Aleksey shrank back to the window, only
to jump away again in terror. Instead of Perkhushkin's garden,

through the glass pane he saw hundreds of grotesquely grinning mirror phantoms floating in the air.

With a single leap, Aleksey reached the door and dashed through it. Horrified, he saw that, instead of the fortune-teller's parlour, which he had only just left, he was in an enormous hall, with huge, dark mirrors set in its walls, in which the turbid waves of strange reflections rippled like the surface of a river. In the air – now here, now there – electric sparks flared, and there was an unbearable stink of ozone. Aleksey felt dizzier and dizzier; circles of fire flickered in front of his eyes, a cold sweat broke out across his brow, and he seized his head in his hands.

In the same instant, he saw in the mirror in front of him his frenziedly leaping reflection, thumbing his nose at him and, laughing wildly, feinting with his fists.

With a howl of fury, Aleksey flung himself at him and struck the hard surface with all his might. Glass shattered. Aleksey hurtled into a dark abyss and found himself crawling head downwards along a gigantic black agate pipe. On the opposite side his double was capering frenziedly, and below them the pipe, glittering with liquid mercury, tapered into the mouth of a well. Aleksey's fingers slid over the agate surface, his nails leaving no trace on the polished stone. He could see his double preparing to deal him a death-blow when he reached the rim of the well of mercury.

By a superhuman effort of will, at the last instant and on the very brink of the pit, Aleksey sprang almost from a kneeling position over the mercury surface and straight onto the back of the hunched glass man. Not expecting an attack, the latter collapsed and toppled heavily, taking Aleksey with him. Struggling desperately, they rolled into a ball and slowly slipped beneath the surface of the melting metal. Suddenly Aleksey felt his knees touch the bottom. With another superhuman effort, he seized the glass man by the throat and, ramming his own head into the other's body, plunged into the depths of the pit of mercury. Keeping his own head above the surface, he continued to strangle his weakening, floundering opponent under the blanket of mercury.

The liquid metal splashed under his hands; he saw nothing except the glittering surface, since *he himself had no reflection.*

The glass man stopped moving, but Aleksey's hands continued to choke him. He felt a bizarre sensation, as though his victim were expanding, transforming into a jellylike substance and dissolving. Aleksey shuddered, watching strange stains appear on the waves of mercury. A moment later he realized that these were fragments of his reflection, still scattered, not yet subdued. And as soon as his fingers met, losing the last traces of the glass being as it dissolved into the mercury, he saw his reflection, once again whole and submissive.

His strength deserted him, and with horror he felt his arms and legs give way; in his exhaustion he was sinking into the hellish embrace of the liquid metal. A moment later his head struck something hard and he briefly lost consciousness. When he recovered, he found himself lying on what felt like a mirror. He managed to lift himself up, and realized he was in the utterly empty hall of the Perkhushkin house, lying on a strange, glassy substance which seemed to have been decanted onto the floor and left to set.

As far as he could tell in the moonlight pouring into the room, the windows had long been broken; they were matted with cobwebs, the wainscots and oakum were peeling from the walls and from the half-collapsed ceiling. Aleksey stood up and satisfied himself that the surface of the mirror obediently reflected him. He walked up and down the room. Through the doorway, which had no hinges, he saw that the house was empty and had evidently been unoccupied for many years. Staggering, he made his way down the half-ruined staircase.

A dog barked at him from the darkness of Perkhushkin's courtyard; a woman who was shelling nuts with a soldier by the gates cast a suspicious glance at him. He dragged himself to a cab and ordered the driver to take him back to his house on the Yauza. He could feel that his face was covered in blood, and his body ached from cuts and bruises.

The Spasskaya clock-tower struck eleven.

The coachman drove slowly, and the twilight of the Moscow streets neither delighted nor oppressed Aleksey. On Pyatnitskaya Street a hairdresser's shining mirror seized his attention. He stopped the cab-driver, jumped out of the carriage and with trepidation made his way to the shop window. The oval mirror obediently reflected his pale, exhausted face, marked by traces of blood. He set off again. It seemed to him that years went by, that entire days passed between one hoof-beat and the next.

Not wishing to wake the household, he stopped the cab-driver beyond the garden, opened the side-gate with a key and went in by the secret entrance. The bookcase filled with Elsevier editions opened noiselessly, and Aleksey was met by a stream of light and the warmth and comfort of his study.

He trembled and stopped dead: in his old Voltaire armchair by the hearth, lit by the rosy reflections of smouldering logs, sat Kate. Hearing a rustle, she raised her eyes.

London, 1922

MIKHAIL BULGAKOV

The Red Crown

Historia morbi

More than anything else I hate sunlight, loud conversations and, of course, the endless thudding. I'm so afraid of people that if I hear unfamiliar steps and voices in the corridor in the evening, I start screaming for help. That's why I now have a room to myself, a peaceful, more pleasant one, no. 27 at the very end of the corridor. No-one can call on me here. But just to make myself even more secure, I spent a long time imploring Ivan Vasilyevich (I even wept in front of him) to let me have a typed certificate. He agreed and wrote out a statement that I was under his protection and that nobody had the right to remove me. But to be honest, I wasn't completely convinced that his signature was enough. So he made one of the professors sign it as well and he sealed it with a round blue stamp: that was quite another matter. I know many cases when men have stayed alive purely because a stamped piece of paper was found in their pocket. True, that worker in Berdyansk, the one with the sooty smear on his cheek, was hanged from a lamppost right after they found a stamped document balled up and crammed down his boot ... But that was a very different case. He was a Bolshevik criminal, and that blue stamp was a criminal's stamp. That stamp sent him to the lamppost, and it's thanks to that lamppost that I'm now ill (don't worry, I know perfectly well that I'm ill).

The truth is that even before what happened to Kolya, something had happened to me. I walked away so I wouldn't see how they hanged that man, but my terror came with me in the trembling of my legs. At that time, naturally, there was nothing I could do, but now I would say to him straight up:

'General, sir, you're a monster! You have no right to hang people!'

You can tell from this that I'm not faint-hearted; I didn't go on about the stamp because I was afraid of dying. Oh, I have no fear of death. I'll put a gun to my head soon enough, because Kolya will drive me to despair. But I'll shoot myself so as not to see or hear Kolya again. And the thought that others might come too is beyond bearing.

For days on end I've been lying on my bed and staring out of the window. A gash of sky yawns over our green garden; on the far side a big yellow building looms, its blank, windowless, seven-storey wall facing me. Right under the roof hangs an enormous, rusty square. A signboard for the dental laboratory. In white letters. At first I hated it. Then I got used to it, and if they took it down I'd probably miss it. All day long it hangs there swaying: I concentrate on it and think about many important things. But then the evening comes. The dome grows darker, the white letters vanish from sight. I turn grey, melting into the murk, just as my thoughts also dissolve. Twilight is a dreadful time, full of meaning. Everything dwindles, everything blurs into something else. The ginger cat begins his wandering through the corridors on velvet paws, and every so often I scream. But I won't allow them to light the lamp, because if it's burning I shall spend the whole evening sobbing and wringing my hands. It's better to wait patiently for the moment when that last, most important image will light up again in the flowing darkness.

* *

Our old mother said to me:

'I won't last long like this. I see madness everywhere. You're the oldest, and I know you love him. Bring Kolya home. Bring him home. You are the oldest.'

I said nothing.

Then she poured all of her longing and all of her pain into these words:

'Find him! You're pretending that this is the way things have to be. But I know you. You're intelligent and you've known for a long time that this is all madness. Bring him to me for a day – just one day. I'll let him leave again.'

She was lying. Could she really let him go, after she saw him? I said nothing.

'I only want to kiss his eyes. They'll kill him anyway. Can't you feel for me? He's my little boy. Who else can I ask? You're the oldest. Bring him to me.'

I couldn't bear it. I said, without meeting her eyes: 'Very well.'

But she caught me by the sleeve and turned me towards her so that she could see my face:

'No, you must swear to me that you'll bring him to me alive.'

How could I make an oath like that? But, like the madman I am, I swore: 'I give you my word.'

* *

My mother was too fearful. That's what I was thinking when I left her. But then I saw the crooked lamppost in Berdyansk. General, sir, I agree that I was no less guilty than you of the crime; I am paying a terrible price for that man with the smear of soot on his face. But my brother has nothing to do with that. He is nineteen years old.

After Berdyansk I obeyed my oath scrupulously: I found him not twenty kilometres off, by the stream. It was an unusually bright day. Throwing up swirls of white dust, a cavalry unit was proceeding at a walk along the road to the village, from which a cloud of ash was rising. He was riding at the edge of the first column, with the peak of his cap pulled down over his eyes. I remember every detail: one of his spurs had slipped all the way down his heel. The strap of his cap stretched across his cheek and under his chin.

'Kolya! Kolya!' I bawled and ran to the ditch by the side of the road.

He started. In the column, the gloomy, sweaty soldiers turned their heads.

'Why, brother!' he yelled back. For some reason he never called me by name; it was always 'brother'. I am ten years older than him, and he always listened to me carefully. 'Wait, wait here,' he went on, 'by this spinney. We'll be right back. I can't leave the squadron.'

At the edge of the wood, at a little distance from the dismounted troop, we smoked our cigarettes greedily. I was calm with him, and firm. This was all madness; our mother was perfectly right.

And I whispered to him: 'Just as soon as you come back from that village, we'll go together to the city. And we'll get out of this place forever, as soon as we can.'

'What do you mean, brother?'

'Don't say a word,' I said, 'don't say anything. I know what to do.'

The troop mounted up. Swaying in the saddle, they rode off at a trot towards the black smoke-clouds. A thudding came from the distance. An endless thudding.

What could happen in an hour? They would come back. And I settled down beside the Red Cross station to wait.

* *

Within the hour I saw him. He was returning at a trot, as he had left, but there was no sign of the squadron. Instead there was just a rider with a lance galloping on either side of him, and one of them – the one on the right – kept leaning over my brother as if to whisper in his ear. Screwing up my eyes in the sun, I stared at this strange masquerade. He had ridden away in a grey officer's cap; he came back in a red one. And the day had ended. His face had become a black shield under a coloured crown. Where his hair and his brow had been was a crimson halo with yellow flecks.

The horseman with the tousled red crown was my brother; he sat his lathered mount rigidly, and if the rider on the right had not been carefully holding him up, you could have imagined he was on his way to a parade.

The horseman sat proudly in the saddle, but he was blind and dumb. Two wet red stains were all that remained of the bright eyes sparkling an hour before ...

The rider on the left dismounted and seized the rein with his left hand, while the man on the right very gently pulled Kolya's arm. Kolya sagged sideways.

Someone said: 'Hey, our volunteer's been hit by shrapnel. Orderly, call a doctor ...'

The other grunted and answered, 'A doctor won't do any good, my friend. This one needs a priest.'

At this point a blanket of black crêpe came down and covered everything, even the headdress ...

* *

I've become used to everything: to our white building, the twilight, the ginger cat that comes and scratches at my door. But I cannot get used to his visits. The first time it happened I still lived downstairs, in room 63: he appeared out of the wall, wearing his red crown. Nothing about him frightened me: he looks just the same in my dreams. But I know perfectly well that if he's wearing the crown, he must be dead. And then he spoke, moving dry lips clotted with blood. He parted his lips, came to attention, raised his hand to his crown, and said:

'Brother, I can't leave the squadron.'

And every time since that first time, the same thing happens. He arrives in his soldier's blouse with the ammunition-belts over his shoulder, with his curving sabre and spurs that never jingle; and he says the same words. First he salutes. And then:

'Brother, I can't leave the squadron.'

How he frightened me the first time! He scared the entire clinic. It was all over for me then. I've figured it out rationally: if he's wearing the crown, he's been killed, and if a dead man comes and speaks to me, I must be mad.

* *

Ah, it's twilight. The hour of retribution. But there was one time when I dozed off and dreamed of a parlour with old-fashioned red plush furniture. I saw a cosy armchair with a broken leg. There was a portrait on the wall in a black, dusty frame, and flowers in vases. There was an upright piano, with its lid open and the score of *Faust* set out on it. He was standing in the doorway, and a wild joy blazed up in my heart. He wasn't dressed as a cavalryman. He looked just as he used to before those terrible days. He was wearing a black double-breasted jacket, the elbow smeared with chalk. His eyes were bright with mischievous laughter, and a lock of hair hung over his forehead. He jerked his head:

'Brother, come to my room. You'll never believe what I'm going to show you!'

The light shining from his eyes lit up the whole parlour, and the weight of remorse inside me melted. That ill-omened day when I sent him off, saying 'Go', had never happened, no thudding, no clouds of ash. He had never ridden away from us, never served in the cavalry. He was playing the piano, the ivory keys were tinkling, the golden thatch of his hair was glinting, and his laughing voice was full of life.

* *

Then I woke up, and there was nothing. No radiance, no eyes. I've never had another dream like that since. And that very night, to make my hellish torment even worse, the cavalryman came all the same, in battledress, stepping silently, and said the words he was destined to say for all eternity.

I decided to put a stop to it. I spoke to him firmly:

'What is this for, my eternal torturer? Why do you come? I admit everything. I take the blame on myself, because I sent you on that deadly campaign. The weight of that other man, the one they hanged, I also take upon myself. And now I have told you this, forgive me and let me be.'

General, sir, he said not a word, and stayed.

Then my suffering made me cruel and I wished with all my heart that he would appear to you just once, raising his hand to his crown in salute. I assure you that that would be the end of you, just as it finished me. In the blink of an eye. However, perhaps you too have a visitor in the dark hours of the night?

Who knows, perhaps that grubby man with the soot-stain comes to you, the one we hanged from the lamppost in Berdyansk? If that's so, our suffering is justified. I sent Kolya to help you with your hanging; you hanged men too. You gave countless orders that were never written down.

So then, he stayed. I scared him away with a yell. I roused everyone. The medical assistant ran in, they woke up Ivan Vasilyevich. I didn't want to see another dawn, but I wasn't allowed to do myself in. They tied me up with a sheet, took the broken glass away, and bandaged me up. I've been in room 27 since then. After they'd dosed me I started dozing off, and I heard the assistant's voice in the corridor. She said:

'A hopeless case.'

* *

It's true. There's no hope for me. Vainly, in the twilight, in my scorching grief, I wait for that dream: the old familiar room and the peaceful light of his shining eyes. None of it exists and it never will again.

The burden is still upon me. And I wait patiently at night for the familiar cavalryman with unseeing eyes to appear and say to me hoarsely:

'I can't leave the squadron.'

It's true, I am a hopeless case. He will torture me to death.

1922

MIKHAIL BULGAKOV

A Seance

Don't summon him in vain!
Don't summon him in vain!
MEPHISTOPHELES in Gounod's *Faust*

I

Ksyushka, the idiot maid, announced: 'That feller has turned up to see yer ...'

Madame Luzina snapped: 'In the first place, how many times have I told you not to speak to me in that familiar manner! What sort of fellow?' And she sailed into the hall. There she found Ksavery Antonovich Vulpinich hanging his cap on a stag's horn with a sour smile on his face. He had overheard Ksyushka's announcement.

Madame Luzina flushed. 'Oh, Lord! Forgive me, Ksavery Antonovich! That country-bred fool ... She's the same with everyone ... Welcome!'

'Oh, please don't trouble yourself!' Vulpinich spread his hands elegantly. 'Good evening, Zinaida Ivanovna!' He placed his feet in third position, inclined his head, and lifted Madame Luzina's hand to his lips.

However, just as he was about to favour Madame with a long and lingering gaze, her husband Pavel Petrovich slithered through the other door. The gaze was instantly quenched.

'Ye-es,' Pavel Petrovich was already drawling, 'a "feller" ... ha–ha! Sa-vages! Positive savages! I always think: there's freedom for you ... Communism. If you please! How can anyone dream about Communism, when we're surrounded by creatures like Ksyushka! A feller ... Ha–ha! You'll forgive us, for heaven's sake! A feller ...'

'Oh, what a fool he is!' thought Madame Luzina, interrupting him: 'Now why are we standing in the hall? Come into the dining room!'

'Indeed, please step into the dining room,' Pavel Petrovich echoed her, 'after you!'

The three of them, crouching low, passed under the black chimney-pipe and emerged in the dining room.

'Just as I always say,' Pavel Petrovich continued, with his arm around his guest, 'as for Communism ... There's no question about it: Lenin is a man of genius, but ... may I offer you a cigarette from my ration ... hee–hee! I got them today ... but Communism – there's a thing, that, as you might say, by its very nature ... Oh, has it burst? Take another, here, from the edge ... In its essence it demands a certain level of development ... Oh, is it a touch too soggy? What dreadful cigarettes! Here, please take this one ... In terms of its social content ... Wait a little, it'll light ... What awful matches! Rationed as well ... a certain degree of consciousness ...'

'Stop a moment, Paul! Ksavery Antonovich, will you have tea before or after?'

'I think ... well, before,' replied Ksavery Antonovich.

'Ksyushka! Put on the primus! They'll all be here any minute! Everyone is terribly fascinated – terribly! I even invited Sofia Ilinichna ...'

'And what about the table?'

'We actually got hold of one! Although, just one thing ... it has nails in it. But still, I hope that won't matter?'

'Hmm. Of course, that isn't good ... But we'll make do somehow or other ...'

Ksavery Antonovich favoured the three-legged inlaid table with a brief glance, and his fingers moved of their own accord.

Pavel Petrovich began again: 'I have to admit I don't believe in these things. I'm not a believer, or whatever you call it. That said, it's true that in nature ...'

'Oh, what nonsense you talk! It's wonderfully interesting! But I warn you: I'll be frightened!' Madame Luzina's eyes sparkled with enthusiasm: she dashed out into the hall, swiftly adjusted her coiffure in front of the looking-glass, and flitted into the kitchen. From there issued the hiss of the primus and the clattering of Ksyushka's heels.

'I'm of the opinion ...' Pavel Petrovich began, but he didn't finish the sentence.

Someone was knocking on the front door. Lenochka appeared first, followed by the lodger. Nor did Sofia Ilinichna, a second-form schoolteacher, hang back. And immediately after her came Boboritsky with his fiancée Ninochka.

The dining room filled up with laughter and tobacco smoke.

'We should have done this long, long ago!'

'I have to admit ...'

'Ksavery Antonovich! You'll be our medium. Surely you will! Won't you?'

'Ladies and gentlemen,' said Ksavery Antonovich teasingly, 'in truth, I'm just as much of an amateur ... Although ...'

'Oh, not at all! You made a table rise in the air!'

'I have to admit ...'

'I assure you, Manya saw it with her own eyes – a sort of greenish glow!'

'How dreadful! I shouldn't like to see a thing like that!'

'The light must be on! There must be light – or I won't agree,' cried Sofia Ilinichna, a solidly built, very material lady. 'Otherwise I won't believe a thing!'

'If you'll allow me ... We'll give you our word of honour ...'

'No! No! With the lights off! Like that time when Julius Caesar described his death to us ...'

'Oh, I can't bear it! Don't ask about death!' exclaimed Boboritsky's fiancée, but Boboritsky whispered languidly: 'Lights off! Lights off!'

Ksyushka, her mouth hanging open in astonishment, brought in the tea-pot.

Madame Luzina rattled the tea-cups. 'Hurry up, ladies and gentlemen, we don't want to waste time!'

And they sat down to take tea ...

The window, on Ksavery Antonovich's direction, was tightly covered with a shawl. They put out the light in the hall, and Ksyushka was ordered to sit in the kitchen and not clatter her heels. They seated themselves, and the room became dark ...

2

Ksyushka was bored and worried at the same time. There was some sort of devilry afoot. It was pitch-dark everywhere. *They*'d locked themselves in. At first there was silence, and then a gentle, regular knocking noise. Ksyushka froze when she heard it. She felt petrified. Then there was silence again, followed by a muffled voice:

'Almighty God?'

Ksyushka stirred on her greasy stool and began eavesdropping. Tap ... tap ... tap ... The voice of one of the guests (a real tub of lard, Lord forgive her!) seemed to be droning: 'A, ba, ba, ba ...'

Tap ... tap ...

Ksyushka was rocking on her stool like a pendulum, veering between terror and curiosity. Now she fancied she glimpsed a horned devil through the darkened window, now she yearned to be in the hall ... At last she could restrain herself no longer. She eased open the door of the lighted kitchen and sneaked into the hall. Feeling ahead with her hands, she bumped into some trunks. She inched further forwards, fumbled around, spied the door, and put her eye to the crack ... But in the crack lay an infernal darkness, out of which voices issued ...

3

'Spirit, who are you?'
'A, B, C, D, E ...' Tap!
'E!' several voices sighed.
'A, B, C, D ...'
'Em!'
Tap ... Tap, tap ...
'Em-per! Oho! Gentlemen, ladies ...'
'Emperor Na-po ...'
Tap ... tap ...
'Na-po-le-on! Good Lord, how fascinating!'
'Keep quiet! Ask it! Ask it something!'

'What? Yes, ask it something! Now, who wants to go first?'

'Imperial spirit,' enquired Lenochka, haltingly and nervously, 'should I change jobs from Glavkhim to Zheleskom, or not?'[1]

Tap ... tap ... tap ...

'F ... O ... O ... Fool!' The Emperor Napoleon answered distinctly.

'Hee-hee!' giggled the insolent lodger.

A ripple of laughter spread around the table.

Annoyed, Sofia Ilinichna whispered: 'Must we really ask such nonsense!'

Lenochka's ears burned in the darkness.

'Don't be angry, noble spirit!' she implored, 'if you're not angry, please knock once!'

Napoleon obeyed the hands of Ksavery Antonovich, who was managing to do two things at once – brushing Madame Luzina's neck with his lips and spinning the table. Napoleon lifted one leg of the table before plunging it down on Pavel Petrovich's bunion.

'Sssss!' hissed Pavel Petrovich in agony.

'Ssssh! Ask it something!'

'You don't have any strangers in your flat?' asked the cautious Boboritsky.

'No, nobody! Ask what you want!'

'Imperial spirit, tell us, how much longer will the Bolsheviks remain in power?'

'Oho! That's an interesting one! Ssssh ... Count the knocks!'

Tap, tap, Napoleon rapped, favouring one of the table legs.

'T ... H ... R ... THREE M-O-N-T-H-S!'

'Oho!'

'Thank God!' exclaimed the fiancée, 'I hate them so!'

'Shh! What are you thinking of!'

'Well, there's nobody here!'

'Who will get rid of them? Tell us, spirit!'

They held their breath ... Tap, tap ...

Ksyushka was bursting with curiosity ...

At last she could hold herself in no longer. Starting back from her own reflection, which had flashed in the gloom of the mirror, she squeezed between the trunks back into the kitchen. Seizing her shawl, she sneaked back into the hall, hesitating briefly before taking the door key. Then she made up her mind, very gently opened the door and, letting her heels do their worst, tripped hastily down to Masha in the flat below.

4

Masha-from-below was on the front stairs beside the lift, with Duska from the fifth floor. There was a small fortune in sunflower seeds in Masha-from-below's pocket.

Ksyushka poured out her feelings.

'*They*'ve locked themselves up, girls ... *They*'re writing things down about the Emperor and about the Bolsheviks ... It's terrible dark in the apartment! The lodger's there, and master, and madam, and that fancy man of hers, and the schoolteacher ...'

'You don't say!' ooh'd Duska and Masha-from-below, and sticky sunflower husks spread all over the mosaic floor.

The door of apartment no. 3 banged, and down the stairs came a gallant in an extraordinary pair of trousers. Duska and Ksyushka and Masha-from-below squinted at him. His trousers were quite ordinary as far as the knees, cut from good cloth. But from the knees down, they widened out until they looked like bells.

A jersey strained across his square, sculpted chest, and on his hip the narrow muzzle of a gun peeped dully and ominously from a leather holster.

The gallant, jauntily cocking his head (gold letters ran across the band of his cap), made his way down to the lift with a slight swagger, making the bells swing. He threw the three girls a scorching glance and turned towards the exit.

'*They*'ve put out the lamps, because they don't want me to see ... Hee-hee! ... and *they*'re writing things down ... and saying that it's all up with the Bolsheviks ... An *imporor* ... Hee-hee!'

Something had happened to the gallant. His varnished shoes suddenly stuck to the floor. His steps grew halting. The gallant stopped abruptly and rummaged in his pockets as if he had forgotten something; then he yawned. Suddenly, appearing to change his mind, instead of going out by the main door, he turned back and sat on the bench, screened from Ksyushka's field of vision by a glass ledge with the inscription 'Porter'. He was evidently intrigued by a red-headed, rather chipped cupid on the wall. He stared hard at the cupid, as if memorizing it.

Having relieved her feelings, Ksyushka clattered back upstairs. The gallant yawned gloomily, glanced at his wristwatch, shrugged his shoulders, and, clearly bored with waiting for someone from apartment no. 3, he rose. With a lurch that set the bells swaying again, he set off a step behind Ksyushka.

When Ksyushka disappeared into the apartment, trying not to slam the door, a match flared in the darkness of the landing in front of the white number-plate – 24. The gallant no longer yawned nor dawdled.

'Twenty-four,' he said purposefully to himself and, with renewed energy and spirits, sped like an arrow down all six floors.

5

In the smoky darkness Socrates, who had replaced Napoleon, was working wonders. He danced like a madman, prophesying imminent disaster for the Bolsheviks. Perspiring but refusing to pause, Sofia Ilinichna was reading out the alphabet. Everyone's hands were numb, except Ksavery Antonovich's. Dim, whitish silhouettes shimmered in the gloom. When everyone's nerves were already stretched to the limits, the table – with the Greek sage seated upon it – rocked and rose upwards.

'Oh! ... That'll do! ... I'm frightened! ... No! Let it be! My dear one! Spirit! Higher! ... No-one is touching it with their feet? ... Of course not! ... Shh! ... O spirit! If you're real, play the note *la* on the piano!'

The Greek plummeted from a height and landed on the floor between their feet. Something broke inside him with a crack. Then he floundered up and, stepping on the toes of the squealing ladies, began to push his way towards the piano ... The spiritualists, bumping heads, rushed after him.

Ksyushka leapt up, as if stung, from her cotton blanket in the kitchen. Her squeak of 'Who's there?' went unheard by the frenzied spiritualists.

Some new, malicious and dreadful spirit had taken over the table, displacing the deceased Greek. The table clattered its feet terrifyingly, like machine-gun fire, flung itself from side to side and uttered nonsense syllables:

'Dra-tu-ma ... by ... y ... y ...'

'Dearest spirit!' the spiritualists moaned.

'What do you want?'

'The door!' the furious spirit finally wrung out.

'A-ha! ... The door! Do you hear that? It wants to run out the door! ... Let it go!'

Tik, tak, tuk – the table limped over to the door.

'Wait!' Boboritsky suddenly shouted, 'you see how powerful it is! Let it knock on the door without walking over to it!'

'Spirit! Knock on the door!'

And the spirit more than fulfilled their expectations. It rapped so hard on the far side of the door that three fists might have been knocking at once.

'Oh!' three voices yelped inside the room.

The spirit, however, was truly endowed with power. It thundered so hard on the door that the spiritualists' hair stood up on their heads. For an instant everyone held their breath; silence fell ...

Pavel Petrovich called out in a trembling voice:

'Spirit! Who are you?'

From the other side of the door a sepulchral voice replied:

'The Cheka.'

The spirit evaporated ignominiously and instantaneously from the table, which landed on its damaged leg and grew still. The spiritualists froze to the floor. Then Madame Luzina groaned: 'Oh Lo-ord!' and quietly collapsed in an unfeigned swoon on the breast of Ksavery Antonovich, who muttered: 'The devil take this idiotic caper!'

Pavel Petrovich opened the door with shaking hands. A moment later the lamps flared up, and the spirit appeared before the pale-as-snow spiritualists. He was dressed in leather – all in leather, from his cap to his briefcase. Moreover, he was not alone. An entire procession of subordinate spirits could be seen in the hall. Among them glimmered a sculpted chest, a glittering gun–barrel, a grey greatcoat, another greatcoat . . .

The spirit cast his eyes over the chaos of the spiritualists' room and, smirking unpleasantly, said:

'Your documents, please, comrades . . .'

Epilogue

Boboritsky got a week, the lodger and Ksavery Antonovich thir-teen days, but poor Pavel Petrovich was locked up for a month and a half.

1922

SIGIZMUND KRZHIZHANOVSKY

The Phantom

No pair of eyes that may accidentally stray beyond the title of this tale will be beguiled by its opening lines. They may as well turn away again, no matter whose they may be. In the tale that follows, you will not find the sort of phantoms spawned by dreams and delirium; likewise, this tale ignores phantoms both allegorical and symbolic. Its subject is as prosaic as possible, a thing made of wood, rubber and leather, the so-called medical 'phantom'. Or rather, one of that phantom's quintessential appurtenances.[1] Well then, don't trouble to read any further, avert your eyes from these lines; leave me alone with my tale.

As it happens, I am no more than the retailer of this tale; I provide only the words, while the facts are his – Twoman-Sklifsky's. To verify his existence, to test the substantiality of my supplier of facts, couldn't be simpler: your imagination need only go as far as that house over there, that conglomeration of bricks and chimneys. Here your imagination must teeter on tip-toe and peer in at a certain seventh-floor window, right under the roof of that huge building. Its eyes, and the dawn, will be met by a still-burning, dull yellow electric smudge, and a square book lying open on a square table. Pillowed on the page lie the cheek and ear, the tightly closed eyelids, and the lax, slumbering lips of Twoman-Sklifsky.[2] Dawn is gathering strength, and already you can descry a few words on part of the flat paper cushion, those not lost in the dent under the sleeper's head:

> … and after the phantom's birth canal is twisted to resemble a fish-hook, the hips and soft parts of the phantom are prepared; they are stuffed with hair and bast like soft furniture, and covered with canvas. After this the model is lined with soaked, softened leather; inside this, to replicate the *labia*

majora, a slit-like, serrated rubber plate is set, with a thickness of 4 or 5 mm. (the rubber is grey and solid, the kind used for attaching soles to shoes). Now that the main component of the model – its soul, so to say – may be considered ready, it is essential to arrange ...

... but the word 'arrange' collides with the crown of the sleeper's head and the remaining text dives under his dishevelled locks. Several more words, 'belong ... although not ... the method of Professor Schultz ... poss ...', skirt the bulge of his forehead and the protruding nose with its rhythmically flaring and subsiding nostrils.

What's this? On the other side of the wall, slippers start shuffling, a primus begins buzzing like a metallic bumble-bee, and a hatchet sinking into a log begins a dull but penetrating racket against the kitchen floor. Twoman-Sklifsky shudders awake, lifts his head from the printed lines, and wipes his eyes. I'll read the last part ... no; Twoman slams the book shut and, yawning, makes his way to the wash-basin. Next, six metal eagles slide their beaks into six clasps on his grey student jacket. On the wall to his left, a clock gives nine rusty coughs. My supplier of facts pushes his slicked-down quiff under the dark-blue band of his cap and shoves the door open. Now your imagination must hunker down and stay alert: for Twoman-Sklifsky, the action is about to begin.

I

A matt board on the door of the auditorium separated crossed-off numbers from those not-yet-crossed-off. A dozen of the not-yet-crossed-off milled around the board, riffling their text-books, propping their backs and elbows against the walls and the window-ledges. At intervals a wrinkled hand would wave, and another examinee would emerge from the suddenly opened doors. 'Next!'

Sklifsky stepped over the threshold. Above him arched the white vault of the ceiling. Before him was a tabletop covered in ink-stained, rumpled green oilcloth. To his left hunched a student, shoulder-blades twitching in agony, bending scarlet ears toward the examiner's questions. His chair, balanced on its front legs, bucked its hind ones in the air. Behind his back, a junior professor was flourishing his cuffs and a rapid flow of words could just be discerned in the rumble issuing from under the twisting shoulder-blades. A chair on the right of the table was vacant. A red, puffy face crested with needles of grey hair winked at Twoman behind its spectacles: Do your best. He stepped forward and flipped over a cardboard square: 39.

'What have you got there? Hmmm ... "The phantom and its appurtenances; basic exercises". So. Nikita!'

The assistant scurried smartly over to the prepared model and rolled the phantom towards Twoman-Sklifsky, castors squeaking, splaying the wooden stumps of its legs, its canvas-covered hips rocking on the screws attaching it to the stool.

'What do you know about obstetric models and their replacements ...?'

Inside Twoman, a textbook flipped open and started tossing out sentences:

'This model, generally built from rubber interlaid with paper, is retained in modern practice. In demonstrating the insertion of the forceps – in cases of cephalic presentation, especially in the anteroposterior pelvic diameter – an ordinary leather ball packed with compressed oakum is employed; to demonstrate still more complicated extractions, the specially injected and prepared corpse of a stillborn child is used.'

'Good. Nikita!'

And Nikita, rushing up from the far end of the table, pushed a glass basin across to Twoman. Over its thick rim, rocking sleepily, agitated by Nikita's shove, the phantom's main 'appurtenance' was visible: a glycerine-infused, bloated little body, soaked up to the crown of its head in alcohol, its purplish-white palms and heels tucked inwards.

The professor kneaded his grey needles:

'Now then. Let's operate. Labour in the fourth stage. A face presentation. Cranial diameter oblique. Prepare yourself – and keep calm.'

Nikita, with an encouraging grin at the student, dangled his long arms over the glass basin and whispered:

'Fifka.'

Twoman understood: even this tiny corpse, born for the hundredth time, passing obediently from forceps to forceps, demonstrating birth, had a name of its own, bestowed by God knows whom. Without shifting his gaze from the child, Twoman-Sklifsky donned rubber gloves and tested the grip of the forceps. In that instant Fifka's head appeared on the other side of the glass rim, its round forehead deformed by previous compressions. Dozens of forceps had evidently dragged it through this phantom already: even before it could begin to live, the head of the fetus bore a martyr's crown of crimson-grey ulcers; its eyelids, ringed by blue lines, were squeezed tight shut; slime and preserving spirits dripped from its slitlike mouth.

Deftly and rapidly Nikita inserted the fetus into the phantom's exposed pelvic basin: its legs stirred and strained, joints squeaking. Twoman, bending over the device, moved – cautiously, feeling his way – towards the crown of Fifka's head, at first with the index and third finger of his left hand, keeping the index finger stiff; at once he felt the sagittal suture and the upper edge of an ear. His right hand brought up first one, then the other blade of the forceps, which instantly gripped the phantom's temples. The lock engaged – and in the same second, Twoman clearly heard something squeak, thinly and pitifully, there inside, under the rubbery crack. Without knowing why, the student released the forceps and looked up at the professor. But the professor was looking past him, and then, abruptly, shaking his beard wrathfully, he broke off to confront some voices outside the door: he poked his head out and barked something about noise, mayhem, 'the devil knows what', science, and the youth of today. Nikita, craning his neck towards the doorway, fretted in sympathy. But Twoman was barely conscious of this sudden hubbub; after looking back at the phantom, he now saw, as if through fog, the locked forceps smoothly revolving in spirals, stretching the rubber, slipping out of the phantom with a soft squelching noise; behind it – pushing it along – was a head, and next came a shoulder, a jutting elbow, a tangle of tiny legs. The little body hung momentarily, swayed back and forth, then, weighed down by the forceps, landed on the floorboards with a damp thud. The student stood in utter bewilderment, understanding nothing, not even trying to understand.

The door slammed loudly, and the professor, having roared his fill, marched triumphantly back to the table:

'What have we here? Aha. All done? We-ell. Is this worth a C, or not quite? Clear it up.'

Pre-empting Nikita, Twoman-Sklifsky, with a nimbleness that surprised even himself, disengaged the forceps and, picking up the small body crosswise, released it between the glass walls of its basin. Something seized him painfully by the finger; he tore his hand away; tiny bubbles gurgled on the surface of the preserving fluid; no-one else had noticed a thing. The phantom was moved back into a shadowy corner of the hall; legs extended, it awaited the next examinee. Sklifsky, clenching twitching jaws, slipped out through the door. The other candidates flocked around him, asking whether the test had been difficult or not; he escaped without replying.

2

Immediately afterwards, the days began to whirl like the vanes of a windmill. That examination was the last. Within two days he had to pack up, settle his affairs, tear himself away from the city, and depart. And now ensued the chaos of farewells, comradely roisterings, and all sorts of traditional nonsense. Twoman-Sklifsky squeezed dozens of hands, pressed boozy lips on other lips, sang 'Gaudeamus', tossed comrades in the air, was tossed himself, was bounced in badly-sprung carriages from pothole to pothole and bar to bar. Towards the end of the second night of their spree they encountered some painted women. And here – to Sklifsky's surprise – through a web of lace clutched in someone's fingers, giggling and whispered words – all at once, bow-legged, slimy and cold, the dead phantom appeared before him. Sklifsky sobered up in an instant, broke off his impromptu romance and meandered home by side-streets, pondering: 'I must have pulled him out, or else he did it himself – by the weight of the forceps, or ...'

Thus the mysterious incident rose to the surface for the first time, presenting face forward and immediately vanishing backward to the depths, to darkness and dreams.

Sklifsky didn't wake until late in the afternoon. All his affairs seemed to be in order. He had three hours before his train left. His temples felt compressed, as if by forceps. His mouth tasted of slime and spirits. He decided to walk off his headache. Down from the seventh floor and along the street, past the yellow dotted line of street lamps, thinking of nothing – wishing only that the forceps might release his head – he wandered numbly, drawn down gaping side-streets, from bollard to bollard, past flickering black and yellow windows. Suddenly the white, faceted stones of the university wall swam up to meet him. Below, in the stone depths where the wall grew into the ground, a light suddenly flashed on. 'Nikita must be here somewhere,' the thought slipped into his brain, and the forceps suddenly relaxed their pressure on his head: the pain disappeared. Twoman-Sklifsky glanced at his watch; it didn't matter now he didn't belong here any more – and besides, he had an hour to while away.

He passed through the gates, looking around for someone to ask about Nikita's whereabouts. Just there, before the first wing of the building, at the corner of the courtyard, he descried through the thick twilight Nikita's contemplative figure, with his long arms and drooping shoulders. Sklifsky called out to him.

'I'm off, my friend. Today.'

'Well, well! Safe journey.'

'I forgot something here.'

'What was it?'

Nikita yawned and turned away.

'You live here in the cellar?'

'I do.'

'And do you live alone, or do you have children?'

'Nope.'

'And what was it you called that phantom, remember: Filka or Fedka ...'

'Fifka,' Nikita corrected him, 'and if you forgot something, you can go back and look for it; nothing gets lost here.'

Nikita dived into his cellar and returned almost immediately, rattling a string of keys. The door creaked open – then another door beyond that – leading from corridor to corridor. Their steps echoing, the two arrived at a low white door in the embryology lab. Nikita groped for the right key:

'Y-yes, Fifka, and you thought he was Fedka. There you go. Hey, the door's open; how can that be?'

The door, sure enough, swung open with a light push. Two rows of glass cubes, bottles, thick-walled vats, retorts and basins were discernible in the gloom.

'On the left. 14-b. Here, behind this glass partition, we'll find the little chap.'

And suddenly the keys clattered to the floor.

'What an extraordinary thing!'

The glass-sided vat contained no more than a shallow pool of preserving fluid, with nothing else inside. They turned on the light: across the floor, running from the vat to the doorstep, lay the damp, closely spaced tracks of a child's bare soles. Even as the two men, bending to the floorboards, examined the prints of its heels, they rapidly dwindled. The alcohol was evaporating; within moments, there was nothing to be seen.

'That means – it only just . . .'

'It only just what?'

'You take a look. He must be somewhere here. He's hiding. We'll track him down. Fif, here Fif . . .'

Both men stepped softly up to the door; to their right and left, under the cave-like overhanging arches, endless empty corridors extended, dully catching their footfalls. Nikita was about to set off into the shadows but, not hearing Sklifsky follow him, he glanced around:

'Are you coming?'

'I've got a train to catch. I'm running late.'

'Well then. Well, well.'

The two of them turned, silently, towards the exit. Within an hour and a quarter, Twoman-Sklifsky was in a window-seat in his carriage. The train set off; the incident of the phantom he had abandoned so abruptly lingered somewhere far behind. But all the same, it lingered.

3

In moving to the country, to a rural district, the young doctor Twoman-Sklifsky intended to divide his time between people and books, between the clinic and his library. He carried several parcels of uncut books around with him. But the war interfered with his plans: and instead of cutting pages, he was busy cutting up bodies. Mobile clinics, evacuation points, medical stations, hospitals. Faces under chloroform masks. Endless numbers of them. From stretcher to operating table – from table to stretcher. 'Next.' The glitter and clatter of pincers and scalpels: dipped in alcohol, then blood, then alcohol, then blood. After that he somehow found himself in the field: there was a flash of light and a rumble – he lost consciousness. Shell-shock, a severe case. He recuperated. And once again the clang and slither of scalpels: now in alcohol, now in blood. But the skin on the back of his head and down his spine felt like part of someone else's body. Now there were dark stains under his eyes, and the ground slid away under his feet like a spinning top. At last, after passing through all the categories of invalidity, Doctor Sklifsky was relieved of active service and could return to his books, now yellowed, to his wooden medicine box mounted on the wall in a gloomy, half-abandoned village, where only the women remained behind. Life, long dislocated, tried to settle back into its joints: Sklifsky read his books, made notes, wrote prescriptions and letters to the front, tried to cure cases of tertiary syphilis and attended services for the 'fallen'; in the evenings he listened to a cricket sing and drank watered-down spirits. But Sklifsky himself, evidently, was not yet cured: sometimes he felt as if bruises were creeping all over his body, as if not just his temples but his entire head was hooded in some sort of dead, inhuman, clinging skin.

Then ... well, everyone knows what happened next. Each man remembered as much as he could, or as much as he wanted to. Twoman-Sklifsky: typhus – fires – blocked roads – no books

– hunger. The spirits bottle had been empty for a long time, but when it was refilled, Sklifsky started drinking without stopping.

4

The enigmatic specimen, after waiting for years, chose an autumn twilight, just before a storm, to stage its return. Rain clouds sailed overhead and stood at anchor. The setting sun ventured a dim, tarry gleam, but its rays were stifled among those heavy bundles of cloud.

Twoman-Sklifsky was unwell: a prickly centipede was burrowing under his skin and had fidgeted several times along his vertebrae. He wanted to pace his room from corner to corner, but couldn't. He stood in front of his bookcase, screwing up his eyes in the gloom at the familiar bindings: a volume by Duhamel, Vaihinger's *Philosophy of As If*, a state-published translation of Feuerbach, Richet's *Metapsychology*.³ He turned away. He took a swig from his bottle, then another and another. Then he went to the table. He sat down. He braced his soles against the wall. The centipede under his skin extended its spines and was still. At first a few grains of dust speckled the window, directly before his eyes; then the first drops struck. The wind tugged the bolt across the door, which gave way, and the tear-off calendar on the wall leapt several days forward. Twoman-Sklifsky, without taking his soles from the wall, glanced at the door: barely visible in the darkness, following the wind, some man-like thing was squeezing through the long vertical crack between the door-jamb and the wall.

Sklifsky rose as if pushed, and took a step towards the threshold:

'Who's there?'

Without replying, the thing continued to squeeze, slowly but stubbornly, through the tight crack in the slightly ajar door.

'No musculature,' Sklifsky thought, with uncomprehending calm, and hurrying over, wedged his palm against the wooden door.

His mechanism of perception received the phenomenon with perfect clarity and differentiation. Even the gusts of wind blowing their soft *f-f-f* through the crack did not escape his senses.

'Who's there?' he repeated more quietly, and with complete calm, as though this were a laboratory experiment, he pressed harder on the door. Between his palm and the door-jamb something sticky and dough-like was feebly crawling through, flattening under the pressure of the timber. And then, from the crack, just as if his palm had squeezed out the word:

'Fifka.'

Abruptly, it became blindingly clear: the crack gaped – a suture under the finger – a head – below and on the floor – he should have pulled, but he ... Sklifsky reached for the door and opened it.

'I ... just wanted ... about the forceps ...' the voice grew steadily more distinct with every syllable, 'why did you ... force me ... and if you went that far ... why didn't you carry on to the end?'

The voice broke off. Without answering, Sklifsky struck a match and raised the burning yellow shred over his head, peering at the phenomenon. He made out an undergrown creature on rickety legs; a huge, pumpkin-shaped head on the shoulders of a dried-out, flattened body; over the bulging forehead, from temple to temple, lay the traces of the forceps' grip – the familiar perfect girdle encircling its crown, a corona of compression; a floppy mouth ... but the match singed his fingers, and through the darkness that fell between them Sklifsky heard:

'Yes, that protects you against wolves and ghosts. But you can't get rid of me with tinder and matches: even the sun is powerless against us, we who call ourselves men.'

Sklifsky was prepared for anything but an argument:

'N-no. That's not why I lit it. There's no sense in expecting a match to do the work of logic. Why shouldn't something I hear cross over to my visual perception? You're a fact, but, how can I put this, a factless fact. In a word: you're a hallucination. And I, I wouldn't be a doctor if I ...'

'And you might well think,' the shape, outlined against the night, wobbled, 'that I will start to squeeze into your being, just as I did through that door. On the contrary, I am the sort of hallucination that must not be realized, that won't put down roots in any perceptive centres: rather, I must de-hallucinate, turn myself off completely, tear free from the forceps. Send me back – into nothingness, under a hermetic seal, into that glass jar from which you – yes, you humans – dragged me into the world by force and trickery. Who let this happen? I'm asking you, who?'

Sklifsky retreated a step towards the table, but the outline of the phantom came no closer, continuing to lurk under the dark lintel.

'Hallucinations,' he pricked up his ears again, 'and what about words – yours and mine – aren't they hallucinations? Or will you start to maintain that our conversation is half real, half imaginary; but how can my words, if they don't exist, reflect your answers, which do, of course, exist; or don't they? Even with a minimum of logic, having admitted even the tiniest thing, the least substantial apparition among an innumerable multitude of others, to be a hallucination, one must extend this term to everything else. Imagine a dreamer who dreams that he falls asleep and dreams. The sleeper, as he sleeps, doesn't take this dream for reality; he evaluates it correctly as imaginary, as a vision. But to maintain that a dream within a dream is more real than the real dream is the same as to say that a circle inscribed around a polygon is more geometrical than one drawn inside it.'

'Wait a minute, enough tongue-twisters, give me a chance to think,' Sklifsky burst out, 'you're saying that –'

'– that you – and everyone like you – dreamed up your world and that you are yourselves dreams, with no awakening: I tried to calculate the coefficient of your reality. It's something like 0.000 over X . . .'

'Hmm . . . That seems like the beginning of some strange new philosophy . . .'

'Perhaps. At least, it's a premise for phantomism.'

'Now what can that be?'

'Phantomism is simple: like locking forceps in position. Men are puppets on strings; constructs of their own nervous tissue. Books are well aware that there's no such thing as free will, but the authors of books have already forgotten this; and whenever what he needs is part of life, rather than between hard covers, man fatally forgets his predetermined condition. Consciousness has locked onto this ludicrous position. Everything is based upon the same fiction: all behaviour, the very possibility of human actions, is founded on so-called "reality". And as nothing can be maintained upon a fiction, so nothing exists: not God, not the worms, not you, not I, not us. Since everything is determined by others, only the other exists, and not the self. But the marionette stubbornly dreams that it isn't made out of cardboard and strings, but from meat and nerves; and that both ends of the strings are in its own hands. It endeavours to contrive philosophical principles and revolutions, but its philosophies are about dead, non-existent worlds, and revolutions everywhere and always ... tear themselves free of the forceps. And so here is the ruptured suture between me, the phantom *qua* phantom, and your dilettantish, phantomizing consciousnesses. Both you and I were dragged by various causes into our pseudo-being, but while you, the phantom-ids, having become citizens of the world of causes all the way to non-being, imagine yourselves rulers of the ludicrous "kingdom of ends",[4] as Kant called it, I, forced into life, know only the will of the forceps which dragged me into being – and no more; and therefore, to be included in the game of intentionality, like you, to sense myself desiring and acting, is never and in no way possible for me; causes act upon me, I feel them and I am conscious of them, but I do not myself desire a single one of my actions or words, and desire seems to me as awkward and impossible as walking on water or lifting myself by the crown of my head.'[5]

'So then you weren't brought here by intention?'

'No.'

'But what about causes ...?'

'You shouldn't rush your questions. I've come here – out of the clamp of the forceps – into the crush of the door ...'

For a moment both were silent. Behind Sklifsky's back, in the square of the window, the night blazed with streaks of lightning. Turning his face towards the dazzling flashes that lit up the shabby room, he said – bypassing his guest, addressing neither him nor himself:

'How strange: some sort of stream of shades that's slipped in, it's not even a phantom – or an "appurtenance" ... perhaps it's a whole chain, cause after cause, link after link. There's a stool by the door,' he finished, looking over his shoulder at the phantom pressed against the wall.

The shape by the door swayed and grew shorter.

'So. Even a multi-volume biography, if you take away all intentions, leaving only causes, would be reduced to a dozen pages. Finding myself trapped inside life, like a mouse in a mousetrap, for a long time I patiently waited, and I still wait, to be pulled out of it and ... but let's begin in the correct sequence. After I got out of the glass basin, I set off for the doorway without knowing where it might lead. I encountered shadows and a labyrinth of empty corridors, which forced me into some sort of dark and stifling lumber-room, piled high with old rags and all sorts of rubbish. Wrapping myself in the nearest rag – I had grown cold wandering the corridors – I began listening in to the space concealed between the thick walls: at first nothing, and then, somewhere far away, two voices and the clinking of keys. I set off towards the sound, but wasn't able to catch up with it. However, the doors were open – they led me first into the courtyard, then through the black hole of the gates – and then outside, to the lights and noises of the city night.

'At first I was afraid I would be spotted and identified: one cry of "Phantom!" and I'd be seized and put back behind glass. I hid my face in shadow and squeezed close to the walls, trying to conceal myself under my rag. But I soon realized that these precautions were unnecessary: people only notice those they need, and then only for as long as they are needed. And as I ... well, in a word, I had no special reason for concern. Hundreds and thousands of pairs of boots trod past me; what was laced inside them interested me very little and took little interest in me. Sometimes, when I walked down the boulevards in the morning, little human children would raise their curious eyes to me. I was still the same height as they were, and on two or three occasions I tried to join in their games. "If I hadn't died then, before I became a phantom," I thought to myself, "I would have been just like them." But, terrified and weeping, the children turned away from me: their nannies and nursemaids waved wooden spades and parasols at me: go away. And so I went on, struggling to bend my needle-punctured legs, on and on, never settling anywhere.

'They hadn't desiccated me properly back in the phantom lab; and here, between the sun-warmed paving stones of the city, this gradually became apparent to me. At noon every day flies clung to me, plunging their proboscos into my dead flesh. I had only to sit down and dogs would run up from every gateway; testing the air with their nostrils, fur bristling, enclosing me in a ring of evilly staring eyes, they would howl. I would hurl stones at them, and breaking through the circle, walk on. Soon the cursed beasts chased me to the outskirts of the city; I would curl up in waste places and cemeteries, only in the evenings venturing onto crossroads. Because of the rain and the damp, my body was softening and dissolving; putrid fluids, accumulating in the sublimate and alcohol, went rancid and tormented me. I could not go on like this. I decided to seek attention from passers-by, reveal myself, and beg that they put me back – behind glass. Baring my hands and face, I stepped in front of passers-by, extending my rotting hand directly before their eyes – but, with pupils fastidiously deflected, they only dropped some kopecks into my palm. Coppers piled on coppers, enabling me to buy another day or two of half-life from the pharmacy.

'The caterpillar of time, looping and wriggling, crawled through the days. The dank autumn drew nearer. People sheltered under their roofs; even I felt nostalgia for my little glass roof. During one patch of bad weather I decided to return: by myself. Crawling over the cracked pavements, shunning encounters, from crossroads to crossroads, I finally reached the gates of the university.

'Through the gates, at the very first corner, I made out, through the twilight, the stooping figure of a man. It was Nikita.'

'Nikita?'

'Yes. I was surprised that I didn't surprise him. He was a strange old man, but a good one. A few years before this (as I learned later), he had lost his wife and child – he was tormented by loneliness. This is the only way I can try to explain why the old man shared his boxroom in the cellar with me, and why we started to live together. However, as I later understood from his lengthy tales, I was not the only one who had played on his paternal instincts. Isn't that so? And another thing: Nikita told me you were afraid of me, the evening when you left the city, remember?'

'Get on with it.'

'After that – life within the four corners of the cellar. I rarely went up to the surface of the earth. Nikita fetched down my sublimate and spirit. In the evenings he told me tales of his dead family. Little by little, I even learned to help him with his chores: sweeping away cobwebs and dust, setting up apparatus, keeping up careful housekeeping through a hundred keyholes. He taught me my letters, and soon I began rummaging through the library shelves and hunting through the pages of books.

'Once, on a holiday, when bells were ringing throughout the city and the university corridors were empty, Nikita decided to bring me to see my "mama", as he called her. After passing windows laced with sunlight, we went through a familiar door: she was standing among cupboards and instruments, still with her legs splayed in the same way, worn and stained by hundreds upon hundreds of palms and forceps. We stood there silently for a moment. It was quiet in the instrument room. Flecks of sunlight made rainbows in the glass curves of the vessels. Nikita placed his hand solemnly on my shoulder, and we walked back through the solemn desolation of the corridors.

'Years passed in this way. At first the town was decked out in the tricolour,[6] then in red. The old man and I rarely left the stone square of the university courtyard. I remember one of those days, when the streets were bloody and noisy, and we were sitting behind the trembling panes of our cellar. Past our windows, which were momentarily in shadow, a lorry thundered – and in the same instant a paper bird pecked the pane. I pulled the sash: outside the window was a gleaming sheaf of proclamations. Without leaving the window-ledge, I started to read them aloud. The old man listened, then said:

'"That's not for you or me, Fifka. Not for the likes of us."

'After that – little by little – came hunger and exposure. At first I was actually cheered by the continual emptying of the university block; you could roam for hours on end, from book to book, without fear of meeting anyone. But the cold penetrated the bullet-holes in the window-panes, and crystals of rime formed on the hot water pipes. Nikita knew that the damp would unpick my stitches and rot my body; with his last strength he made an iron stove and dragged himself to the market for firewood, trying to protect me. Age and hunger did their work: I buried the old man and stayed on quite alone.

'His bunch of keys, my inheritance, led me through a hundred doors. My life was caught up in small, petty tasks. No-one appointed me to fill the vacant post of cleaner and watchman, but ghosts and phantoms – you may rest assured – lead an impromptu existence. There were a dozen or so professors and a half-blind librarian, still shuffling among their instruments and books, absorbed in their thought processes, never noticing the famulus creeping silently along the walls, offering their instruments at the right moment and shivering in dark corners while they rustled their papers. I filled out employment forms. Under "social origins" I always wrote "appurtenance of a phantom"; in the space for "current position", I inscribed elegantly: "human". Not bad, eh? And then I signed them.'

'I'm curious to know what name you signed.'

'Twoman-Sklifsky. Or aren't you willing to acknowledge me?'

Silence fell for a minute. Through the fading night beyond the window the outlines of poplars could be traced. The cracks in the floor began to stand out from the white glimmer of the walls. The doctor went over to one wall and rooted among his bottles. Something gurgled. The cork was reinserted in its glass nest.

'Actually I'm not fully lubricated,' he heard a voice say behind him – a heavy, viscous voice, as if forced through saliva.

Sklifsky's hand sorted through the glasses, reached to the left and, finding what was needed, passed it to his guest. Standing a step away from the table, Sklifsky could almost make out the round lips of the phantom, thirstily fixed on the bottle's neck. He clearly heard the rhythmical suction of its breathing. At last lips and glass were separated:

'Excellent stuff,' tittered Fifka, tapping a nail against the bottle: a cloyingly sweet aroma wafted from its neck. Sklifsky took it away and stoppered it:

'That's enough. What happened next?'

'Next ... I couldn't see any "next" in front of me. No visitors came downstairs to the cellar. Even my dreams were sightless and empty. Whatever I dreamed came to pass: instead of a glass cage I had a stone one. In the evenings I sat on Nikita's empty pallet, training my pupils on the trembling yellow wick of the oil lamp, and watched streaks of shadow fall upon streaks of damp. Neighbours, when they met me, always looked away, and the bony floor-cleaner from the next cellar once shouted at my back: "Eeee, monster!"

'Only sorrow, every evening, silently descending the slimy steps, visited me in my low-ceilinged, dark little box. Sometimes I considered: if you take the minus of a minus, the non-being of non-being, wouldn't you be left with – being? And I lingered ...

'This was how it ended: one night, entering the instrument room, I stole my mother and hauled her down to my cellar. There had to be some way to darn the gaping void in my existence. Now I could study her often and at length – my wooden birth-mother, her headless body tilted backwards, frozen in an extended spasm of labour. This brought back too many memories. And sometimes, as I told her about books I had just read, about phantomism, which sooner or later would overcome the Kingdom of Ends and extinguish all those will-o'-the-wisps, the agonized sprawl of her legs prevented me from finishing my thought or my sentence: seizing the ends of her stumps in my hands, I tried to push them together, but the stumps didn't obey, threatening me instead with more births, new lives – and more often than not I broke off my deliberations.

'Another winter was approaching. My logs wouldn't last long. I would have tried, as others did, to filch planks from the neighbours' fence, but I didn't have the strength to rip them away from their nails, and the sound of an axe would have attracted attention. A monster like me could hardly beg for alms on the street. And the frost grew fiercer. For several days in a row I gathered wood-chips frozen into the snow, but they were more ice than wood. My body became blue, like mercury squeezed by frost into the bottoms of street thermometers. And on one of those evenings when the wind beat against the glittering windows and gusts blew through the cracks and seemed about to tear the flame from my long-hoarded wick, I broke her up; I burned my own mother. The stove gave off heat together with the smell of rubber and burnt hair. That was all she could give me – besides life, as you call it. I can't recall how I survived to the end of that winter. Cooped up inside the blind walls of the basement, I didn't notice how everything around was gradually renewing itself and assuming fresh features. Painters appeared on the sooty bricks of our courtyard; the smell of fresh asphalt wafted over the potholes in the paving-stones; bullet-holes in the window-panes were masked with putty; the empty corridors became busy again; the grime-dimmed windows admitted light once more. None of this was to my taste: without waiting for the questions and stares – where did I come from, who was I – I left, I took myself off, as quietly and unremarkedly as I had lived there. Anyone venturing down to my mouldy cell in the basement would find nothing except a bunch of keys on the table and, in a cobwebbed corner, a row of empty bottles that had once held sublimate and spirit.

'I am clumsily formed and stitched – as you can see. Owing to various encounters with sun and showers I am beginning to give at the seams and go mouldy. As you see. I would soon have sunk to the most pathetic condition had it not been for a single incident. Once, when I'd found shelter from a cloudburst by huddling under a gable, a door opened suddenly, struck me in the back and knocked me clean off the steps into a puddle. Lifting my head, I beheld a screwed-up face with benevolent eyes and a tiny freckle on the right cheek. On the spot – splashed and thundered upon by the gutters – I dragged out my old attestations and was appointed errand boy at the clothing store run by this sympathetic lady, who took me under her wing. And I swapped my books for a new burden – cardboard boxes and trunks which I carried from street to street, from customer to customer. I was still strong enough to carry light fabrics in these boxes. Along the way I concealed as much of myself as I could under my cardboard load: when I arrived, I didn't ring at the street door but would go to the back entrance and, after thrusting my boxes through the open doorway, I would try to retreat as soon as possible. But no-one ever even noticed me: hidden under the ribbons of my parcels were crudely designed "phantoms", after a fashion; imitations of the body, some plump, some skinny, some elongated and some foreshortened. In a word, they counterfeited form no worse than I imitated life. I enjoyed watching, cramming myself into a dark corner somewhere, how the scissors and cutting machines of the finishers travelled over the paper surfaces, tracing the correct line between dream and fact. In the workshop, hanging from rows of hooks, spilling off narrow wooden shoulders, there were always dozens of gauzy, silky, velvety body-husks: women, women, women. There was a smell of glue, perfume and sweat. This harem of fabrics needed its eunuch: something faceless and bodiless. A man would have been out of place in that little world where they planned the ensnarement of men. But my appearance seemed to have won me the right to play this role. Moreover, whenever I watched the measuring tape creep over the nude torsos of live women, warm and soft, I experienced nothing – except revulsion and fear. We phantoms have our own tastes and our own opinion of what you call love.'

'Indeed,' smiled Sklifsky, 'Just a moment. I'll be back directly.'

Glass once again rang against glass. As the dawn's blue luminescence saturated night, Sklifsky saw clearly before him, eyeball to eyeball, the freakish face: unblinking eyelids, a forehead dented by the blades of the forceps, a sticky crack for a mouth.

'Now then, let's begin with your opinion,' Sklifsky stooped towards that hole of a mouth as it began trembling again; the rising rumble of blood in his ears muffled the words.

'My opinion reduces to the fact that you humans are irreducible. You are mere lookers-on, you spy on the rendezvous of spectres. You invent each other from the very beginning. A man always loves a woman as if she were a phantom, a piece of equipment for his two-backed, four-handed pleasure. Hence any "he", before enduring a lingering embrace, thus or otherwise protects some immaterial "her" from an all-too-material "she". Take the most vulgar thing about it: the night. After all, the majority of you make love in darkness, when the wooden mannequin beside you may be sheathed in the most surpassingly beautiful body, and that body in turn can be wreathed in the most fantastic of souls, that phantasm of phantasms. Your confused nocturnal fumble fails to infuse the brain with spectrality; it uses your yearning to prepare the way for a crude fact, such as ... In a word, because men imagine "her", "she" gives birth. And if ...'

'Wait a minute,' Sklifsky interrupted, 'you've addled my brain already. You seem to have imagined – quite accidentally – that the act of love, well, you know what I mean, is a backwards birth; that it draws you backward, bizarrely, to the place from which the forceps pulled you. And that's all. I seem to be mixed up. My head is buzzing.'

And at that moment, almost pressing their faces together, Fifka tucked his mouth under Sklifsky's very ear: around his eyes leapt blue-black dots of morning light, the air hummed, and a mysterious heat simmered. Between the dots and the humming, Sklifsky made out the following:

'No, no, you must hear me out right now. We haven't reached the bottom of this. Don't spill your drink. So. Where was it we stopped? Yes, my practical attitude to love. I've already explained that all these females made of crinkled flesh were inexplicable and even horrifying to me. But above the workshop ceiling, up seven bends of the spiral staircase, I discovered something I'd often dreamed of behind the door of my narrow box-room: there, upstairs, was a sort of archive of mannequins. I had the key to it. Few people went up the creaking stairs to the cardboard manne- quins. But it was better to be cautious. I always chose night as the time for my secret rendezvous, when no-one was in the workshop and all the doors were locked. Then, candle in hand, I would climb the stairs: through the chink of the doorway I could see rows of one-legged female figures, the candlelight silently exposing the lifeless infolds and outfolds of their bodies. I walked past without touching a single one. There, at the end of the row, against the left wall, my chosen one was waiting. Placing my candle on the floor, I walked up to her, breast to breast. She had no arms to defend herself, no eyes to reproach me. Tenderly, my fingers slid over the frigid lines of her hips; my chest rubbed the empty bulges of her bosom. Her slender leg squeaked pitifully and helplessly, and I fancied ... but, you understand, this, even this did not bring me to the peak of passion, but rather to this thought: for a man to be born, two living beings must make love; but in order – listen to me, listen – for a man to die, two phantoms must fall in love. And there ...'

'Wait, wait,' Twoman-Sklifsky placed one palm against the wall and tried to raise himself, but the black dots, proliferating wildly, had merged with the gloom – 'that means, you came to me so you could ...'

Through gaps in the gloom he glimpsed the small movements of Fifka's mouth once again, but the swarming dots forestalled any reply: they closed ranks and ... really, that 'and' is needless, and we could simply conclude here; but tradition – I didn't begin it, I'm not ending it – demands some sort of bookish rounding-off and referral to sources. As you will.

5

The walking wounded arrived – complete with hernias, rashes and boils – for Doctor Twoman-Sklifsky's morning surgery and waited a long time, sighing decorously and glancing furtively at his door: not the faintest stir. Someone had the idea of looking through the windows of the house next door, where the doctor lived: perhaps he had overslept or gone out. After standing for a minute with his face pressed to the glass, the information-seeker waved his arm as if demanding assistance. A moment later a multitude of faces appeared at the window. The door was half-open. Everyone went in, to be met by a smell of alcohol and sublimate. On the floor, his palms scorched and his cheek in a semi-evaporated puddle of preserving fluid, lay the doctor. They lifted him up: his eyes were squeezed shut, but his lips were mumbling something incoherent and his entire body rattled with shudders. The patients, exchanging looks, diagnosed typhus.

I myself was a patient of Dr Twoman-Sklifsky nine years ago. We were brought together by a grenade fragment which had settled in my hip. Dr Sklifsky, as I knew him then, gave the impression of being a gloomy man who avoided friendship and meetings. It is unlikely that he remembered me in the intervening years, but I took longer to forget him: the dull pain, constantly revisiting my unhealed wound, always carried with it the associative thread of Dr Twoman's image: his long face, the bold arch of his brows, the lips hidden under red overhanging whiskers, the brief, sure touch of his hands.

Not very long ago, searching in the lists of patients at Moscow sanatoria for a name I needed, I happened upon the unneeded (as I first thought) Twoman-Sklifsky. After some hesitation, I decided to pay the invalid a visit, since I was only a few doors away from his bed. Sklifsky recognized me immediately: the grip of his hand was different – softer and more lingering – and not only were his eyes, which burned and glittered like those of all fever patients, less reserved with me, but … in a word: having called in for a minute, I sat with him a full two hours, until the nurse whispered in my ear that long conversations were bad for the patient. I left, promising to return and hear out his story, for it was during this meeting that Twoman-Sklifsky began the tale of his encounters with the phantom.

My second visit brought me to the end of the story. True, in the three or four days since we had last seen each other, Sklifsky had managed to become even more gaunt: his eyes were like ashes, his face waxen; he spoke raggedly, in fits and starts, losing the thread in his confusion. Nonetheless, as soon as I got home I immediately made notes. At first nothing would come: then my pen began stumbling over various obstacles. After all, we brotherhood of writers, on receiving a fact, always manipulate it in some way or other, searching in it for that 'correct line' between facts and dreams, as Twoman's spectre expressed it. I was not remotely concerned about the coefficient of reality in the data I had obtained; rather, I was flummoxed by the tale's lack of structural coherency. For example, I had to explain Fifka's gradual transformation into a person, the imperceptible trend of phantomism towards teleology, the collapse of causes into ends, and the consideration that all this was the result of consequences which, one might say, had been invented by Twoman's sensations, or had it all arisen directly from those sensations, which he had confused with a phenomenon?

The simplest solution to this confusion was to approach the original source. But I was not admitted to Twoman's ward.

'He's in a bad way. No visitors.'

After waiting another two or three days, I made a second attempt. Without venturing any needless questions, I made my way down the hospital corridor to the familiar door. It was half-open. I was met by a light odour of sublimate. I stepped into the ward: his bed was empty; under the plumped-up pillow lay a neatly folded blanket, the white square of the little table was pushed against the bedhead – and that was all. I heard footsteps behind me. I turned: it was the nurse.

'All over?'

'All over.'

Returning to my manuscript, I decided – after hesitating for a while – to grant it authenticity: let Twoman–Sklifsky answer for every word. It costs him nothing to do me this service; he's dead, after all.

1926

ALEKSANDR GRIN

The Grey Motor Car

I

On the evening of July 16th I went to the cinema, hoping to banish the unpleasant impression lingering from my latest conversation with Corrida. I had encountered her as she was crossing the boulevard. From some way off I had recognized her energetic stride and her distinctive way of swinging her left arm. I had bowed, trying to discern a shade of friendliness in those large, slightly surprised-looking eyes, gazing so sternly from under the proud curve of her hat.

I turned back and joined her. She walked rapidly, with an even gait, sometimes glancing in my direction, but always past me. I observed and relished how passers-by often turned to look at her. 'Some of them probably think we're husband and wife, and they envy me,' I reflected. I was so entertained by enlarging on this train of thought that I didn't hear what Corrida was saying until she shouted:

'What's the matter with you? You're so distracted!'

I answered, 'I'm only distracted because I'm walking with you. No-one else's company crushes me like this; no-one else inspires me with the profound and ancient harmony of life's fullness and perfect peace.'

She didn't seem particularly pleased with my reply, since she asked: 'When will you be finished with your project?'

'That's a secret,' I said. 'I trust you more than anyone else, but I don't trust myself.'

'What's that supposed to mean?'

'Only that an imprecise explanation of my idea, which is still hazy in many respects, could damage the idea itself.'

'The thousand and second riddle of Ebenezer Sidney,' Corrida commented. 'At least can't you explain what you mean by an imprecise explanation?'

'Hear me, then: we remember best of all the words we say ourselves. If these words depict something intimate or secret, they must echo perfectly both the reality and the mood that inspired them; otherwise our memory or impression becomes distorted. A dash of distortion lasts a long time, if not forever. That's why one shouldn't explain complex phenomena hastily, in any old way, especially if they're still taking shape: you'll bring confusion into the very matrix of the idea.'

She heard out my tirade with a kindly smile, but stayed on her guard; I sensed that my company was palling on her. We fell silent. I didn't know whether to excuse myself or to accompany her further. I could see no encouragement for the latter course; on the contrary, Corrida's expression suggested that she might have been walking alone. Finally, she said:

'My brother has given me a new Excelsior.[1] A big group of us are taking it out the day after tomorrow: it'll be a pretty brisk jaunt. I'm going. I'll bring you along if you like.'

'No,' I said in a stern tone, although she must have caught the pained way I said it. Not wishing to appear rude, I added:

'You know how much I hate that sort of sport.' I almost said 'those machines', but I preferred to be vague.

'But why?'

'I allowed myself to speak my mind on that topic in your presence once before,' I said, 'I provoked amusement, excessive amusement, and I would not care to suffer the experience a second time.'

'You're definitely trying to bamboozle me.' She stopped at the door of a clothes store, screwing up her eyes to glance at the shop sign, and I realized I had bored her. The sign was only an excuse. 'Yes, you are bamboozling me, Sidney, and I think that only the poor state of your nerves can explain such a strange hatred for . . . for a carriage.' She burst out laughing. 'Goodbye.'

I kissed her hand and walked off hastily, to avoid accidentally catching this young woman in the act of deserting me – she might have walked right back out of the shop without checking whether I was still there. I wasn't ashamed of what I had told her. I could have lied politely, gone on the excursion with a bunch of fools, and gazed at her all day. But I had already given my word not to lie: I was so tired of lying. Like everyone else, I lived enmeshed in lies, and they had exhausted me.

As I crossed the street on my way to the cinema, a wavering, growing, brightening beam of light was flung at my feet. Turning my head, I froze for the brief fraction of a second necessary to fix an impression of this onslaught by the blind white headlamps of a motor car. It rushed past, slashing my eyes with a stream of wind, blaring the yowls of phantom felines across the roadway; it whined, wailed, and vanished, bearing off with it some blank-faced people in bowler hats. As ever, each new motor car added several fresh features and details to my revulsion. I memorized them and went into the theatre.

It was a squalid, third-class little establishment, with a grubby screen and a fake pianola playing crackling arias. The film, like thousands upon thousands of others, was insipid and void of content, but I was afforded immense satisfaction precisely because so much energy had been squandered on generating the constant, flickering motion of onscreen life. It was like watching a gambler wager and lose vast sums. The camera, the actors' talent and skill, their health, their nervous energy, their private lives, the machines, the complex technical equipment – all of this was transformed into a convulsively jerking shadow thrown on a screen so as to briefly titillate an audience who would leave after scarcely an hour, already forgetting what the performance had been about – unnaturally out of pace as it was with the tempo of their lives, as it swept through a string of attacks, kidnappings, celebrations and dances. My satisfaction in observing this was indistinguishable from malicious pleasure. Before my eyes, energy was being converted into a shadow, and thence into oblivion. And I knew very well how all this had to end.

Meanwhile, the greater part of my attention was devoted to the large grey motor car – a landaulette – which occasionally appeared in the film. I scrutinized it each time, trying to remember whether I had seen it somewhere before or whether I was deceiving myself, as often happens when an object before one's eyes evokes some other, long-forgotten thing. It was the usual type of metallic monster, with a six-sided, projecting snout, like a galosh on wheels, toe-cap pointing forwards. The driver wore a fur coat that bristled like a hedgehog. The upper part of his face was hidden behind glasses and, thanks to these and the flickering of the image, his features were indecipherable – yet I could not overcome the feeling that I had met him before; I was firmly convinced that I had once seen this very driver, in this car, under circumstances I had long utterly forgotten. Of course, with the innumerable standardized similarities between such objects, I had no solid evidence to go by, no distinguishing marks on the vehicle, but its licence plate, *C.C.77-7*, had at some time – and I felt this strongly – been linked to a specific memory, the details of which I could not recall in spite of my efforts. My memory retained not the actual number, but a faint impression of its former significance.

And yet this was impossible. The film had been made by an American company, and to judge by the appearance of the streets, it had been shot in New York. It followed that all props would have been local; and I had not left Alambeau for five years and had never been to America. Consequently, my imagined recollection had to be nothing more than coincidence. But all the same – I *had* seen that motor car and that chauffeur before somewhere.

When we are ruled by a conviction about something, even if it is poorly or not at all substantiated, it is difficult to resist; as with glue smeared on leaves to trap a perching bird, each effort to escape makes it stick harder. Such are the phantoms of jealousy or of persecution, of illness – of everything that menaces us in any way. Efforts to think logically lead in such cases to fresh apparent proofs, based on nothing. The conviction that filled me in the cinema was not at all frightening or unpleasant, apart from my repugnance for the motor car, but I sat out the show with a strange intuition that some new development was already weaving its invisible web.

I am not referring to the characters in this empty and exploitative drama, which dragged the pitiful imagination of the audience forwards through ludicrous leaps and satanic crimes, evidently catering for that part of the public which gains its thrills and ideals from this sort of thing ... But I followed the motor car

C.C.77–7 with the closest attention, growing tense each time it appeared, which it did six or seven times. The last time it was descending a hill; from far-off it resembled a grey stain on the picturesque roadside scene. As it plunged downhill towards the viewer, it swelled almost to actual size. It rushed upon me. At one moment there was still a strip of landscape at the edge of the screen; at the next, darkness covered everything, and two lamps bore down on me like fangs; then the vision disappeared, and only its shade – the fancied continuation of motion – swooped over my head in a silent convulsion of shadows. Once again the landscape filled the screen.

I had nothing left to do in the cinema. Yet another feature had been added to my impressions of the motor car; perhaps a valid clue, one of those that inform so-called coincidences. I did not linger on this thought, leaving the future to develop it – if necessary – but a dreadful suspicion suddenly chilled me. Surrendering to an inexplicable urge, just as if someone had turned to stare at me, I read the yard-high letters on the brightly lit signboard adorning the cinema entrance. They ran:

'*The Grey Motor Car*: a world-class drama in 6,000 metres! The best thriller of the season! Lots of stunts!'

2

I had a very unpleasant sensation, just as if someone had trodden on my foot, laughed rudely, and walked off snickering behind my back. I walked away hurriedly and tried to banish my vile mood by setting a brisk pace and glancing at the street traffic, but at every pause in my thoughts the words 'grey motor car' appeared before me once more, in the middle distance. After I had walked two blocks, however, the letters lost their graphic clarity; they were replaced by a sound, as though someone were repeating these two words far-off, softly and firmly. I have always avoided alcohol, turning to it only at exceptional times, but now I needed a drink.

Everyone knows that modern city streets anticipate our every possible desire with an always aptly-designed sign or window display. I have no doubt that a man passing the fruit stalls on the

Dutch Exchange, were he suddenly to crave a geodesic instrument of some kind, would inevitably spot the necessary device in the window of a specialist store appearing from nowhere.

Wine lies in wait for us in what might seem the least appropriate places. There could hardly be a less profitable spot for a vintner than the hidden recess between the wall of the Institute of Geography and the Boulevard of Secrets, where even in the daytime the shadows of enormous trees lie so densely that the entire wall feels damp and cold; this spot almost completely lacks that frenzied street traffic which rattles the gold plate and crockery in innumerable restaurants. This time, as I turned the corner, I glimpsed a small stone annexe, which had either not existed before or which I had never noticed. It was a small trellised restaurant with a glass door between two windows; I sat down in a rocking-chair at a table by the door.

There were few customers here. Glancing through the window into the interior, I saw two stout men playing dominoes; a steamship mechanic dozing with his legs stretched out, one hand trailing over the edge of the table, holding a smouldering cigarette on the point of crumbling away; and three women with their legs crossed. They were smoking, tossing back their heads and releasing the smoke in slow, identical rings.

The waiter poured me some liquor: a special herbal extract, very strong. I swallowed two shots and lingered over a third, pushing the carafe away.

I soon felt its effect: a warm glow all over, and I could sense the precise rhythm of each moment, defined perhaps by the speed of my pulse, or perhaps by my mental acuity, which had effortlessly sharpened. My thoughts flowed abundantly and blithely. After this drink, I laughed at my state of mind of a short while before. As I listened to the occasional hiss of passing tyres, I realized plainly that no connection could arise between myself and the grey *77–7*; no such connection existed. In that moment each of my clearly defined impressions was equally sharp and precise: this state of being afforded me incomparable satisfaction, and I made use of the moment to think over certain aspects of my project.

Corrida El-Basso, a woman of unknown nationality – I can state this confidently, as I possess solid evidence – took an interest in my project out of politeness. It was up to me to transform this feeling, the pleasant but meaningless smile of a well-fed dinner guest, into emotion, perhaps even passion. I still had hope of this. But I had to catch her unawares, make her react spontaneously, instantly, perhaps even at one of those times when she was barely suffering my presence. When that moment came, the project – or, rather, what she thought of as a project – would strike her with all the brilliance and forethought of its extraordinary, overwhelming boldness, would inspire a profound and glorious renewal. So much the better. Only then would I find out the true nature of the woman called Corrida El-Basso, the woman I loved. I would discover whether her face – the colour of yellow chalk – had any other shade. I would hear the timbre of her voice when she spoke to me affectionately. And I would feel the strength of her hand – that uniquely feminine strength which, melting warmly and silently into our own hands, can slow our breathing as if by electric control.

Swaying agreeably, I was already – mentally – in my 'laboratory', in the Callot Gorge, probably so named by a relative of the famous artist[2] or one of his admirers. A light, nervous hand was laid on my shoulder. Without turning, I knew it was Roncourt. Indeed, he sat down opposite me, asking me what I was up to.

'This is a lovely spot for a date,' he added, 'or for a suicide. The light in the windows, the mysterious pattern of the leaves on the pavement, the solitude, the wine. Sidney, I'm going to Lercat's Casino; there's going to be a rather unusual contest there today. It's just your kind of thing. Have you heard about the mulatto Grineaux's unlikely run of luck? This is already the third day in a row he's been winning at poker, piling up cheques, gold and jewels. Do you want to watch the game? There's lots of people there.'

No-one could have made me a better suggestion. When struggling to resolve an awkward real-life problem, it's splendid to relax and enjoy an engrossing spectacle; still better if the spectacle is spontaneous, if you're seeing the dénouement of a real event complete with chorus, extras and speeches by the principal actors. Roncourt took my arm and led me off.

3

The Casino Lercat is famed as a first-class haven for all sorts
of crime. By night, a marble statue of Pallas Athena gleams
palely, mysteriously and sorrowfully on its pediment; vendors of
cocaine, opium and risqué photographs throng around the steps
descending fanwise to the square.

A long line of motor cars was halted here on both sides of the
road. From time to time one of them, shuddering and blowing its
horn, would leave the line, describe a semicircle, churn up dust
and, rumbling, disappear into the distance; each time I watched
this there rose in my heart an impression of a cynical, insolent
being, alien to everything, cold-heartedly pursuing unknown
purposes. Usually the elongated cavities of these massive,
mindless machines were full of people who had chosen this or
another route of their own free will – but my vision imposed its
own reasoning, independent of abstract logic. I could never tell
myself, 'They are driving'; instead I would say, 'They are being
driven'; our ordinary familiarity with the internal rhythm shared
by everyone could not reconcile this rhythm with the unnatural
speed of these beings, which coexisted in tested and accustomed
harmony. When walking in the street, I was always perturbed
and oppressed by the atmosphere of violence that these complicated conveyances generated, rattling and scuttling with the
swiftness of gigantic beetles. Truly, all my senses felt violated;
not to speak of the exteriors of these nightmarish machines, I
had to abruptly interrupt my private internal life every time the
savage, inhuman shriek or whistle from a motor car lashed my
nerve-endings; I had to leap aside, stare around me, or hastily
flatten myself when, rudely pushing through the street traffic,
one of them threatened to cripple or kill me. Besides all this, the
motor car retained to a bizarre degree a lifelike appearance, even
when standing silently, lying in wait. For some time I had begun
to suspect that its nature was not as innocent as well-intentioned
simpletons suggest when they sing the praises of culture or, more
accurately, of the degeneration of culture, its horrible parody . . .

'Come back from the fourth dimension!' said Roncourt,
seeing that I had stopped silently on the pavement. 'The fairies

are fleeing from you, the lamps here in the doorway give them insomnia.'

This gambling den specialized in an oppressive, vulgar luxury – skilfully aimed at the unconscious mind – illustrating the riches to be won. We walked upstairs, passing shiny pools of sickly bluish light and female bodies draped in billowing cloth, posed against huge paintings. We crossed carpets, so deep that our feet lost all sensation in the pile, and pushed our way through the exquisitely dressed crowd under an awning of palm leaves; here, against the backdrop of a marble fountain group, seated opposite a newly bankrupt gambler whose hands were shaking, the mulatto Grineau was putting on a brilliant show.

4

I stood on a dais by the wall, with Roncourt beside me. From here we had an excellent view of both the table and the faces of the gamblers: they were seven, including the mulatto.

People surged feverishly around the table, placing their bets.

The mulatto was sitting with his elbows splayed, his shirt-sleeves rolled up, without a jacket. A light sweat shone on his full, coffee-coloured face. A black beard, fiercely ringing his cheeks and chin, twitched with each clench of his jaw as he mulled over an additional draw or a raising of the stake. He very often declared a flush or a full house, but he also often passed. Before my eyes, he won pots of ten and then twenty thousand showing just three queens, while his opponent showed two pairs, seven high, and then three jacks. Once he topped a four with four cards and a joker. The game was being played with the joker, which I noticed he drew fairly often.

On my way over to the table, I noticed the losing gambler furiously toss down his worthless cards, conceding final defeat. I had a fair amount of money on me, and I kept an eye on this player, meaning to take his place if he decided to leave the table. This he soon did. Forcing a yawn, his face pale, the gambler rose; the crowd gave way and closed in once again after he had pushed his way through the tightly pressed circle.

His chair stood empty. Glancing at Roncourt, who responded with a smile of cool approval, I took the seat, which happened to be directly opposite the mulatto. He did not even glance at me. The croupier dealt new cards.

My cards were of different suits and not in any sequence; in a word, they were no good at all. However, rather than passing I discarded them and drew five new ones. Now a full house was taking shape, thanks to the joker which turned up in this draw with its picture of the devil. I had a ten, three sevens and the joker; and by counting it as a fourth seven, I had a powerful combination of four of a kind.

'A thousand,' I said when it was my turn to raise. The player on my left folded, the second did the same, the third said, 'Two.' 'Five,' said Grineau. At the beginning of the second round, as almost always happens unless a third player refuses to fold, Grineau and I were the only ones left in the game.

'Ten,' I said, with the fervent look of a newcomer hoping to frighten his opponent. Grineau stared dully at me and responded, 'A hundred.'

I now had to agree to his wager and show my cards, or name a still higher sum, after which he could, if he wished, refuse to compare cards, giving up his hundred thousand without further ado. And the same for me. Such is the nature of poker: two players, never showing each other their cards, take turns to name ever higher sums until one loses his nerve, fearing that he will lose even more if his opponent's cards turn out to be stronger than his own; or until, having agreed to the last figure named by his opponent, he shows his cards at the same time.

Naturally, I did not know what the mulatto held in his hands. He could have a stronger four than I had, of higher cards than sevens; or even a straight flush. If this happened he would win – if, of course, he did not fold, fearing whatever I might have, if I assumed a look of complete confidence in my own victory and constantly called higher stakes. But he could well not take fright, and thus, when we finally showed our cards, it could turn out that I myself was obliged to pay him a bigger stake than he had counted on obtaining.

It was equally possible that his cards were weaker than mine;

they could have been absolutely no good at all, if when he bought new cards (he had discarded and bought four cards) his hand didn't include even the minimal single pair – with which, if you are brave, or more accurately reckless, you can sometimes win large sums if your opponent imagines you have four of a kind and folds with what might be a full house.

Thus neither of us could tell the strength of the other's cards. Having heard about the mulatto's audacious style, I at first imagined that he was simply bluffing: but the size of his wager suggested that he must have some basis for playing so high. I weighed the three possibilities: showing my cards and losing if his beat mine; reraising more than one hundred thousand, thus allowing Grineau to raise again; or folding and paying out ten thousand.

I was planning to take the latter option, not having any particular reason to risk a large sum for the sake of four sevens. I examined my hand again, and was startled that I had miscounted the sevens – there really were four of them. One of them, the seven of hearts, I had mistaken for a ten; I could not explain my confusion. So of course my joker now became a *fifth* seven. This was the most powerful hand in poker: five cards of the same rank, a very rare event. If you have four cards of the same rank as well as a joker in your hands, you can clean out any opponent to his last kopek, however strong his hand.

So I decided to play on. But it was vital not to betray myself: I had to make Grineau believe that the strongest hand I could possibly have was a strong full house. I reasoned that my opponent's hand had to be at least a full house. Touching my index finger to my brow, I sank into contemplation – pretended, naturally – of my five cards; I compressed my lips, the better to display tense calculation. At the same time it suited my plan for Grineau to see that I was pretending, but ineptly; let him think that I had a weak hand, since one often pretends hesitation over poor cards, hoping to instil the opposite supposition – that the hand is strong. This contradiction makes sense if I add that a player with a genuinely strong hand acts firmly and decisively, planning on obtaining his expected payout. My behaviour was designed to lead Grineau to a conclusion precisely opposite to the truth. And I began with a prolonged hesitation.

Now that he was evidently thinking that I was making the best of a weak hand, I had to act out something else – the concealment of a powerful card. If he guessed that I was likely to beat him, he would fold instead of raising any higher. But I said:

'Three hundred thousand.'

This sum equalled three times my entire fortune. But I was playing a certainty: I could raise millions, without risking anything in real terms.

Silence fell, the sort of silence that settles after a room empties. But lifting my head, I saw an endless portrait gallery of greed in the burning eyes of the lookers-on; the features of their faces had become a forest, quivering with excitement. To them the mulatto and I were deities, with thunderbolts in our fists.

'A cheque,' said the mulatto hoarsely, throwing me a sharp, concentrated glance.

However hard I thought about it, I could not guess his strategy. He looked on, giving nothing away, steepling his fingers over his cards and staring dully at a spot on the table midway between us. Laying aside my cards, I began to write a cheque, slowly forming round letters, even lines. Before signing it, I wrinkled my nose and glanced vaguely at the mulatto, then scribbled: Ebenezer Sidney.

When I looked up at him, I saw that the little finger on his left hand was trembling treacherously. Now everything was clear to me. He was trembling with agitation because he probably had a four. He was agitated by greed; he counted on ruining me. As you know, I had no need to worry, and I could keep up the appearance of a man 'diabolically in control of himself' as long as I wished. After writing the cheque, I gave it to the croupier.

'A cheque for three hundred thousand dollars, drawn on the Royal Bank in Antway,' the croupier said loudly. Grineau brightened visibly.

'Five hundred thousand,' he announced carelessly, pushing all the money and cheques which were lying in front of him to the centre of the table.

'I'll see you,' I said coldly.

A rumble of delight passed round the table. A stake of half a million dollars! Roncourt was staring at me like a bird watching a snake. The gamblers at the other tables, having made their bets, held their breath as the moment came to show our cards.

'Well,' I said, chuckling, 'show us your four, Grineau!' He turned his cards over, tapping them with the edge of his hand so that an ace flew out at the side. But there were three more of them – four aces, that was what he'd had! A maddened roar greeted this gesture, a furious burst of relief from Grineau's supporters. It was as though a whirlwind had swept the crowd, shuffling people around with the speed of an assault. Roncourt paled regretfully; I saw in his elegant face great and genuine sorrow. A hand such as that is virtually never beaten. He knew my financial position and therefore, quietly getting out his cheque-book, he asked softly: 'How much do you need, Sidney?'

'You are mistaken,' I said, showing my five cards with the grinning devil and spreading them out in a fan. 'Grineau, how do you like this gentleman?'

Such a moment defies description. I did not even hear the groans and exclamations, so deeply was I enjoying the expression on the face of the astounded mulatto.

'Your ...' he said, with a faint whining sound. Then he collapsed backwards and his eyes rolled up ... He had fainted. While they were carrying him away, the croupier counted the money and gave it to me, observing that it was ten thousand short. He volunteered to make enquiries, and left; I was already chatting to Roncourt, surrounded by a multitude of well-wishing flunkies, those exquisitely dressed outcasts to be found chasing gold dust in every big casino.

Meanwhile the croupier had returned, and I read the wine-splashed note he brought from Grineau: 'I'll send some of the money tomorrow,' he wrote, 'but I don't have the lot. However I'll send you, to settle up, a new motor car, registration *C.C.77–7*; I bought it not long ago. Take it if you want it; otherwise you'll have to wait till the next time the devil calls on me.'

'What's the matter?' asked Roncourt, seeing me rise to my feet. There was a mirror opposite and one glance into it showed me why he had asked. But I couldn't care less what he thought of me. A profound, deadly, numbing cold was rising slowly from my feet. My enthusiasm had vanished. I studied the note again, wondering why Grineau had taken it into his head to write down the registration number. Roncourt, glancing attentively at me again, took the note.

'Well, what of it?' he asked. 'Now it's plain that you'll have to cure yourself of your dreadful prejudice; fate herself is sending you a vehicle, and a smart, fast one.'

'Why do you think he wrote down the number?'

'A mere reflex,' said Roncourt.

'You know, I think you're right. Why don't we roll it over a cliff in the mountains?'

'Now why should we do that?'

'It strikes me as the necessary thing to do,' I said, mastering myself. That evening the dark powers had hold of me – my thoughts and my wishes were hopelessly confused.

'Look, something's happened. Everyone's started rushing around.' Roncourt took me by the arm. 'Let's go and see what they're looking at.'

The hall around us was certainly emptying. Many had remained, but plenty of others, after exchanging a few words, were raising their brows and swiftly disappearing into the blue haze of the flashing main doors. I strode quickly after Roncourt, but our curiosity was immediately satisfied: three habitués, waving from a distance, called to us:

'The joker killed Grineau! He's died of a brain haemorrhage!'

'What!' I exclaimed. Instead of the excitement I might have been expected to feel at this news, it revolved coldly inside me; it acted on me much more feebly than had the note with the registration number – a number so rich in meaning, so deaf, so dumb, and so eloquent in the language of objects, which escapes our understanding – I noticed with horror that I was talking complete nonsense, chuckling and making incoherent replies to those standing around me. Meanwhile, tragic grimaces went round the hall; the superstitious and those whose hearts were not quite dead were momentarily confounded; then everyone began to listen attentively to the orchestra, as before, and people started circulating again. Bets were laid, with laughter. A swarm of women was clustered around a fat man floating oilily amid their overblown blooms. He smiled like an innocent who had just frisked his way into heaven.

5

Seeing that I was overexcited, and interpreting my state of mind in his own way, Roncourt did not restrain me when I made for the exit. I wished him swift success. He stayed on for baccarat.

An oblique black line edged my mood, put there by the mulatto's note. This line cut sharply though the blaze of my excitement: however strange or repellent my project might prove to be, my unexpected wealth would not only bring me closer to Corrida, but would make me her equal. It was inevitable that this unhealthy attitude should be rooted in her very nature. She lived in a vile way: that is to say she was an utter and obedient slave to the objects surrounding her: toiletries, carriages, motor cars, drugs, mirrors, and jewels. Her conversation entailed a litany of useless and even harmful things, as if her life would offer nothing of interest without these essentials. As far as entertainment went, she liked exhibitions of paintings best of all, since in her eyes paintings were above all *objects*. She didn't like plants, birds or animals, and her favourite reading was Huysmans, who perverts objects, and detective novels, where the plot inevitably rests on inanimate items. Her day proceeded like a wound-up machine, and I feel sure she dreamed of shopping lists of objects. Bidding at an auction was a joy for her.

In spite of everything, I loved this woman. She had appeared in Alambeau not long ago; first her brother had arrived and opened an office; then she came, and I made her acquaintance thanks to Roncourt, who had had some business with her brother. And around this vapid being, my immense, unrequited love curled up, like a big dog. All the same, I preferred to picture her as a mannequin with a peaceful smile, shining behind glass.

Yet I loved in her the person I wanted to see, if her beautiful form were left untouched and a soul infused into it. However, I lacked the self-reliance to place all my faith in my own capabilities and trust that my attempt would have a favourable outcome.

I felt only that I could and should do whatever was possible. Unfortunately, I was well aware of the limited power of homilies in the ears of a creature regarding herself as no more than a source of physical satisfaction, mentally translating all your passionate conviction into cynicism, sneering at your powerlessness over the situation. Thus my assessment of whether renewal would be possible was based not on her words, but on those feelings she showed. I wanted so little – oh, so very little; a vivid blush with just a trace of excitement, a shy smile, a shadow of pensiveness. We rarely know the identity of the second person that dwells within us, and the second soul of my tormentress might be revealed as a good angel in real life, and like beauty, a good unto itself, might inspire others.

I put down my thoughts on this sacred subject precisely as they were, without trying to colour my impressions with that scholastic tone so useful in a literary context, since it compels the reader, already confused, to suspect the devices of the author. I had always had warm feelings for this woman, but I know that a love exists which is ready to face death even when it is filled with hopeless, sorrowful malice. I had no reason to hate Corrida El-Basso. Had I hated her, I would have been lost to myself forever. All I could feel was pity.

I had time to think all this over as, swiftly and with relief, I walked away from the casino under the light of its electric moons, extremely content that I could not reply to the mulatto, as I should have been inevitably obliged to say 'yes' to taking the car, from contrariness and as a challenge to myself; something always lures us to gaze farther than we are able to look with safety. Thanks to his unfortunate demise the car would remain his, even if he no longer needed it. The freshness of the sea wind, buffeting my face with strong gusts, settled my mood somewhat; a smile brimming on my lips, I crossed the street, almost empty at that time of night, with an elastic, unhurried stride. The sound of scattering sand somewhere nearby caused me to turn. I slipped, which saved me; my body, losing its balance, staggered convulsively aside just in front of the wheels bearing down on me. The visual impression of terrifying proximity had still not faded when, with a piercing, high-pitched bark, a huge grey motor car glittered in the street-light at the corner and disappeared with a fading hiss of tyres. Its headlights were dimmed and it was empty. I could not make out the driver. Nor did I manage to note its number.

During the extremely careful scrutiny I gave myself after this incident, I observed that my pulse had scarcely speeded up. I had barely been frightened at all. Somehow I was even a little glad that I had received such a warning. Just then I could not isolate a single distinct thought about what had happened: all my thoughts, manifold and clamorous, resembled a cacophony of stringed instruments, approaching a melody but decipherable only to an ear which already knew the motif, as I did not. You know when you try to cling to a dream in the moment before waking, when its scenes are still clear in your mind, and when you understand them but cannot at once translate that understanding into thought; while the idea slips away as fast as a handful of water and evaporates completely when full consciousness has returned? The same or very similar sensations took shape inside me. I hailed a cab, ordered it to drive to my house, and entered it at four o'clock after checking that someone was still awake.

I lived here as a guest of the Collemonce family. Our fathers had built their wealth together. Now their children lived together, behind the same walls, living for pleasure and for a vague but pleasant future. I entered, knowing I would happen upon an argument, a dance, or a concert.

6

I first returned to my room, opened my desk and placed my winnings there. I did not wish to tell anyone about them, at least for the present.

'In that case,' I heard, as I approached the door of the dining room, Hopkins's familiar voice – Hopkins was a lawyer –, 'he has been run over by a motor car. You know how careful Sidney is about such things. All the same, cautious people often fall victim to the very thing they try to avoid.'

'You're nearly right,' I said as I entered. 'It was sheer luck I wasn't run over.'

There were no ladies present. My sister and my older cousin's wife, Yutetsiya, had gone to bed long ago. My older cousin
Kishley and my younger cousin Thomas were sitting with their
guests, Hopkins, Sters and 'Nikolay'. The last was a newspaper
critic who had recently started building his career: his surname
was so long and clumsy that it had slipped my mind.

They were drinking. The windows were wide open. Having
recounted my near-accident with the motor car, I listened for
a while to the lawyer's thoughts and arguments as he explained
lengthily why it was needless to dodge backwards to avoid an
oncoming motor. I said 'Yes' and fell silent. The conversation,
without lingering on me, took up its thread again, which was
futurism, bitterly rejected by Hopkins. Nikolay was making
fun of him. They were both opposed by Thomas and, strangely
enough, by Kishley, whose full, good-natured face, as he smoked
his cigars methodically, thoughtfully and with relish, represented
the embodiment of healthy, axiomatic wisdom.

'Innovators have always been persecuted and ridiculed!' said
Thomas.

'A few of these people do have talent, of course,' Hopkins
retorted, 'and they, as one can judge from certain features of their
work, probably follow a special path. As for the others – all sheer
epilepsy of technique and taste.'

'I'm outraged that I'm being openly and impudently called a
fool,' said Nikolay, 'as if I'd accepted a painting or a poem that
was a planned attempt on my pocket, my time and my imagination. I don't believe in the sincerity of futurism. They're all good-
natured kids, ringing your doorbell and running away before you
can scold them.'

'But,' objected Kishley, 'mustn't there be some reason why the
movement has become so popular? The reasons must be rooted
in the way we live. You react to futurism the way Sidney does to
motor cars: he won't ride in one for anything, although tens and
hundreds of thousands of people use them every day.'

'Kishley is right,' I said, 'futurism must be studied only in
relation to other things. I suggest examining it in relation to the
automobile. This is a phenomenon of a certain type. There are

many other phenomena of the same type in existence. But I don't want to simply make a list. Not long ago, in a shop window I saw a piece of china that had been designed by some Cubist or other. It was decorated with coloured squares, triangles, oblongs and lines, combined in various ways. Now as far as art is concerned – from our point of view, from a human point of view – there's no more to say. Another way of looking at things has to exist. After considering this, I adopted the point of view of the motor car, and presupposed that besides the power of motion, it has some kind of unexpressed consciousness. Then I found the link, I found the harmony, the order, the idea, I understood its sinister dismissal of everything in our visual world. I understood that those coloured lines, parallel and close together, combined in a triangle, reflected its perceptions as it drove down a street, merging innumerable cornices, drain-pipes, doors, signs and corners, with one powerful gleam of its headlamps, into a single image. Press yourself flat against the wall of any house and look down at the pavement. Before you is a simple outline of the street where you are standing, compressed into an extremely narrow angle of vision. It will be a multi-coloured medley of lines. But, if we presuppose that the motor car is capable of vision, we cannot avoid also assuming an aesthetic – that is, a preference, a choice. If phenomena have a humanlike face, we credit them with human nature too; we see a link with living things. A machine cannot see this way. Its vision must be, by its very nature, exclusively geometrical. And so this vaguely humanlike mixture of triangles and squares or semicircles, surmounted by a single eye, over which simpletons puzzle themselves and screw up their eyes, must be taken as the Machine's visual impression of Man. It sees everything in its own terms. The ideal of elegance, to its perception, must be the triangle, the square and the circle.'

'The devil take you!' Hopkins shouted. 'You don't really believe that a motor car possesses consciousness and a soul?'

'Yes, it does,' I said. 'To the extent that we endow it with that part of our being.'

'Explain,' said Kishley.

'Gladly,' I answered. 'By accepting the motor car, by including it in our thoughts and actions as a part of our life, we accept its

nature absolutely: external, internal, and potential. This would
be utterly impossible if a tiny part of our nature were not also
mechanical: otherwise the motor car would never have existed.
And I suspect that this part of our consciousness composes its
consciousness.'

'What proof have you got?' cried Nikolay.

'You would be equally justified in demanding proof if I insisted
that a cat sees different colours from those that we do. Nonetheless, neither I nor the cat could be publicly interrogated, since
we have no common understanding, and no means of achieving
this. However, animals must have their own physical sensations,
perhaps utterly different from our own. Take, for example, the
dragonfly with its tens of thousands of eyes. You must agree that
its perception of light, with such a visual apparatus, must diverge
from ours.'

'Inanimate matter,' said Kishley. 'Iron and steel are dead.'

I made no objection to this. I seemed to hear the snort of a
motor car outside the window. Indeed, the sound was repeated
close by, and then right under the window.

'Do you hear it?' I said. 'That's its voice – a howl, distantly
reminiscent of crude words, full of enmity. And thus it possesses
a voice, the power of motion, vision – perhaps even memory. It
has a dwelling of its own. I recommend calling in at the wholesale
motor car stores on rue le Boc-Metaigne and observing them in
their domestic setting. They stand there shining, gleaming with
oil, on an extremely spacious cement floor. Their portraits hang
on the walls – photographs of different models and prizewin-
ning racers. They have their own music – several new com-
positions painstakingly conveying the dissonance of street traffic
or the random noises they make when they move. Finally, they
have their own gramophone, their cinema, they have doctors,
panegyrists, poets – those same individuals you were speaking
about half an hour ago, people with a strongly developed feeling
for the mechanical. They even have lovers, those ladies whose
waxen faces smile out from the windows of fashionable stores.
Doesn't all this amount to living? I'd call it a reasonably full
existence. Added to that, they play sports, they commit murder
and they wage war.'

'Makes perfect sense,' said Nikolay. 'But I'll tell you briefly. A certain motor car, covered in filth and scratches, returned from the battlefield. It had a shave at the barber's and made for home, where it played a gramophone recording of the "Fame and Glory" march and ordered a private screening of the film "Motor Races Between Liss and Zurbagan". It got so excited that it burst a tyre.'

'Your caricature proves that you have understood me,' I went on. 'The mutual relationship between objects, which might be quite insignificant to me, can take place through their very nature, in ways we can't comprehend. But when these interrelationships impose a particular pattern on the pattern of my life, adding useful or harmful elements to it, then it is vital to trace the connections between these phenomena, in order to know what kind of danger we are dealing with. Beware of objects! They can enslave us in no time.'

'What sort of harmful elements?' asked Thomas. 'Life is becoming more complex, faster-paced, constantly more intensive. Technology facilitates this intensiveness. Surely you don't want us to return to savagery?'

7

From that moment my companions took over the conversation, and I patiently heard out their defence of the motor car. This was how they justified it: the speed of the motor car enables the fastest possible exchange of goods, the lightning resolution of business, and the potential to travel to a distant place almost as fast as reading about it. I heard them out and left, laughing. Alone in my room, I counted the money again. It was a fortune. I was mildly troubled that I wasn't reeling with elation, intoxicated by my winnings. All my recollections echoed dully within me, like axe-blows on a solid tree. As I held the money in my hands, I also grasped that I had been transformed from a prosperous man into a rich one; but I thought this as though I had read it somewhere in a book. Perhaps all my desires were at this moment overshadowed by my main desire, my chief and inescapable idea

– the girl. Moreover, I was very tired, after thinking about the same thing for so many days. Nor was there any way I could express, in any of the world's languages, what this one thing was that was gnawing at me and destroying me. I understood it as an excruciating obstacle to comprehending my own thoughts. But I could not define it.

I dozed off, warmed and lulled by the sunlight stealing under the roof. Tomorrow, or more accurately that day, I ought to begin putting things in motion. I gave orders to be woken at three o'clock. My project was waiting, calling to me and to her. After a long hesitation I had made up my mind. I would confront her, Death-in-Life, face-to-face with Life-in-Death.

8

My acquaintance with Corrida El-Basso was extremely strained. If I went some time without seeing her I was able, despite all the love I felt for this girl, to think about her dispassionately, as you already know; I could even casually carry on a conversation quite unrelated to her. But in her presence I felt a tension that made me timid and inhibited. This was caused less by her beautiful and dainty appearance, which made an overwhelming impression upon me, than by my own awareness of the dissonance between the rhythms of our two souls. Hers was full of irregularities and disharmonies, while mine was slow-moving, with marked and regular vacillations, irreconcilable with anything that did not happen to accord with my mindset or simply with my current mood. While others quickly and easily communicated and joked with her, I was obliged to remain in the shadows, as I wanted to see her only in that complete, concentrated, private mood of love which I felt myself; interrupting that mood with empty chatter struck me as unnatural, even unlawful. Doubtlessly, as a result, I often bored her. But I had no other course. I was well aware that it was beyond my power to act a part so skilfully that my pose would not at once be revealed and provoke an answering pretence. Unconsciously, I wanted her never to forget my love for an instant, I wanted her to sense that my constraint, distraction and clumsiness arose purely out of love for her.

Because of all this I found it difficult to remain long in her presence if she was not alone. The tension I felt at such times often expressed itself in profound sorrow, after which there was no point in lingering: my saturnine face inspired only fear and revulsion. Yet I knew how different I could be if she stopped resisting me, if she used the familiar 'thou' when we spoke.

At half past four I picked up the telephone. I felt gloomy, but I had to assume the glee of a court jester as I spoke. I managed to sustain my role.

When she answered, I envisioned the pained expression on her face, her lips parted with annoyance, her always slightly sleepy, vague eyes. Thinking of her childlike forehead, on the other side of the town, I had an impulse to stroke it.

'So it's you,' she said, and I shivered; her voice sounded so welcoming. 'Oh, I'm so glad. I must congratulate you!'

'On what?' But I already knew what she meant.

'They're saying you won a million dollars.'

'No, only half that.'

'Even so, that's not bad! Now you're sure to go off travelling?'

'No, not at all. But I want to offer you what I swear will be an exclusive treat. I have completed my project. If you have no objections, you can be the first to see it; nobody knows anything about it.'

'Oh, I'd love that!' she cried. 'And as soon as possible!'

'In that case,' I said, 'if you're free, I have a short horseback ride into the Callot Gorge in store for you. It's no more than five miles away. I've got a horse, and my cousin Kishley will give me a second.'

'Wonderful,' she said, after a short pause. 'I agree. You are truly very kind. I'll be with you in half an hour.'

'I'll be waiting.'

So our conversation ended. While the horses were being saddled, I wondered how all this would turn out. It struck me that I had no right to behave as I did. But that didn't deter me. On the contrary, I became still more fixed upon my decision, for I might regret any weakness all my life. Matters could get no worse; I believed they might get better.

Just then the telephone rang. Its clamour burst in upon a pleasant, tender and pensive reflection. I raised the receiver.

Who was this speaking to me? A strained, ingratiating voice, like someone pleading for mercy, softly spoken and so distinct that it seemed it would continue to sound after the receiver had been replaced. I had woken that day with a sense of cloudy confusion: the weather was triumphantly bright, but an invisible, stagnant fog might have been weighing on my brain. Now this unusual idea gained strength.

What I heard resembled the end of a conversation, as can happen if your caller starts by finishing an exchange with someone else. That distinct voice was saying, as it spread across invisible airwaves: '. . . it will need very little time.' Then he addressed a remark to me: 'Is that Ebenezer Sidney's apartment?'

'Speaking.' Involuntarily, I moved the receiver away from my ear so that it wouldn't touch my skin, so unnaturally and repulsively close did this metallic voice sound, as if it were issuing from my own hand. I repeated: 'Sidney speaking: who are you and what do you want with me?'

'You don't know my name; I am calling you at the request of Emmanuel Grineau, the mulatto who died yesterday. He entrusted me with a few small matters he had left unsettled. Among these was a request to send you the four-seater Levand motor car which you won. Therefore I would like to request you to name a time when your humble servant can discharge this duty.'

An irrepressible rage struck me so suddenly that I yelled and stamped my feet. As I shouted, I shuddered all over with malice towards this unknown individual. If I could have done so, I would have beaten him with pleasure.

'Stay the hell away from me!' I roared. 'Go to the devil, I'm telling you! I don't need a motor car! Grineau owes me nothing! Take the car yourself and smash your head open on it! You worthless scoundrel, I can see through your schemes!'

But through my shouting, and when I ran out of breath and fell silent, I heard the uninterrupted flow of the man's speech, which continued to pour out at the same time as my maddened words; he was evidently completely untouched by this tempest in the telephone cable. Dispassionately, persuasively, his thin, steady voice ratcheted into my agitated mind. Wrung out by my fury, I heard 'take into consideration', 'from a sense of delicacy', 'the very nature of the case', and other similar expressions: as methodical and steady as the rope binding the hands of a man struggling to escape its loops. I threw down the receiver and walked away. Some minutes later a servant announced that the horses were ready.

What a beautiful day it was! Even the fog I have mentioned seemed to have dissolved by now, so that I could breathe deeply; although I hardly ever ceased to feel its steady oppression. I wanted to rub my head to expunge this sensation. The servant rode behind me on the second horse. As we approached the house where Corrida lived, I glimpsed her beaming face: she was on the balcony, looking down leaning her cheek on her hand, tightly gripping the balcony railings. She started to wave her handkerchief when we were still far away. I rode up in the elated and somewhat foolish state of mind of a man whose company people enjoy because, being rich, he may come in useful. I was not deceiving myself. Corrida El-Basso had never before been so friendly to me. But I did not want to dwell on that: my goal was near, even if I owed my success to the fascination imparted by a large win at gambling.

Leaving the horses, I walked in with a calm and assured step. Now that I was master of the situation, that inhibiting depression suddenly disappeared – that cursed feeling of loneliness which weighs upon us in the presence of a loved one. I began to allow myself to hope that my undertaking might succeed.

I kissed her slender hand and looked into her eyes. She smiled.

'You look pleased with yourself,' said Corrida, 'it isn't hard to guess why – you've had two successes – which of them do you count the more important? But perhaps your project will make you even richer?'

'No, it won't bring me a kopek,' I contradicted her, 'in fact, it may ruin me.'

'How can that be?'

'If it doesn't justify my hopes; it hasn't been tried out yet; there haven't been any tests.'

'What sort of thing is it? And what is it meant to do?'

'You'll see for yourself in an hour. Wouldn't it be better to wait?'

'True,' she said, vexed, lowering her veil and picking up her whip. She was in a riding habit. 'Is it pretty?'

'That I can tell you with complete sincerity. It's beautiful.'

'Oho!' she said, sensing something in my tone. 'And so, we're off to your workshop?'

'Yes, indeed,' and I couldn't resist teasing her, 'to nature's workshop.'

'You truly are a hoaxer, just as they say about you. Hoaxers aren't gallant. But let's go.'

We walked out and mounted; I helped her up.

'I'm feeling splendid,' she announced, 'and your horses are splendid too. What's mine called?'

'Change.'

'The name is as strange as you are.'

'I'm very simple,' I said, 'the only strange thing about me is that I always hope for the impossible.'

9

After riding beyond the outskirts of the city we started to gallop, and within half an hour we reached the start of the hilly track leading to the Callot Gorge. Our conversation was so trite, so insultingly and unnaturally trivial, that my spirits sank several times. However, there was no way I could direct our talk even to the relative closeness between us – if only to arouse a mood in harmony with the landscape, which assumed an ever more captivating character as we went on. To everything that failed to interest her she responded, 'Oh, yes!' or 'Really?' in an indifferent tone. But my winnings continued to intrigue her, and she kept mentioning them, although I had already told her everything of importance about my contest with Grineau. 'Oh, I understand how he felt!' she said, when she learned that the mulatto had had a stroke. But my refusal of the motor car inspired deep and contemptuous surprise – she looked at me as though I had done something extremely, unpleasantly funny.

'This is your mania again,' she said, after some thought. 'I've heard so much about it already! But I adore that enchanting speed, I love it when my lungs fill up with air. That's living!'

'It's the speed of decline,' I countered. 'Savages also love speed. What you seem to consider a sign of your unique refinement is simply atavism. All entertainments of this type – water sports, cycling, races of all kinds, skiing, funfairs, carousels, carriages, horse-racing – this is all a contagious enchantment with the dizzy sensation of free-fall. Speed has a limit beyond which movement along a horizontal plane becomes free-fall. You take pleasure in the sensation of free-fall. And those who think like you want to create a motion that's just like free-fall. What could be more primitive? And, one might say, pointlessly primitive?'

'But,' she said, 'the entire pace of modern life ... Variety has become part of our nature.'

'Quite true, and it is deeply unfortunate that this is so. However, precisely because this process takes place slowly (of course, relatively slowly, as the standards of speed are different for everyone and depend on every individual's kind of motion), precisely for this reason it is most valuable. The speed of an agent of a company that conducts trade increases the quantity but not the quality of its products – take the sale and manufacture of calico; but just let that agent, with his automotive swiftness, try to assemble and distribute an oak, a simple oak tree. That tree takes hundreds of years to grow. A cow grows up in two years. A fully formed human being matures over thirty years. Diamonds and gold are ageless. Persian carpets take years to make. A man comes to understand science still more slowly. And as for art? It's hardly necessary to say that some artists begin their masterpieces when they start shaving, and have grey beards before they finish. You claim that rapid movement speeds up trade, that it stimulates culture? It crushes it. It moves so fast because it cannot restrain itself.'

'I don't know,' Corrida objected, 'you may possibly be right. But life should be lived fast, don't you think?'

'If you were to die,' I asked her, 'and if you were born again, remembering the way you were – would you live as you do now?'

'I don't like your question,' she answered coldly. 'What's wrong with the way I live? Even if I am wrong, what right have you got to needle me?'

'No right at all, I simply ask because I care. However, I am at fault, and I must therefore make amends. In just ...'

'No, you're not to wriggle out of it!' she shouted, pulling up her horse. 'This isn't the first time. What are you leading up to with these questions?'

'Corrida,' I said softly, 'if you will be so good as to stop being angry long enough to answer a single question – with complete honesty – I give you my word that I will respond just as sincerely.'

We were already approaching the gorge; a ghostly lilac light, shaded by far-off greenery, spilled from the vast fissure. As I looked at it and recalled my intentions, I realized immediately that I had asked my question too soon, greedy for certainty. The fog was thinning a little (I mean that internal fog which misted my brain), and I could see all the wonders that would follow from my scheme as if in the light of a huge, blazing candle. Therefore I did not hesitate.

'I'm waiting,' said Corrida.

'Tell me,' I began, 'and this will remain between us, why and with what aim in mind did you come out of that ... shop?'

As I spoke, I could feel myself turning pale. She might guess. Inanimate things have a certain instinct which, for example, helps them to fall in such a way that other objects collude to hold them in the new position. But if she pretended surprise, I was ready to translate my words into a joke – to pass them off as sheer distraction. I watched her narrowly.

'Out of the *shop*?' Corrida said slowly, turning on me such an unflinching, searching and cunning look that I shuddered. No doubts remained. Moreover, her face had unexpectedly turned a paler shade of white, the same matt shade of white found in wax mannequins. That was enough for me. I chuckled; I had no wish to trouble her further.

'I have no more questions,' I said, 'I meant our meeting yesterday, when you went into a shop. You came straight out, and I didn't wish to go up to you yet again.'

'Yes ... but that's very simple,' she answered, trying to think of an excuse. 'I didn't find the salesgirl I wanted. But that's not what you meant to say.'

'You just muddled me with your fierce rebuff. I asked the first thing that came into my head.'

Then, without allowing her to dwell on her suspicions – if she had any – I returned to the topic of the game with the mulatto, and recounted the details of our duel so amusingly that she laughed until tears came. We rode along the gorge. At right angles to it on our left stretched a deep crevasse. I rode over to this and stopped my horse.

'It's here,' I said.

Corrida slipped out of the saddle, and I tethered the horses.

'I'm a little worried by all this mystery,' she said, glancing around, 'do we have far to walk from here?'

'A hundred paces.' To stop her from fretting, I began joking again, likening our stroll to the dog-eared pages of crime novels. We walked side by side; the smooth floor of the lateral crevasse did not impede our steps, and soon the shadow of the walls lightened – we reached the far end, a precipice hanging steeply over a valley flooded with sunlight. Far below, farms and villages spread out like flocks of birds. The wind blew the huge blue emptiness into our faces. Just here I stopped and pointed over the edge.

'Do you see?' I asked, looking into her lovely face, contorted by peering downwards.

'The view's not bad,' she answered impatiently, 'but perhaps, all the same, we should be getting on for your laboratory?'

A crazy joy overwhelmed me. I took her hands and kissed them; she was too surprised to struggle. An internal urge drove me on; unthinkingly, I looked behind at the crevasse, where she could escape in no more than a second, and blocked her way to it. But we made for the crevasse at the same instant – at least, when I caught her by the waist she was already halfway past me, pushing me off with one hand. Her face was pale, like a corpse's, her eyes huge and round. Her other hand was doing something rapidly at her side, by her pocket. Panting, I dragged her towards the precipice, shouting, persuading, pleading.

'It will take one moment! One! And then a new life! Your salvation is out there!'

But alas, it was already late – too late. She broke free in a whirlwind of unbelievably swift movements, and raised her revolver.

I saw it jerk in her hand and realized that she had fired. It felt as if a pebble had struck my left temple. Unaware – against my will – convulsively struggling not to fall – I fell, and as I did so I saw her tiny lacquered shoes leap back hastily. But I managed to grab hold of them and tug.

She toppled down beside me; as she fell, the revolver sprang out of her hand. I could see it by turning my head. If she hadn't hindered me by catching my arms, I would certainly have grasped it. But she had a feline resourcefulness. Seizing her by the waist and holding her close to stop her jumping up, I was already touching the revolver with my left hand, trying to scrape it towards me with the tips of my fingers, but she struck my hand at the wrist, deflecting my fingers. Finally a blow from a stone defeated my hand. It slipped away like a boned fish, and Corrida took the revolver. At this point my strength deserted me. I could only lie and look on.

While she scrambled away and got to her feet, the revolver stayed constantly trained on me. A silence followed, broken only by the sound of both of us breathing, as loud as screaming.

'What's all this about?' she said. 'Now you're going to talk, do you hear me?'

10

I lost no time in telling her what she was missing.

'Yes,' I said, 'this is indeed my project. Did you see the radiant world? It's calling. So let's fling ourselves into it and be instantly reborn. It's what we both need. You don't have to pretend any more. The cards have been revealed, and I see yours clearly. They're stained with wax. Yes, the wax is dripping from your beautiful face. Your face is dissolving. It had to reflect rage and terror before the wax remembered its previous life in colours. But the real, the true life will kindle in you only after destruction, after death, after renunciation! I tell you that I meant to jump too. There's nothing to fear! We must die and be reborn!'

'Where are you wounded?' she asked harshly.

'On the head, by my ear,' I said, touching my damp and sticky hair with my wet fingers. 'Leave me! What am I to you now; your place in my life is empty.'

Hitching up the edge of her dress, she walked round behind me, and I felt a small, cold hand lifting my head. There was the sound of her kerchief ripping. She bound my head tightly, then stepped once again out of the shadow into the light. I lay there, utterly weak from loss of blood, and listlessly accepted her care. I felt sheer horror that I had failed.

'Can you walk as far as the horses?' Corrida asked. 'If you wish, I will help you stand up. If not, lie still and try to be patient; I'll send someone for you.'

'As you will,' I said. 'Do what you want. I can't walk to the horses. Now it's all the same to me whether I live or die, since I've lost you forever. Perhaps I'll die here. So let's speak plainly. Our first meeting you must remember not from Alambeau – no, it was in Glen-Arrolais. Do you remember Glen-Arrolais? An old man parted the muslin curtain to show you inside your case; wax with a mechanism inside – that was you – you slept, breathed and smiled. I paid ten cents entrance fee, but I would have paid with my life. How you escaped from Glen-Arrolais, how you came to be here, I don't know, but I discovered the secret of your mechanism. It gave the outward appearance of human life, thanks to all the mechanisms clattering around us. But to become a woman, you must understand, to become a genuine living being, you must first be destroyed. Only then, I know, will your heart beat with my love. I am half-dead myself, I move and exist like a machine: the mechanism is already growing, creaking inside me; I can hear its iron. But in self-destruction there's strength; instantly resurrected, we shall deafen the entire world with the beating of our hearts. You will become human and blaze a line of fire. Your face? How beautiful it is; you would enter the gardens of the earth armed with the desire for real beauty. Your eyes? The shine of your hair? The quality of your smile? Your power to attract would shine through in your way of living. Your voice? It's alluring and tender, and you would become the person your voice suggests. How much you have been given! And yet how dead you are! How badly you need to die!'

I spoke without looking at her. Opening my eyes, I looked

around with an effort and saw no-one. Damnation! Her heart could have changed from a simple system of levers and cogs to a full, flourishing pulse – to tears and joy, to ecstasy and upheaval – it could have started loving me at last, I who would have been consumed in the blaze of the impact and transformed into a laughing little boy – and that heart was gone! I knew she did not want to remember Glen-Arrolais. True, in that little town only hideous pretended people had seen her, but nonetheless ...

With an effort, I rose to a sitting position. My head wasn't whirling, but it felt awkwardly suspended, as if it might roll off. I made an attempt to bend my legs, hoping to make further movement easier, and this worked ... Finally, I stood up, holding onto the wall, and took a step. I wanted to go home in order to calm down and think through whatever lay in store. As far as I could tell, my wound hadn't affected my brain; therefore I had no fear of collapsing on the way in an even more serious condition. I dragged myself along, holding onto the jagged rocks in the crevasse; every so often I stumbled and had to pause.

As I went on, the impenetrable shadows of twilight (it was already growing dark) gave way to that mysterious, thrilling glow shed by the moon, between daylight and magical, ghostly darkness. Reaching the end of the crevasse, I glimpsed in the gleam of the full moon the enchanted chasm of the ravine: the bottom, strewn with rocks whose round shadows resembled the brims of white peaked caps, was like the bed of a gigantic river, dried up forever. The horses were gone. The wax woman had taken my horse, doubtless assuming I had died. I had not believed her promise to send help; she was more likely to dispatch assassins.

I touched the bandage, then took it off. A mild heat, some pain and a sensation of stretched skin still lingered where the bullet had grazed me, but it had stopped bleeding. Suddenly suspecting that the blood-soaked fabric might tell me something, I peered at the markings in the light. They were her initials. I saw symbols unknown in any of the alphabets of our planet –

ᗡ Ǝ B

– and realized that I would never discover the nature of the creature that used such symbols.

'Corrida!' I yelled. 'Corrida! Corrida El-Basso! I love you, I love you, I love you, mindless as you are in your cold glitter, unobtainable, for you're not even alive – no, a thousand times no! I wanted to give you a little life from my own heart! It wasn't me you shot – you shot and wounded life itself! Come back!'

And an echo, taking the *rri* from her name, resounded persistently somewhere beyond the high rocks: the sounds resembled the popping of a far-off motor. I kept remembering Glen-Arrolais, where I had seen her for the first time. Yes, there on a dais she had lain under glass in a wide white case, legs extended and crossed, covered with gauze, surrounded by dusty flowers. Her quivering eyelids were lowered; her soft, petal-like bosom breathed peacefully as if living. It was as if her eyes, radiant and smiling, might open; bending modestly yet charmingly at the waist, she might rise and speak the great word that had been trapped in silence. Now, with the silent consent of certain individuals, she was among us, promising so much and slaying so certainly, so slowly, so hopelessly.

Exhausted, shaking and wobbling, I made my way down the gorge, only noticing where I was when I reached the end. Among the green and silver sea of hills several paths wound away: I stumbled down the steepest one to the roadway below. Here, at a little distance from the road, stood a house which, in the words of the poet, 'was poor and slumbering'. Stepping over the narrow stone wall, I spied out an open window and pushed my winnings through it, knocking something over in the process. Who lived there? What power would I awaken in the morning with the gift I had not needed? I can only say one must leave clear traces on earth: a faint trail is quickly overgrown by grass. The next morning there would be cries, noise, arguments and howls from the astonished inhabitants, perhaps sudden illness from ecstasy: what of it? Such is life, with its convulsions, grimaces, wails and smiles – any kind of life is good.

The moon rose higher; its round skeleton sent the eye downwards, blanching the road all the way to the horizon. Here it stretched out like the Roman letter V, resembling the double curve of a bow. Standing on a rise, I saw a dark line in the distance moving over the next incline. A point emerged from the line and grew, like an ink blot spreading across paper; the blot crawled to the centre of the nearest hollow with a speed that disturbed me. I walked towards this phenomenon, but it soon brought me to a halt. I was not mistaken – a grey motor car was already approaching me with that repulsive automotive swiftness which obliterates our ordinary perception of effort. Turning aside to the bushes, I hid in their damp shelter: now there was such a short distance left between me and the motor car that I could see and even count those inside it. There were four of them, besides the same bespectacled driver whom I had seen the day before. They were glancing all around; one spoke to the person beside him as the car crackled past me.

Everything was clear to me now. The hunt had begun: there might even be an inevitable, ghastly revenge. The letters and the number I had seen when sick with fury hung in the air as if printed there: they were *C.C.* and *77-7*. I was truly on the verge of madness. Shaking as if I were already a prisoner, I searched confusedly for a different road from the one my enemy controlled: I floundered into bushes, but I could not make progress. Roots were so tightly woven into hollows in the ground that I was forever on the point of tripping between piles of brushwood: dry blackthorn snagged my coat. Moreover, I made my way noisily, which risked exposing me to my pursuers: some of the hollows were so deep that when I fell my entire body was painfully rattled.

After stopping and catching my breath, I again approached the road and looked around. It was empty. Neither from left nor right came the slightest sound; therefore, knowing that I could always find cover in the bushes, I walked out onto the road with the aim of making up as much distance as possible.

And so I began to run. At one time I had been a good enough runner to win races. My running ability did not forsake me now; the road sped by behind me with the regular impact of my feet; the swift motion of the air cooled my burning face. Although I was very tired, I did not allow my exhaustion to rob me of strength.

My rhythm was broken by a pothole – a small black cavity which I noticed in front of me and which, to my astonishment, I did not reach as quickly as I should have done. Although it was not far away, it came closer so slowly that it might have been able to increase the distance at will. And then, sadly looking back once more, I realized that I was not running but walking, and barely dragging my feet at that. This reverse finished me off. I sat down, but I couldn't even sit; leaning on my hands, facing the gorge, I could tell by the reverberations in the ground that the pursuit was returning. Not two minutes had passed when the grey motor car appeared in the distance, heading towards me, ready to land the final blow.

I felt unable to stir. I was so numbed, so impossibly weak, that I could not even feel fear. My terror could crouch peacefully on my back for as long as it wished, without the slightest hope of contorting my face or my spirit. I was immobile, relaxed, I was like the road itself. I met the oncoming, whistling wheels with a firm, fixed smile. Instead of the sunny, vital cliff of joyous immortality, Death was already touching my face with the shining scythe of light thrown by the approaching headlights – when suddenly this iron cat, about to run over my body, uttered a muffled thunderclap, swerved and stopped. The four men hurried out of it, lifted me, and placed me on a seat. Barely able to move my arm, I crawled off it at once, having ceased to see and almost ceased to hear – I had the sensation that thick tarpaulin was ripping, deep under the earth.

II

I came to in a small, high-ceilinged room; the door was closed and the place was suspiciously quiet. I was lying in bed; on my left was a small table with some flowers. They were an extremely skilled imitation; their petals (I smelled and touched them) had exactly the same moist chill and slippery softness as real ones; they even smelled like the real thing. Touching my head, I felt bandages. A green ceiling lamp threw a round shadow. I already felt strong enough to speak and demand an explanation for my captivity. Noticing a bell-wire, I pressed the button.

The door opened, and a man appeared whom I had certainly never seen before in my life. He was solid and upright, with a square, decisive face and unpleasantly bright eyes behind spectacles. His patronizing smile was evidently directed at me, as if my helplessness and weakness pleased him.

'Whoever you are,' I said, 'you have a duty to tell me at once where I am.'

'You are in Dr Emerson's clinic,' he said. 'I am Emerson. Are you feeling better now?'

'I was kidnapped,' I answered in a tone meant to make plain my urgent wish to know what had happened while I was unconscious. 'Who are you – a friend or an enemy? Why was I brought here?'

'I ask you,' he said with surprising imperturbability, 'to be perfectly calm. I am your friend – my only wish is to help you get better as quickly as possible.'

'In that case,' and here I rose, swinging my legs off the bed, 'I am leaving here immediately. I am sufficiently well. Your actions will be reported to the Royal Prosecutor.'

He rose also and rang so quickly that I was too late to catch him by the arm. The immediate appearance of three strongly-built men in white caps and aprons obliged me to lie back against the pillow in my former position – resisting four men would be unthinkable.

As I lay, I looked at Emerson in despair and irritation.

'So you are in on the plot with all the rest,' I said. 'Very well, I am powerless. I ask you to leave me.'

'What plot are you talking about?' he asked, making the men a sign to leave. 'There's no plot here; all you have to do is rest and get better.'

'You're pretending not to understand. I mean,' and I traced a circle in the air with my hand, 'the plot by the circumference against the centre. Imagine an enormous disc revolving on a horizontal plane – a disc on which every point is filled by thinking, living creatures. The closer any particular point is to the centre, the more slowly, within the same revolution as all the other points, that point will revolve. A point on the circumference describes a circle with maximum speed, simultaneously with the stillness of the centre. Now let's interpret the metaphor: the Disc is time, the Movement is life and the Centre is truth, while the thinking beings are people. The closer to the centre, the slower the movement, but it takes the same time as the movement of the points on the circumference; consequently it reaches its goal at a slower rhythm, without diminishing the overall speed of attainment of this goal, which is a circular return to the point of departure.

'Along the circumference, whistling and rattling, as though chasing the inner beings (those closer to the centre) but in deadly simultaneity with them, a false life makes maddened circles, infecting the people of the inner circles with its own feverish abundance, interrupting their progressively calmer inner rhythms with the thunder of motion that is far removed from truth. This impression of fevered brilliance, at the very limit of happiness, is actually the suffering undergone by frenzied motion, hurtling around its goal but never coming close. And the weak, those like me, no matter how close they are to the centre, are forced to take in this outer whirlwind of mindless haste, beyond which lies emptiness.

'However, there is one dream that never leaves me. I see people who don't hurry, like those points closest to the centre, with a wise, harmonic rhythm, fully alive, masters of themselves, smiling even when suffering. They don't hurry, because their goal is nearer to them. They are calm, because they are satisfied with their purpose. And they are beautiful, since they know what they want. Five sisters beckon them from the centre of the great circle – unmoving, for they are the ultimate goal – and they are equal to the sum of every movement in the circle, for they are the source of all motion. Their names are Love, Freedom, Nature, Truth and Beauty. You, Emerson, told me I'm sick: oh! if that's true, I am sick with a great love. Or ...'

Glancing at the door, which squeaked, I saw that it had opened a crack. A whiskered face looked in and chuckled. One eye met mine. And I fell silent.

This manuscript, enclosing an order to the Commander of the Centaurs to capture the grey motor car immediately, and also the wax mannequin calling itself Corrida El-Basso, which has escaped from a panopticon, I will place tonight in the requests box.

1925

GEORGY PESKOV

The Messenger

At that time we were already living in the annexe rather than the big house. Aleksandr Glebovich, after his second stroke, had taken to his bed; I pushed him around in a bath-chair. We had no logs for the fire. When the evenings grew short, I gathered brushwood in the forest. We had no fuel for the Dutch ovens. With difficulty the priest prevailed on Pakhom to build me a brick oven: it smoked, but it was warm. But Aleksandr Glebovich's legs still got chilled through and through. I would wheel him right up to the stove and deal out his favourite Rouge et Noir solitaire on the table. Sometimes he stayed up in his chair all night long.

We never spoke about our son, our Glebushka. We couldn't bring ourselves to talk about him. We didn't even know what to wish him when we prayed: good health, or eternal rest. All things are known to God; He will do what's needed.

We had no callers, apart from Father Agapit. I was glad we were left in peace. It's already hard enough to grow accustomed to new ways in old age. What's more, we chatted as much as we wished with our own people – those who had passed away – and that eased our hearts. Before, when we were young things, Aleksandr Glebovich used to laugh at me; he'd say I had taken leave of my wits, and quote science at me. But later, when so much had happened to us, he seemed to have started believing in it, sometimes at least.

The priest scolded me, saying, 'You must know that the Holy Fathers of the Church won't hold with this.' But what was I to do? I know it's a sin, but I'm used to it; all my life I have spoken with the dead and I won't stop now when it's become our only source of joy. And it's not as if we pester them. We always ask, 'Who is able and willing to talk to us?' 'Well,' says Father Agapit, 'in that case it's not difficult to guess *who* answers!'

And what of it? Of course, it happens sometimes. A troubled spirit is always idle and, from sheer idleness, curious. But you can tell straightaway from the conversation whether a spirit is mischievous. If you read a prayer aloud, it'll leave you alone. And then the joy is all the greater when you chat with your dear ones. Aleksandr Glebovich's mother often came, and his uncle Pavel Kirillovich, and our daughter, little Natasha; she wasn't two years old when she left us. 'Papassa,' she'd lisp, so sweetly and amusingly. Aleksandr Glebovich would be in better cheer after hearing her and he would sleep more soundly at night. Glebushka never came. I was glad of that, thinking it meant he was still here on earth. But Aleksandr Glebovich would say 'There's no telling why he doesn't come' and frown. I asked no questions.

Then one evening Aleksandr Glebovich was dealing his patience and I was peeling a potato for supper. And he glanced at me over his glasses – which fitted him badly – and said, 'Leave off that rubbish, I won't be eating anyway. Your hands are like a cook's already.' He never could accept the way our life had changed. Suddenly I remembered how the old Count would always kiss my hands – like an elderly Don Juan.

'Something reminds me of the Count,' I said.

'Perhaps he wants to have a chat,' Aleksandr Glebovich said, shuffling his cards. 'What do you say, Marie, shall we give it a try, all the same? We might be lucky today.'

We sat down. I picked up a pencil.

'Count Pyotr Sergeyevich, speak to us, if you are willing and able,' said Aleksandr Glebovich, laying his hand over mine. The pencil never moved. 'My old friend doesn't want to talk,' muttered my husband, aggrievedly. 'No-one wants to know us, Marie, we're no use to anyone!'

The pencil suddenly made a loop and sketched out: 'I, I, I ...'

Aleksandr Glebovich gave a short, cross laugh. 'It's another of those rascals: your docker from Hull or that multiple murderer they strung up in Hanover. They're the only ones that stay around.'

I crossed myself.

Again: 'I ... I ... I ...'

'Who are you?'

The pencil scraped the paper sharply enough to rip it, and in the far right corner – my hand barely reached across – it printed clearly and firmly: 'A messenger.'

'Who sent you, and what is your message?'

Endless loops. We waited. The only sound was the steady rubbing of pencil on paper. Suddenly, letters of a sort started appearing with great speed, one after the other. My hand wasn't fast enough.

I dropped the pencil. On the paper we read: 'A blessing.'

'It must be a priest,' Aleksandr Glebovich said light-heartedly.

We took up the pencil again.

'No, no, no.' That meant we had misunderstood.

'Then what are you? Please explain.'

Once again, 'I ... I ... I ... a messenger ... a blessing,' and then a word beginning with the letter G which we couldn't make out. But we both knew and grew anxious.

'Start again, please!' asked Aleksandr Glebovich.

The second time it was perfectly clear: 'Glebushka.'

'Do you mean to say that we will hear good news about our son?' Aleksandr Glebovich asked, scarcely breathing.

'Yes, yes, yes.'

I could contain myself no longer: tears poured down my cheeks. My old husband was blinking crossly.

'God has had pity on us ... God has finally had pity on us ...'

I was already certain: my boy was safe, God had saved him from the hands of the evildoers.

'We must ask who he is ... This "messenger" is too mysterious. He should tell us his name,' Aleksandr Glebovich fretted.

'There's no need, Papa; you shouldn't ask for too much.'

'No, I want to.'

We took up the pencil again.

'Tell us your name!'

'If you wish to and if you can,' I added.

Circles, spirals, arabesques; not a single letter. It was gone! It did not want to give its name, or to say any more about our poor boy. Aleksandr Glebovich pushed his chair away with great feeling. He was crimson all over. It had been a long time since I had seen him in such a state.

'Once again ... pranks played by some scoundrel!'

'May God forgive you, Papa!'

'No, I've had enough! You may have the patience of an angel, but I'm tired of it. All these nights without sleep ... praying for my son. And then ... some Hanoverian murderer!'

He turned away, and I knew that not even all his willpower was enough to control his feelings.

'Papa, St Thomas said: "Lord, we know not whither Thou goest".'

He turned back to me. His face looked so guilty; it was pitiful.

'And Christ answered: "I am the way, the truth, and the life".'

'You're right. Thank you, Masha.'

And so we sat, wordlessly asking for absolution from the sin of Doubting Thomas. Outside the window a white wall of snow was whirling and the wind was howling in the chimney. We might have been the only living beings left in this chaos. But I knew we were not alone.

Suddenly something rapped on the window-pane. Aleksandr Glebovich shuddered and crossed himself. I went to the window. There was nothing visible in the darkness. I sat down again and waited tensely for something to happen. Then there was a firm knock on the door. But not from the veranda; from the servants' entrance.

'Who can this be? At this time of night? In a blizzard? Make sure you don't open up without asking who it is!'

The knock came again. I went into the kitchen. With difficulty I opened the small window, which was frozen shut. There was a man standing outside, a complete stranger, as he seemed to me. He was tall and thin.

'Who are you looking for?'

He turned and stared at me silently, without answering.

I understood immediately and rushed to the door. I tried to open it; there was so much drifted snow outside that it wouldn't shift. 'Tell me just this, is he alive or not?' I called through the door.

'He's alive and thriving, put your mind at ease.'

He started scooping the snow away with his foot. I could feel him straining to pull the door outwards. I can recall everything as though it happened yesterday. I remember the glowing joy and the tenderness that welled up within me. He wrenched the door; it opened, but not very far, so that he struggled to squeeze through. He was powdered all over with snow.

'I've barely made it this far,' he said, taking off his fur hat and brushing himself down. His voice had a touch of hoarseness.

'You must have caught a cold. Come into the room as quick as you can. You should drink something hot.'

'In God's name! No need to take any trouble on my behalf!'

He quickly took off his overcoat and we went into the room. He was wearing a British-style service jacket. Epaulettes shone faintly on his shoulders. From my old husband's face and the tenseness of his neck, I could see that he had already guessed. In silence, they shook hands firmly.

'Papa, our Glebushka is well,' I said, weeping.

Our guest glanced around the room.

'It's grim for you here.'

I gave him a chair, poured tea, and served what little we had. We didn't ask him questions; we had to let him gather his strength. He sat without touching a thing. Then I noticed that he was trembling all the time, in the strangest way.

'Are you feeling unwell?' I asked him.

'I have a fever.'

'Oh, Lord above! You've caught a chill for our sake.'

He looked dreadful, just as if he hadn't eaten for days. Where his cheeks should have been were hollows; the skin clung to his jawbone. His nose and his long-unshaven chin were bluish-grey. His eyes seemed to have fallen in, and they stared motionlessly at a single point.

'You don't look well at all.'

'I have typhus,' he said indifferently.

'What? Typhus! Good Lord, how did they ever let you go?'

'I was sent,' he corrected me.

'This is terrible! You must rest straightaway, and I'll try to fetch the doctor.'

'There's no need. What are you thinking of? The doctor can't help, and I certainly can't stay. Allow me to pass on what I was sent to tell, and I'll be off.'

'There's no way I'm letting you leave!'

'It stands to reason, it's impossible,' Aleksandr Glebovich supported me. 'At least stay until morning. Apart from anything else, you need to be cautious. I'm amazed how you managed, in that uniform ...'

'*Now* I can travel in any uniform I wish.'

'You're mistaken. If you came from that place ...'

'That's precisely why I can.'

'They'll arrest you immediately. It's strange they haven't arrested you yet.'

'Let them try!' He laughed contemptuously, but with a note of bitterness.

'We must unpick those epaulettes,' Aleksandr Glebovich persisted. Our guest made an impatient gesture.

'Trust me, it won't matter. Here is what I was charged to tell you. I – forgive me for not identifying myself earlier – I am a lieutenant of the Drozdovsky Regiment; my name is Serikov. I was a friend of your son, Gleb Aleksandrovich. I saw him for the last time at Simferopol just before the Reds turned up. For reasons that I'm not going to mention, I remained in the city when our forces were evacuated. We parted there. There is no reason to doubt that your son left the Crimea and is now in safety. That's all I know. However, if you wish to know more, then I can let you have the address of one of the White Cross sisters. The field hospital for the "hopeless cases"' – he curled his pale lips unpleasantly – 'was abandoned. Yes, abandoned to the tender fury of the Reds. So this girl – Sister Shirintseva – refused to be evacuated and remained behind ... with us ...'

'Lord above, what a terrible thing! What did the Bolsheviks do to you?'

He looked at me with his dull, almost unseeing eyes.

'I wasn't there at the time ...' He trailed off and then added jerkily: 'Well, as for the rest ... they were dealt with as always happens in these cases: the sick and wounded were shot, and as for the sisters ... Sister Shirintseva works for them now, against her will, of course. Yes, strange how things turn out. She ... she was your son's fiancée.' His mouth twitched again, as if a spasm had seized him. 'He tried to persuade her ... he begged her ... he threatened to shoot himself. She wouldn't leave. Nothing worked! She would comfort him . . . She was so cheerful, so pretty . . .' He was speaking almost deliriously, as if in the grip of a high fever. 'But she . . . she had a different destiny in store for her. She did not leave with the man she loved . . . She stayed behind to give her blessing to a dying man she didn't love . . .' He suddenly fixed us with a queer stare, as if he had only just noticed our presence. He stood up and gave a forced, unpleasant laugh.

'Well, it's time for me to go. Take down her address, if you want it.'

I wrote it down.

'And won't you stay, after all?'

'Out of the question.' He shook hands with us. I remember the damp and slippery feel of his chill fingers. He had gone to the door, where he suddenly hesitated and stopped.

'When you write . . . please send her my respects.' He almost added something else, then said, 'Well, it makes no difference!' and walked out.

When I had closed the door behind him and come back into the room, Papa was sitting and staring oddly at the chair from which our guest had just risen.

'Has he gone?' he asked. 'You must write to that sister right away. Perhaps she knows something about Gleb. And as for this fellow . . . you must ask about him too.'

'What should I ask?'

'"What should I ask?" Who he is! Why he stayed with the Reds, where he went when they came. You heard him say it: "I wasn't there at the time". He might be some sort of spy, or a deserter.'

'Don't tempt God, Father. Didn't he bring us good news about Glebushka?'

'We should know who we are dealing with!'

The next morning Father Agapit came to see us. When I told him about our visitor of the night before, he shook his head doubtfully.

'Unlikely, my dear Maria Stepanovna, if you'll allow me to say so. Where could a messenger like that have come from? Wearing one of those English uniforms with epaulettes ... How could they not have caught him, at a time when you and I, who have never so much as held a sword in our hands, walk around looking over our shoulders and expecting our end to come every minute! Why, there weren't even any tracks in the snow in front of the porch. Could they really have been covered up by snow?'

'He came in by the servants' entrance.'

'By the back way? And however did he get into the garden?'

'True enough, Marie,' Aleksandr Glebovich put in, 'however did he get in? Did you unlock the garden gate for him?'

'No.'

'How could she unlock it?' said the priest, 'she could hardly have found the gate at all under the snowdrifts.' Then he added sternly, 'My dear lady, it is wrong of you to occupy yourself with all this devilish sorcery. You pay no heed to the Holy Fathers; now you see that it doesn't lead to any good. You're letting the Enemy in to see you.'

When he was gone, I didn't say a word to Papa about what had happened the night before. I sat down immediately to write to Sister Shirintseva.

Two weeks later a letter arrived with a Simferopol postmark. It was painful even to open it. Later I had to destroy the letter; but I read it over so many times that I remember it almost word for word.

'Dear Maria Stepanovna,

'It gave me great joy to receive your letter. I can even say that it was my first happy moment since our forces left. But there is much in your letter that isn't clear to me. I cannot tell you more about your son than you already know. It's difficult for me to talk about my relationship with Gleb Aleksandrovich – and what good will it do? Now, whatever may be, he won't come back. I don't regret what happened, and I have never regretted my decision. I could not have acted otherwise. But as for what you write about Lieutenant Serikov, there is plainly some misunderstanding: Lieutenant Serikov died of typhus in my hospital on the very same night that our forces left. It's true that he and Gleb Aleksandrovich were friends. Not long before the evacuation they quarrelled. It's too difficult for me to write about this as well. When

Gleb Aleksandrovich came to say goodbye to me, Serikov was already lying unconscious. Camphor no longer had any effect. At this point Gleb Aleksandrovich and I had the conversation which you mentioned. But how could you know anything about it? There was no-one in the ward besides the three of us. I must not write anything about the way I live now … Please forgive me if you can. Yours, Zoya Shirintseva.'

I gave Papa the letter. As he read it, he went dreadfully pale. Then he suddenly turned purple.

'So that's the way of it! Didn't I say so? Clearly a scoundrel!' he shouted.

'But, Papa, he died!'

'Yes, he died, and some charlatan made good use of that, wanting to find out about Gleb from you. I'm not such a lunatic as to think dead men are paying me visits. However, you could drive anyone out of his wits!'

That evening the priest came to see us again.

'Well, Father Agapit,' Aleksandr Glebovich greeted him, 'I've had enough; I've sworn to give up spiritualism.'

'That's a wise course, Aleksandr Glebovich, and it's about time. If you're tormented by boredom, it would be better to play cards: it's the lesser sin.'

'It's not that it's a "sin", Father Agapit; I'm afraid even you would go mad here. Especially if you were in my position. She forced me to talk to Julius Caesar. In Latin. I swear to God that's no lie. How does that strike you? And now she's dragging spies into our house, and what's more, she wants me to believe they're spirits from another world. She takes offence if you argue with her. Who knows, a man could really go out of his mind.'

'May God have mercy!' The priest crossed himself. 'You should put mustard plasters on your temples, Aleksandr Glebovich.'

That same evening I wrote again to Simferopol, but I never got a reply. I tried to send a registered letter to the hospital manager and the senior doctor. It might as well have vanished into thin air. I never did find out what became of Zoya Shirintseva, who had loved my boy, but who loved God more. Nor have I learned anything about Glebushka to this day. Every time I unburden my soul in a secret chat with the departed, I ask them to call Lieutenant Serikov to pay us another visit. But he never comes.

Doubting Thomas did not believe until he saw for himself. And we still doubt after laying our fingers in the wounds. Lord, forgive us, we of little faith, for sharing the sin of Thomas!

1925

GEORGY PESKOV

The Woman With No Nose

I'm in a bad way. My head's like a cauldron, my ears are howling, everything aches. And I'm terrified.

There's typhus in the city. I've heard that dead bodies are piling up like logs in the hospital mortuary. They strip them naked and stack them up. Yesterday I saw ten sick men in the station. They were lying right there on the ground, delirious. Begging for water.

Before, I always used to think that nothing like this would happen to me. Now, on the other hand, I'm certain that it's bound to. Entirely certain. And I'm going out of my mind with terror.

The main thing is not to give up. I'll get a permit and take my seat in the carriage. After that it's easy; they'll hardly throw me out along the way. But I mustn't give away how dreadful I feel; they mightn't let me on the train. And there's no way I can stay behind.

I got separated from my own people. I'd thought I'd feel better after lying down; in the meantime they evacuated our offices. Yesterday I had this foolish delusion again; it's truly unpleasant. Can it be delirium beginning?

I went to the station yesterday to watch people boarding. At the entrance to the platform I asked a porter: 'Is that the train for Rostov?'

'That's right.'

'Why isn't it leaving?'

'Well, you see what's going on here. That one's still to leave – and tomorrow's train will leave too. And there'll be no more trains after that.'

I walked into the hall and stopped in the middle of the commotion. I stood there, plunged in thought. I glanced to one side – and there she was again. The devil knows what she is! She turns up everywhere. Even at the manager's office, or in our courtyard. Everywhere. It's a coincidence, of course – but a queer one. Yes, a very queer coincidence.

Every time I see her I feel much worse. And a sort of dread comes over me, that she might see me too. It's not at all like delirium – how could I be delirious when other people see her too? An old woman beside me threw a glance after her and spat in disgust:

'Ugghhh, a woman with no nose!'

Truly, her face is dreadful! Even apart from her lack of a nose, her eyelids are crooked. But she has curls on her brow, deliberately trained around a hairpin: this is peculiarly vile, as if she hasn't noticed that her nose has rotted away. Her cheeks are blue with powder, her lips painted red. As she walks by she smiles at the men she passes. There's something especially horrible about that. It makes it twice as bad for me. I don't know why.

What do I need her for! And yet I can't get rid of her. I saw her before, a long time ago, many times. I've only the vaguest impression where ... 'The woman with no nose' ... I've heard that phrase somewhere too, without a doubt. In childhood, from my nurse. She always used to frighten me with some sort of noseless woman: 'Here comes the woman with no nose to take you away.' I didn't understand, but I was scared. When I think about her I try to remember where I saw her, which makes my head hurt even more.

However, I must be firm with myself. I can't carry on like this. That's the end of it: I won't allow myself to think about any more irrelevant things. Especially about that.

Once again there was a crowd around the colonel. Tobacco smoke swirled in the air; wet clothes stank. People sat on tables, on window-sills, on the slime-stained floor.

The colonel's eyelids were grey. He opened his door and said:

'There are two seats as far as the Crimea.'

Here the shouting started. Someone said he needed three seats, not two. Someone else said he was going to Rostov. A lady was trying desperately to explain about her children. And absolutely none of it went into my head. It was as if I'd been struck deaf: I could see the colonel's lips were moving, but I didn't hear anything. Someone asked me, 'Are you ill?'

Everyone looked at me fearfully.

'Not at all, I'm quite well.'

'You wanted a seat, so what's the matter with you? Take it!' Joy at getting a seat made my mouth and throat feel completely raw. The room started spinning.

I was walking out of my office. Thoughts were swirling in my head like ripples through water. I was holding lots of documents, all of them extremely important, essential. They must not be lost; I had to hide them. But where? The main thing now was to think everything through. I'd wanted to sew the money into my overcoat. Yes, that would do. And I'd hide the documents in my wallet and my inner pocket.

I had to train myself to be sure to remember it all: the first thing to do was to hide the money and documents. The second thing to do was to be at the station by ten. By ten on the dot.

Now these two things are all I need to do. The rest can go to the devil. And I mustn't think of her. Not that I am thinking of her ... it's just that that ulcer instead of a nose and that curl on her brow might as well be right before my eyes. However, that's not what matters now. It doesn't matter a bit. And now which two things is it that I need, what was I thinking? Yes, I must hide my papers. And the second? What was the second? To be at the station – now I remember – by ten. There's Vera Vasilyevna standing in front of her door, dragging a loaded toboggan. She has a lamp in her hand, a big kerosene lamp, with a green glass bowl. And then, as I stare steadily – very steadily – at this lamp it suddenly bursts into flame ... and Vera Vasilyevna's face ... but none of this has anything to do with the matter in hand, it just gets in the way. I got a bit distracted, and now I can't tell for sure where I've come out. If this building in front of me is the station, then why is it on my left, instead of my right, like yesterday evening? These symptoms are all so vile. Well, to hell with them.

I go in. There are even more people than yesterday. I squeeze through to the wall, lean on it and stand in line. A shabby little old man keeps turning around to stare at me. But his face isn't bad at all; it inspires trust.

'Are you going to Rostov?'

'To Rostov … to Rostov …' I look around, wondering where I've ended up.

I see a large church candle sitting on a tall candlestick. There's an icon. If I'm not mistaken, it's Alexander Nevsky. In armour – well, he was a warrior. A woman is placing a small candle beside the big one. I must take off my hat. Although, I have to say, church isn't where I need to be.

But this is our church, the parish church. And this is our priest, old Father Nikolay. That means everything is all right … I remember when Father Nikolay married my brother in this very church …

'Isn't she here yet?'

They're waiting for the bride. What a strange idea to get married on a day like today!

How dark it is. There are just a few little candles, and the icon-lamp in front of Alexander Nevsky.

'Why haven't they lit the candelabras? That seems only right at a wedding.'

'They're not well, you see. And they don't have any luggage at all. And they've no coats on their backs. Wouldn't you say they're cold?'

'Yes, I'm very cold indeed in just this tailcoat. And have they gone to fetch the bride, then?'

All the same, this is rather odd; I've absolutely forgotten who the bride is. What unforgivable carelessness! But my head aches pitilessly, so perhaps that's why I forgot. Who could I ask, after all? What a silly situation.

I was wrong to come here. Something tells me I should never under any circumstances get married. At this point everything can still be made right. But later … later will be too late.

The most important thing is that I have no time. They must take this into account. I can't stay; I'd be shot. I must be there by ten. There were two things I have to remember. What was the second? There, I've forgotten. Vera Vasilevna with her lamp? No, what has that to do with anything? That wasn't it at all.

The priest takes me by the hand. We walk forwards. The choir sings. All this is just as it should be. If only I could remember who the bride is! I must clear that up as soon as possible …

A pink satin rug lies before me; I face the lectern. How well Father Nikolay speaks, with simplicity and solemnity at one and the same time!

'The servant of the Lord Andrey is pledged in marriage ...'

Now here is where I will find out who she is. There! ... Why are the words suddenly so hard to hear? He must have said her name, but I didn't catch it. No harm done, he'll repeat it any moment. It's unpleasant how my temples ache when I listen closely ...

'The servant of the Lord Andrey is pledged in marriage to the servant of the Lord ...'

Once again I didn't hear it! Perhaps he deliberately pronounced her name in a whisper. I had a feeling he would ... I should have left immediately. Now it's too late; I'm lost. I know for certain I'm lost. If not, why do I feel such inexpressible horror?

For the third time:

'The servant of the Lord Andrey is pledged in marriage ...'

I look Father Nikolay in the face. I can clearly see his lips trembling under his whiskers. And I hear every word now with complete clarity:

'Let the documents be prepared!'

The best man behind me kneels and whispers:

'Any moment now he'll come out onto the platform, there's more space there.'

'Oh, that's got nothing to do with it! Please leave me alone! Can you really not understand? I need to find out her name straightaway.'

All the same, fear still prevents me from looking at her. Nor would I recognize her if I did; it's dark.

Here I am, a groom ... Or rather, not a groom, but – what's the word? – doomed? Just as I think this, I notice a curious phenomenon; as soon as I glance into any dark corner of the church, a lamp is lighted there. Many of them are alight already, red ones, green ones, all kinds. It's very useful. I look upwards. The ceiling forms an immense dark arch. And there the candles in the lamps begin to light one after another, like stars in the heavens at night. In front of me an enormous round lamp blazes up, unbearably bright.

If only it wasn't for this cursed terror, distracting me! After all, what can it be that I fear so dreadfully? I'm frozen all over with horror. Pain in my back, in my head, in my whole frame. When I turn my head towards her, I feel a terrible ache in the bones of my neck.

I sneak a glance her way; I see, clearly, a hand in a kid glove, holding a candle covered in gold braid; I see a white satin bow and a wreath of orange blossom.

Now I must try to raise my eyes. Although this is difficult; my lids are heavy ... Here we go.

No, in spite of everything I don't see her face, only a lace veil. So that's it! Instead of tulle – lace! She's a widow! I think this with a shudder. But then why is she carrying orange blossom? If she's a widow, she isn't allowed to have orange blossom. However, lace ... I know only widows put on a lace veil for their wedding.

A widow! My vague terror has begun to gather around this word. A widow ... a widow ... She had another man, this must mean. They were married once too. Where is he now? Why hasn't he come? What did she do with him?

And perhaps ... perhaps she hasn't had just one, but several ... many husbands! And she exchanged vows with all of them. She stood with them before the altar, just as she stands there with me now. And then ... No, better not to think of that.

I have to run. If I slip away now, no-one will notice; there are so many people, and all of them are shoving.

'Where do you think you're going? They're telling you not to! What are you doing?'

The best man restrains me from behind and whispers something anxiously.

Father Nikolay's eyes protrude oddly from sunken sockets. They are lightless, red-veined, completely round. They glitter like soap-bubbles, becoming bigger and bigger. They could burst at any moment.

But his lips are moving:

'Anyone who pushes his way into the coaches will be hanged on the spot!' He indicates the crucifix with one hand. Already it's no longer a crucifix but a lamppost. And it's not Father Nikolay at all; it's someone wearing a military greatcoat. A tightly packed chain of soldiers is cutting us off from the coaches. We press close together with our bags and papers. Everyone proffers their papers to the soap-bubbles. I can't look that way; I'm afraid the soap-bubbles will burst.

'Go on, what's the matter with you! I've blocked the ramp; no-one else move from their place!'

'Please do not interfere with the document check!'

Someone is shouting. Someone else tears my papers out of my hands.

The best man is fussing about and holding me tightly by the sleeve. Now here is the step under my feet ... Finally I have escaped from this dark place to the front porch.

In honour of the ceremony, the steps are spread with red cloth. How fortunate that I put on a tailcoat and a white tie. But it's devilishly cold without a hat. The wind ruffles my hair. My head feels fresher. The porter rushes out onto the porch and shouts:

'Up you come!'

He's calling for my carriage. I hope to God they don't really get me a carriage. It's impossible for me to stay with the Bolsheviks, but I won't get into that carriage. Not under any circumstances.

I hurry forward; my feet won't move. And again I hear from behind me:

'Up you come!'

'There's no need!' If only I could walk away. If only they hadn't managed to call the carriage.

Before me is a narrow, dark street. Behind me, something is rumbling. A carriage can't rumble like that. I'm not brave enough to look behind. My feet are moving yet staying in the same place. The rumble is deafening. It's like blows falling on my head. Such unbearable pain!

Now the horses are coming up out of the darkness: a black pair in harness, pulling a carriage. Whatever is this: a wedding carriage or ... The lanterns gleam dully, as if blackened by smoke. The coachman seated above can't be seen in the darkness. The bony black nags barely trudge along at walking pace. The door of the rickety old carriage is half-open. There is an indescribable horror in this half-open door.

They draw level with me and stop. Settling awkwardly on

elderly springs, the carriage sways in my direction. The door opens wider, as if in invitation. I have one thought only: to walk on as far as the turning. There it is. Now I turn the corner. Again, the rumble behind me. The unseen coachman is lashing his horses with a whip. The nags lurch into a heavy, uneven trot.

They catch up with me. Again they stop. The door yawns wide.

Now I am almost running. Sharp stones tear my feet. The old carriage can't be shaken off; it gains on me again, and again stops. Someone shoves me through the open door. It's all the same: no way to escape. No good trying. I'm pushed harder from behind. I climb up on the footboard. And suddenly I see: the lanterns are covered with crêpe.

'What's the meaning of this? I don't want it!'

But the door has already slammed behind me.

'Let's go!'

The nags plunge into a wild gallop. I fall onto the seat; the carriage is shuddering, jouncing on its worn-out springs.

Nor am I alone. Opposite me, a white figure is squeezed into the corner. I can't make out whether it's wearing a wedding dress or . . .

My bride. In her regalia. My plighted one.

Once again, this terror.

'Are you . . . a widow?'

She keeps silent.

'Admit it, have you had other husbands?'

She nods her head.

'How many?'

She whispers dully:

'Many.'

'Tell me, how many?'

'Do you really want me to count them? . . . Many. All men.'

'All men?'

'All.'

'And you . . . all of them?'

'All of them.'

The horses bear us off. The wind rips through the open window. I am drawn irresistibly to look into the face of my bride.

As if reading my thoughts, she moves forwards. I have already changed my mind; I try to move away. She comes still closer. The white blur is directly before my eyes. Even if I wished to see, I could not. Her face is covered with the lace veil. But I know the lace is about to fall.

Then, in some sort of inhuman, final horror, I stretch out my hand to push her away.

The lace falls. In the dull light of the crêpe-veiled lantern I see her face, made hideous by some vile disease. Instead of a nose, there's a dark ulcer. Her toothless mouth is smiling, baring repulsive, pale gums. She is making herself up, fixing her curls across her brow. Over her forehead is a white wreath of orange-blossom ...

'Can there truly be no salvation?'

The doors are firmly shut. The wheels rumble heavily. White flakes of snow fly through the broken window. The wind sets her veil trembling and flings it into my face.

'Lord, grant me the strength to break free!'

There she sits. She looks at me with her dreadful, evil eyes. She is saying something ... What is she saying?

'Now all of us here are doomed! This is utterly intolerable ... in a public coach! It's infectious!'

'Blame me, if you must, madam. If a man is, as one might say, seriously ill, he can't be thrown off the train just for that reason. He wouldn't travel with typhus unless he had to; so he must be desperate. You must try to understand.'

'That man covered him up with his own coat – he's not afraid. And you talk about "infection". You should be ashamed!'

The carriage is weakly lit by the crêpe-covered lanterns. The black nags bear us headlong into the deep, damp night. Someone's hand carefully, like a mother's, settles my pillow.

And the woman with no nose hides in the dark corner under the seats and, from there, keeps watch over all of us.

1927

PAVEL PEROV

Professor Knop's Experiment

A key rattled in the lock, and the face of the prison warder appeared in the open doorway of the cell.

'You have a visitor,' he said, addressing the prisoner in that subtly polite tone which even seasoned employees at Sing-Sing assume before an impending execution.

Gibbs, seated on his bunk, lifted his head. His thoughts had been so far away that he took some time to return to reality. When he understood what was happening, he wanted to yell: 'Get the hell out of here!' But the warder had already stepped aside to admit the visitor. He then returned to the corridor and shut the door.

The two men who remained in the cell took stock of one another. Before Gibbs there stood a dwarfish old man, bald apart from the grey forelocks clinging to his temples like twists of oakum. His entire head seemed to consist of an even, shiny hairlessness, stretching from the nape of his neck to his nose. The remainder of his face was comically squashed together, as though hastily moulded from leftover clay. His poorly shaven chin disappeared into a high collar. Under his arm he carried a red briefcase, and in his hand was a soft-brimmed hat. As he stood there, he tilted his head slightly to one side, examining the prisoner through the spectacles which glittered under his brow, with the interest of a naturalist encountering a rare type of beetle.

He was facing a perfect specimen of *Homo sapiens*: a tall, well-built young man with black eyes and a dynamically defined jawline. The visitor's gaze seemed to palpate him from head to toe. The low forehead and grown-together brows of the prisoner indicated leanings towards crime; the uneven skull outlined under the closely shaven hair revealed imagination, while the thick lips implied good nature and sensuality.

The visitor pursed his lips, muttered something to himself, took a few short steps forwards and, extending his hand to the prisoner, said: 'I am Professor Knop.'

Mechanically, Gibbs stood up.

The professor's small, cold hand slithered against the prisoner's powerful palm like a captured frog. This sensation finally returned Gibbs to reality.

'The hell with it!' he shouted. 'Can't they give me a chance to be alone on my last day?'

'My dear young man,' the professor spoke insinuatingly in his high, rather forced voice, 'don't you think you're anticipating your solitude just a little?'

And before the prisoner could make sense of this hint, the old man burst into cheerful laughter.

'Listen,' he said, becoming serious as quickly as if he had exchanged one mask for another, 'the State Governor has rejected your lawyer's appeal. Out of a hundred chances to live, you don't have a single one left!'

Having said this, he retreated a step, as though to admire the effect he had produced.

Gibbs swayed on his feet. Unconsciously, a faint hope of mercy had survived in his soul: only now, as he hung over the abyss of nothingness, did he realize how desperately his entire being had clung to it.

'Not one chance,' he muttered, bewildered. So it was true then that he, George Gibbs, would be forcibly deprived of life, light and pleasure, and flung into the cold darkness of the grave? For an instant, his feverish brain touched the thin wall separating him from madness, and his overheated imagination blazed through it.

'I'm going out of my mind,' he thought, with a mixture of terror and joy.

But the old man's steely gaze penetrated his burning brain, like a jet of cold water on a blazing building.

'I want to make you a proposition,' said Professor Knop. 'It will give you ten chances of remaining alive. The prison management has already consented. The decision depends on you.'

Gibbs stared dully at him. This ray of light, flickering in the gloom, pierced his consciousness with difficulty. Not rationally, but with a kind of animal instinct, tearing greedily at life, he sensed a new hope. He seized the old man by both hands and cried brokenly: 'I agree to everything! Just don't let them kill me!'

A few hours later Gibbs was sitting in the professor's enormous office, sprawled in a soft armchair, sipping a whisky and soda and looking around curiously.

Professor Knop's office gave the impression that it had been occupied first by an antiquarian before a mechanic had moved in his workshop; then a chemist's laboratory, in which an astronomer had abandoned several instruments, had been installed by mistake, while a second-hand bookseller, hastily collecting his possessions, had scattered books, engravings and drawings everywhere. In the middle of the office stood a long table. To its right a powerful electric machine was placed; to its left, on slender legs, stood extraordinarily shaped instruments with concave reflectors, in the centres of which superheated wires were shining. The remaining objects were plunged in darkness, casting unnatural shadows on the walls and tossing brilliant sparks out of the gloom to gleam on the metal parts of the instruments.

Gibbs was aware that the three policemen who had accompanied them from prison were standing guard in the next room and that escape was impossible. But deep inside, he laughed when he thought that he might now have been sitting in the electric chair.

'I tricked you, you old witch!' he chuckled silently, addressing the misty spectre raising its deathly face from the depths of his mind.

Professor Knop was speaking. And his voice was sweet music in Gibbs's ears: his words created images very different from the terrible nightmares that had haunted him in prison.

'Gibbs, I chose you for three reasons. Firstly, you are young and strong; secondly, you are sufficiently intelligent to understand me; and, thirdly, you are in a situation that allows you no other escape.'

Gibbs nodded.

'The third reason would be enough all by itself,' he commented, helping himself to more whisky. 'It seems to me, Professor, that you're a pretty big cheese. How that old devil of a warden agreed to release me to you – it beats me!'

'Oh, there's nothing strange about that,' said the old man calmly. 'The idea of using condemned prisoners in scientific experiments has been put into practice already more than once. The first trepanning of a skull was carried out on a criminal in Paris: the first heart surgery was also performed on a man condemned to be hanged.'

'It's still better to be alive with a glued-on skull or a stitched-up heart than to lie in your grave with all your organs in working order,' remarked Gibbs philosophically, raising his glass to his lips.

'I quite agree with you,' said the professor, 'but the cases of which I spoke ended fatally for the patients.'

Gibbs choked a little.

'I hope you'll be more successful, Professor?' he asked. 'And what is it you're planning to do with me?'

He was struggling to speak calmly, but his voice was trembling. The whisky he had drunk had evaporated somewhere without achieving the needed effect.

His host rose and took a turn around the office.

'Gibbs,' he said, stopping in front of his visitor, 'the experiments I intend to carry out on you are utterly unique. I will not touch a single one of the organs of your body. They are useless to me. I need only your soul.'

The glass of whisky crashed to the floor.

'Devil take it, Professor!' Gibbs shouted. 'I don't see the least bit of difference between your experiment and the electric chair. Those gentlemen at Sing-Sing also don't want anything but my soul. But that's the very thing I don't want to lose!'

'I'll give it back to you,' Knop said, as simply as if they were discussing the loan of an old hat.

Gibbs stared at him fixedly. The old professor's face was serious, and he began to speak in a dry, even tone, seating himself opposite his companion.

'The nature of my experiment requires that I acquaint you with my theory beforehand. I will try to explain it in simple terms so that you can understand me. Only then can the experiment be effective. You are not, for my purposes, merely an experimental subject. Were that the case, I could use an animal instead. I need an organism with a lively and rational intellect. Now, I said that I needed your soul. And what is a soul? Something that we distinguish strictly from the body. And because we have souls, we separate the entire world into the material world, which we experience with our sensory organs, and the spiritual world, perceived by the soul. But this is not reality. The world, by its very nature, is completely unitary. If we suddenly began to perceive flowers with our souls, and love and hatred with our eyes, then for us, for humans, the world would take on a very different appearance, but would its essence actually have changed?'

Gibbs nodded.

'True,' he said, 'but if we could see love and hatred with our own eyes, those lawyer fellows would be out of a job – since all they do is muddle our ideas!'

'I see that you are following my argument,' Knop observed, nodding his bald head. 'So, let us proceed from the assumption that the nature of the world is unitary. That part of it which is perceptible to our sensory organs has been quite thoroughly studied; that part which our soul perceives remains largely obscure. But once we accept the fact that the world is in essence unitary, does it not cease to matter what we use to investigate it and how we study it? And what prevents us from approaching the spiritual world with chemical formulas? Nature is conservative. Those laws which affect heavenly bodies and those laws to which minuscule bacteria are subject are in principle completely identical. Let us therefore try to apply to the spiritual world our knowledge of the material world, proceeding from the concept that both are made of one and the same dough, as we might say. What is the material world made from? Chemistry has shown us that the basic unit of any matter is the atom. Put crudely, each atom is nothing other than a solar system, on an extremely small scale. Each of them contains its sun, the nucleus, around which revolve the planets – the electrons. All this is immeasurably small. The nucleus of an atom is as many times smaller than your head as your head is smaller than the Earth ...'

The professor fell silent for a moment, as though giving his listener time to digest this comparison.

Then, pacing up and down the room, now appearing in the lamplight in front of Gibbs, now disappearing into the gloom and merging with the silhouettes of his instruments, Professor Knop continued expounding his theory. And the old scientist's ideas, like the man himself, now appeared plainly before his listener, now disappeared into the gloom of cloudy concepts.

Knop was speaking of the universe. Not the kind that Gibbs knew about, decked out in splendid robes, with music; but a universe broken down into its tiniest component units. Before Gibbs's eyes a sort of ocean of atoms was taking shape, a sea in which objects, living beings, emotions and thoughts were simultaneously dissolving. Everything in existence, the whole world – physical and spiritual – was composed of these atoms.

'What kind of force gives them life?' Professor Knop asked, and answered his own question:

'Opposition. The world lives through opposition. Light – darkness. Warmth – cold. Good – evil. Stillness – movement. To destroy oppositions would be to destroy life itself. To use the language of atoms, these oppositions consist of the positive charge of a nucleus and the negative charge of electrons. In mutual equilibrium, these forces move the atom, just as centrifugal and centripetal forces move the earth through its orbit, just as love and hatred drive man along his life's course.'

Gibbs grasped that he – George Gibbs – a tall man with black hair and a birthmark on the right corner of his mouth, did not exist and had never existed. Twenty-eight years ago a nucleus had been born, with a charge of positive electricity derived from its mother, and as it came into existence, it began greedily to trap the electrons circling around it. When it had caught sufficient electrons, it formed an atom, an independent atom, the nucleus of which grew, feeding its charge from its environment and constantly trapping more electrons.

'But sooner or later there comes a time when the nucleus of the atom begins to age,' said the professor. 'The reserve of positive electricity inside it starts decreasing. The electrons, no longer held by the positive charge, drift away one by one. The entire atom falls apart. Nothing is left after the death of the nucleus. The electrons scatter into space. What happens to them? They are attracted to a new nucleus, inside which the positive charge is growing and trapping the electrons around it! A new atom takes shape. And in the phenomenal world, a new organism appears. Perhaps this will be a plant, perhaps a human being. Like air or sunlight, electrons are useful for everything. And does it make any difference to the sun whether a flower turns to it or towards an astronomer's telescope? Thus electrons pass from a dying nucleus into one newly born. There's a chemical explanation of the mysteries of life and death for you. Try to disprove it! Even the most stubborn pope couldn't find anything in it contrary to religion!'

The professor once again paced around the office. Gibbs remained seated, his thoughts swirling chaotically. He fancied that the old professor was unpeeling life one layer at a time, rummaging through it as though dissecting a frog.

'Gibbs,' said the professor, walking up to Gibbs and sitting beside him, 'we come now to the most important point, the actual reason why I brought you here. I have discovered a way to separate the nucleus from its electrons. I can compel the electrons of a single atom to abandon their nucleus and join the nucleus of another atom. In other words, I can transfer the soul of one living creature into the body of another. Do you understand what this means?'

The professor leaned close to Gibbs and thrust a wrinkled finger into his chest.

'I can take electrons from your soul and unite them with the nucleus of any plant or animal and then restore your atom as it was! I can make you see the world from the same perspective as that palm tree there, or that horse which is just now pulling a cart down the street! You are young, Gibbs, but a time will come when you will age. Your nucleus will not have the strength to retain its electrons. So, before your atom dies, I will take your electrons and unite them with the atomic nucleus of a newly born infant! And you will be resurrected into a new life, Gibbs! Do you understand the essence of my experiment? I want to overcome death! And I will accomplish this! I will send your electrons into other organisms, and when I restore the integrity of your being again, you will retain memories of what you saw, and you will relate them to me in human words and concepts. Now you see why I need you, Gibbs! A great role lies in store for you. Columbus's travels are nothing before the journey you will make! A flight to the moon or to Mars is a child's stroll compared with the flight you will make without leaving this room. I won't hide that there is a possibility you may not return. It is possible that your soul will remain in a plant or an animal forever. I am giving you fair warning. Make your choice – it's not too late to choose the electric chair!'

The little withered old man was trembling all over with enthusiasm. Bending over Gibbs, he stared greedily into his eyes with his aged, rheumy, dim gaze.

Gibbs got to his feet.

'Devil take it, Professor!' he exclaimed. 'I'm still a sporting man! Where there's still the ghost of a chance of winning – that's where you'll see George Gibbs. And you're offering me all of ten chances. Stow me wherever suits you – in a flower, a horse, a dog or a cow – I guess even they get some fun out of life! I'm at your service. But first of all, one question. You said that you could carry out a similar experiment on an animal. May I ask you whether you have already tried this kind of experiment, and how it turned out for your patients? You'll understand, Professor, I have to ask this question. Of course, I don't doubt your skill for a moment, but . . .'

Knop stopped him with a gesture.

'My dear fellow,' he said, 'not only have I already made a series of successful experiments, but, moreover, in commencing this current experiment with you, I am allowing you to witness its preparatory stage, so to speak.'

With these words he walked over to a cabinet placed in a corner, withdrew from it a square object draped in black material, and returned to Gibbs. The cover was removed to reveal a cage; behind its solid bars an enormous rat was running to and fro, startled by the light and the nearness of people. Its eyes – tiny and bloodshot – burned with such terrified panic, and at the same time with such near-lunatic hatred for its captors, that

Gibbs involuntarily shuddered. In his heart he could not avoid sympathizing with the animal, in whose position he had been only a few hours before.

The old professor good-naturedly slapped the roof of the cage.

'I have already made several experiments on it,' he remarked, 'and I fear that the patient's brains are not in perfect order.'

He poked a pencil into the cage, and with a savage squeal the rat sank its sharp fangs into it.

'Where did you put its soul?' Gibbs asked, regarding the animal with a shiver.

'Initially I transferred it into a flower, but the plant immediately withered. Then I successfully united its electrons with the nuclei of the simplest kind of organism – molluscs ... But let us continue with our experiment.'

Gibbs once again sank into the chair and observed his host's actions attentively.

'First of all,' said the professor, 'it is essential to firmly retain in the animal's body that portion of its intellect formed from the positive charge of the nucleus. This nucleus forms the centre of any living organism and it is directly connected to the body. The destruction of the nucleus kills the body, and vice versa. Our simplest actions, controlling the organs of sensation and voluntary actions, depend on the nucleus. I have succeeded in strengthening the nucleus within the body by surcharging the entire organism with positive electricity ...'

Saying this, Professor Knop placed the cage with the rat on a table in the centre of the room and lit a lamp above it. Then, soaking a piece of cotton wool with chloroform, he tossed it into the cage and once again lowered the cover. When he raised it a moment later and rolled the rat out onto the table, it showed no signs of life.

'You are unlikely to form an entirely happy impression of this experiment,' the professor continued, going over to the electromachine and turning the switch which activated it. 'We are going to electrocute the rat in a manner similar to that which you have so successfully evaded. With the sole difference that no energy will be discharged from the rat's body because it will be saturated with static electricity.'

Opening the animal's mouth with a lancet, the professor slipped the end of a wire under its tongue, connecting it to the electro-machine. The animal's entire pelt gradually rose on end, so that the rat began to resemble a monstrous hedgehog.

'You can see a similar effect at the theatre,' Knop commented meanwhile, 'when a magician charges himself with static electricity until sparks leap from his body.'

He switched off the light above the table, and Gibbs saw that the entire rat was radiating a bluish light; tiny streaks of flame were rising from its fur.

'A hundred volts,' muttered the professor, turning on the light again and glancing at the dial of the electro-machine. 'That has always proven sufficient. Now, when we are satisfied that the positive nucleus of the atom is firmly lodged in the body, we must, in a manner of speaking, chase out the rat's negatively charged electrons. These electrons, my dear Gibbs, are an extremely interesting thing. On the one hand they are devoid of any connection to the body and, as you will see, they can be removed and exchanged for others without harming the body's health. It is important only that the equilibrium between positive and negative charges in each atom remains the same. Where electrons come from and where they vanish – that is a puzzle whose solution would reveal the secret of birth and death. Electrons are immortal. They fly away from a dying nucleus, they attach themselves again to newly-born nuclei, forming new atoms and serving, in this way, as a sort of link not only between separate species of living organisms but also between living and dead creatures. The more powerful the positive charge of the nucleus, the more free electrons it can attach to itself. Our human body indisputably possesses the most powerful nucleus of all creatures on this planet. As the human mind has evolved, the positive charge of its atomic nuclei has strengthened and it has attracted more and more electrons. Every newly born human organism requires billions of electrons in order to establish equilibrium with its positively charged nucleus, and it attracts these electrons from the air, which is saturated with them. I have no doubt that among the electrons in your soul there are electrons from animals and plants that existed thousands of years ago. From these billions of electrons, the nucleus of your intellectual atom attracts as many as it needs to create a balance. These captured electrons make up your soul. In combination they create, strictly speaking, your personal, original "I", which is unique in this world. Although electrons are immortal, their combination is, of course, mortal, and it decays with the body's decay. Your electrons will separate, and your soul, Gibbs, will perish, because it was never more than an accidental combination! I want to transfer this combination as a unit into a different body and make it immortal!

'And so, let us turn again to our experiment,' the professor continued, taking from a cabinet a small instrument shaped like a magic lantern. 'We must now drive out all the negatively charged electrons from the rat's atoms. How shall we do this? Very simply, my dear Gibbs! We extract them forcibly, exchanging them for others, also negatively charged. This, for instance,' he indicated the instrument, 'contains a tiny quantity of radium. Radium, as you may or may not be aware, breaks down into three types of ray: alpha, beta and gamma. Of these three rays, the alpha has a positive charge, while the beta is negative. The gamma rays do not currently interest us. We use only the negative beta rays. We place the instrument just here, at a certain distance from our patient, and we place this electronic magnet on the rat's body. The beta rays, being negatively charged as they pass through the magnet, bend to the right. We move the rat into the path of these rays. With what result? Our patient's organism, overcharged with positive electricity, absorbs the negative beta electrons and once it has accumulated too many of them, the radium electrons, being considerably more powerful, begin to drive out the rat's own electrons.'

'And what will you do with them?' asked Gibbs, scarcely believing his ears.

'Why, we will capture them!' cried the old professor, rubbing his hands. 'We will capture them inside one of these magnetic receivers,' and he pointed at the instruments with concave reflectors, in the foci of which white-hot wires were gleaming.

Gibbs shook his head.

'Just listening to you, Professor, it's clear how useless our organs of sensation are. Here you are, planning to play out right in front of me a whole battlefield of rays, electrons, nuclei and God knows what else, and I can't see anything except electric wiring, a bunch of tools and a dead rat!'

The professor broke into his familiar giggle and then again switched from a mask of amusement to one of seriousness.

'My dear fellow, your choice of words is perfectly apt. Here a battle will indeed take place, and the size of the armies will be many times greater than the total number of people who have ever lived on this planet. However, you are not quite accurate. It is true that our organs are less than perfect: but to assist them, we have sensitive instruments. We can follow the progress of this battle with the help of photographic film and a microscope.'

He turned off the light, leaving on only a small red lamp on the table. By this sinister light, the office was plunged into semi-darkness. The shadows of the instruments and the cages changed places, throwing monstrous silhouettes on the ceiling. The elderly professor's enormous forehead, already shiny and red, moved like a Chinese lantern through this crimson murk. Only the rat's body glowed brightly, like a chunk of rotten wood.

'Look here,' said Knop, placing a microscope on the table. 'The rays from the radium initially pass through in a single un-divided beam.'

Gibbs looked through the microscope. Before his eyes there lay the black blot of the film. Gradually, a perfectly round stain became outlined upon it. The rays of radium, concentrated by the instrument, were falling like the light from a projector.

'Now we take a new film and examine what kind of imprint is made by the rays of radium after they pass through the electric magnet,' said Knop, changing the film and adjusting the micro-scope. 'As you see, the rays of radium have separated; alpha rays on the left, beta on the right. Our little patient's body is gradually beginning to absorb the negative electrons.'

'How long will it take to become fully charged?' Gibbs asked – whispering, for some reason.

'Oh, not more than a few seconds ...'

Once again the professor changed the film in the microscope and transferred it to the lens of the receiver. For a little while he looked into the microscope by himself, before calling Gibbs over.

On the black background of the film, one by one, tiny, shining points were falling. As they appeared in different places, they genuinely resembled a battlefield, scattered with the bodies of fallen soldiers.

'Each point contains millions of electrons,' observed the professor.

The entire surface of the film was gradually covered by them.

Knop changed the film again. Only a few points showed on it. None at all appeared on the third film.

'We have captured all the rat's electrons!' Professor Knop announced ceremoniously.

Gibbs rubbed his chin.

'I wonder how our little patient is feeling?' he asked. 'You understand that this question is pretty close to my heart.'

The professor switched on the light. As before, the rat lay unmoving on the table.

'I hope it hasn't croaked?' Gibbs asked worriedly.

Instead of replying, the professor took a stethoscope and, placing one end on the animal's body, passed the other to Gibbs. The rat's heartbeat resounded distinctly in his ears.

'Our patient is in fine fettle,' said the professor. 'I advise you to make its acquaintance thoroughly, since in half an hour's time you'll be inside its body.'

The stethoscope fell from Gibbs's hands.

'What?' he asked. 'You're seriously planning to put me inside that revolting creature?'

'What difference does it make to you?' the professor replied calmly. 'Surely you're not planning to look at yourself in a mirror?'

Gibbs scratched his head. 'That's for sure,' he muttered, 'but all the same, you know, you can't help feeling sort of disgusted to think your soul is going to be inside that repulsive animal.'

'My dear chap, when did you start feeling such concern for your soul?' asked the professor mockingly. 'And is the rat worse than hell?'

Gibbs knitted his brows briefly at this remark, but then he laughed and clapped the old man on the shoulder.

'Very well,' he said. 'Put me wherever you want. I only hope that none of the young ladies I know see me in that get-up!'

The professor scuttled around the office, slamming cupboard doors, and returned to the table with a number of instruments. He seated Gibbs in the chair and painstakingly measured his temperature, pulse, blood pressure and respiration, making notes in a book and muttering something to himself.

'Well then, my dear Gibbs,' he said finally, 'the next part of our experiment will proceed as follows: to start with, you will undergo the same process as the rat. Your body will be charged with positive electricity, and then the negative beta rays will drive out the electrons of your soul, which I will collect in a new receiver. These electrons I will then introduce into the body of the rat, regulating the difference between the charges with an electric pulse from the electro-machine. I will give you the opportunity to remain in the animal's body all night until morning, releasing you to roam freely, and you will familiarize yourself with the world in whatever form it appears to a rat's vision and a rat's psychology. But you must give me your word that you will return to the cage, and that you won't try to escape!'

Gibbs burst out laughing.

'Professor,' he said, 'I'll still choose being a man over being a rat! But when you let me free, I'll hardly deny myself the pleasure of biting the leg of one of those police sleuths standing guard there behind the door. Well, what do I do now?'

'Undress and lie down on the table,' said the professor shortly.

Gibbs obeyed. Now that the moment of truth was upon him, he felt as though his courage was deserting him. His body was seized by shudders, and his jaws began to chatter.

'Would a drop of whisky do any harm?' he asked.

The professor nodded his permission. 'Just one glass,' he added, 'after all, what use would a drunk rat be to me?'

Gibbs drank off a small glass of whisky, undressed, and stretched his powerful body.

'In the name of God, Professor, I'm sorry to be swapping my skin with that animal, even for a couple of hours!' he remarked, lying down on the table.

Professor Knop placed the chloroform mask over his face. Suddenly, Gibbs lifted his head and asked nervously:

'Say, have you got any cats?'

'Cats? Ah, I see,' sniggered the old man. 'No, I don't keep any cats.'

Gibbs gave a sigh of relief.

'Well, thank the Lord,' he said. 'It seems I'm already starting to get inside a rat's psychology. So, until we meet again,' he added, extending his hand to the old professor, 'and I hope it'll be in this world and not the next one!'

Knop shook his hand.

A few drops of chloroform fell on the mask. Gibbs's breast rose heavily; his body shuddered and relaxed. The professor listened to his pulse.

'Everything in order,' he muttered and went over to the electro-machine. The motor was running. Knop placed the end of the cable under Gibbs's tongue and took a step back from the table.

Standing with his arms folded, the old scientist observed his experiment. His cold, dry intellect was calculating the chances of success precisely. If Gibbs died, Sing-Sing would give him fresh material. Sooner or later his experiments would be rewarded with success. And then? Knop's heart involuntarily beat faster when he thought about the One Whom his experiments challenged. Himself standing with one foot in the grave, he was audaciously twitching the curtain that already fluttered before him, attempting to look beyond it with mortal eyes. If his experiment were to be successful, death would be overcome. Men could choose a new body for themselves, while they still lived. Old Knop's own soul would pass into the rosy little body of a newborn infant. But how was one to ensure that the soul retained its memories of its previous life? This Knop did not know, and it was Gibbs's task to tell him.

'I believe I've thought of everything,' the professor whispered, glancing at the dial. The arrow stood at ninety volts.

'I'll raise the charge to fifteen hundred,' Knop decided.

His patient's body began shining feebly.

The professor stopped the machine and turned his attention to the instrument with the radium. A slender beam of rays fell on the electric magnet; there they separated, and the beta rays, bending to the right, began penetrating Gibbs's body, attracted by the excess positive charge.

'Everything is going perfectly,' observed the professor, approaching the receiver. Glancing into the microscope, he saw that electrons, flying out of Gibbs, were settling on the film. Knop observed them with interest. They were brighter than the rat's electrons and they swiftly covered the entire film with shining points. He had to change the film a dozen times before new electrons stopped appearing on it. The professor adjusted the receiver and increased its charge to almost a thousand volts once the movement of the electrons had completely stopped.

For a short time he stood quite still, tilting his enormous head to one side and, rubbing his hands, looking at his patients. The bodies of the rat and of Gibbs lay near each other on the table. Their souls were in the receivers. All it would take to revive or to kill them forever would be one motion by the professor. A sensation of pride swelled in his breast. Nature lay exposed before him, revealing to him the secrets she had jealously guarded for thousands of centuries.

'The human mind has penetrated everywhere,' muttered the professor. 'What difference is there between me and a god?'

He sniggered and threw a defiant glance into a dark corner, as though the One Whose secret he had stolen and Whose mightiness he had usurped were standing there.

'Very well, and now for the next step,' said the professor.

He attached an electric cable to the focus of the receiver where Gibbs's electrons were stored, connecting the other end to the rat's tongue. Then he released a weak current, directing it from the receiver to the animal's body.

Bending over the rat, he observed it closely, as usual muttering his impressions to himself:

'The body of the rat is overcharged with positive current by a hundred volts ... The positive charge of its nucleus is about two hundred. Gibbs's electrons have registered at a thousand volts. I'll clearly have to charge the rat's body with another eight hundred positive volts ...'

Alternately loading the rat's body with Gibbs's negative electrons and with positive ones from the electric magnet, the professor worked on for twenty minutes. Towards the end of this stage the animal began to show signs of life. A few minutes later the rat was standing on the table, staring around in confusion.

'Well, greetings, my dear Gibbs!' the professor called, chuckling and rubbing his hands. 'How are you feeling? You look rather confused! Would you perhaps like a piece of cheese?'

The animal raised its head and looked at him. The professor shuddered. Its eyes were those of a terrified, suffering human being. The lamplight showed that the rat was shivering all over; tears glittered in its eyes.

'Now, don't worry,' the professor said, 'in just a few hours I'll give you back your body, and you'll be a free man. And for now . . .'

A strange noise interrupted him. Gibbs's body, lying beside the rat's, had moved. The professor jumped backwards. A whirlwind of thoughts passed through his head. Whatever could have gone wrong? Gibbs's electrons, after all, had been transferred to the rat. Suddenly a cold sweat broke out on the old scientist's brow. He rushed to the receiver which held the rat's electrons and focussed the microscope lens. There were no electrons to be seen on the film: the receiver was empty. The rat's electrons had escaped.

He turned around slowly. Through the crimson murk of his study he saw Gibbs sitting on the table, staring at the red bulb. A faint, hoarse squeak sounded in the room.

'Gibbs's nucleus attracted the rat's electrons,' thought the professor, from old habit formulating an explanation. 'But the nucleus was surely neutralized by the beta rays. What sort of force could have remained inside it to attract these electrons?'

Knop felt as though he had struck a wall. The mystery whose solution he had almost held in his hands had suddenly slammed shut in front of him, like the door of a fireproof cabinet.

'What is still inside Gibbs? The nucleus has been neutralized. His electrons were transferred into the rat's body . . . What, then, remained inside Gibbs?'

The old scientist stood shaking. He knew himself for a small, insignificant mortal, hurled backwards into the dark ages, when nature's terrifying secrets loomed fatefully over mankind.

'What is still inside Gibbs?' his dry lips muttered mechanically.

He heard the hoarse squeak again. There was no doubt that Gibbs was squeaking – the very same Gibbs whose body contained the rat's electrons. Gibbs had become a rat ... And the rat had become Gibbs ...

The professor looked at the rat. It was racing around the table in terror, as if afraid to jump to the floor. Gibbs sat beside it. He appeared not to be fully aware of his freedom, as though he had sat in a cage for so long that he was now afraid to move in case he hit the iron barrier ... Then he jumped to the floor ... sniffed the air ... squeaked hoarsely ... With short, rapid steps, on all fours, hitting the floor with its nails, the Gibbs-thing moved around the room and stopped in front of the professor, fixing its wild eyes on him – the eyes of a hungry, insane, enraged rat ...

If Professor Knop called for help, no-one heard his cries. His gnawed body was found the following morning. Gibbs was sitting in a corner, naked and covered in blood. He made no resistance, said nothing, and only squeaked quietly. An enormous rat was running around him. It got underfoot so insistently, rushing around the room in a kind of panic, that one of the police officers was obliged to shoot it with his revolver.

Gibbs was executed in the electric chair the following day. He never came to his senses, and an electric current twice as powerful as usual was needed to separate his soul from his body.

1924

NOTES

Introduction

1 Konstantin Fedin, cited in Literaturnaya gazeta, 23 August 1934, p. 2.

2 For more on Soviet Gothic, see the present translator's Stalin's Ghosts: Gothic Themes in Early Soviet Literature (Oxford: Peter Lang, 2012).

3 Bryusov's 'In the Mirror' and Bulgakov's 'The Red Crown'.

4 For more in-depth discussion of the origins and history of Gothic literature, see David Punter, The Literature of Terror, 2 vols (Harlow, Essex: Longman, 1996) and Fred Botting, Gothic (London and New York: Routledge, 1996).

5 Charles Crow, 'Introduction', in American Gothic: An Anthology, 1787–1916 (Oxford: Blackwell, 1999), pp. 1–2 (p. 2).

6 Bulgakov received a copy of 'Venediktov' as a gift from their mutual friend Nataliya Ushakova (who was one of Chayanov's illustrators) in 1925. He subsequently collected all of Chayanov's short fiction in his personal library. For more on how Chayanov influenced Bulgakov, see Marietta Chudakova, 'A Vital Necessity: About Mikhail Bulgakov's Personal Library', translated by Vladimir Leonov, Soviet Literature, 2 (1977), pp. 142–49.

7 Sigmund Freud, 'The Uncanny', in The Penguin Freud Library, edited by James Strachey, 15 vols (London: Penguin, 1985–93), XIV (1990), pp. 339–76 (p. 358).

8 Botting, p. 1.

9 See Joanne Turnbull's acclaimed recent volume of Krzhizhanovsky's selected stories, Memories of the Future (New York, 2009); Barry Scherr and Nicholas Luker's translations of Grin, published as The Seeker of Adventure (Moscow, 1978) and Selected Short Stories (Ann Arbor, 1987); and reissues of early translations of Bryusov (the novel The Fiery Angel, translated by Ivor Montagu and Sergei Nalbandov [1930], Sawtry, Cambs, 2005; and the selection of short stories published under the title The Republic of the Southern Cross (unidentified pre-1923 translation, Charleston, sc, 2010)).

Aleksandr Chayanov: The Tale of the Hairdresser's Mannequin

1 Chayanov's pseudonym, which may have derived from a character in the botanical horror story 'Datura fastuosa' (1821) by his hero E.T.A. Hoffmann.

2 Konstantin Yuon (1875–1958), a Russian artist famed for his impressionistic scenes of urban nightlife.

3 The great and undervalued Ivan Lazhechnikov's The Ice House (1835) is a historical novel in the style of Walter Scott, set during the reign of

Empress Anna Ivanovna (1730–40).

4   In this passage Chayanov is indulging his specialist knowledge of
    agronomy.

Aleksandr Chayanov: Venediktov

1   Lutskoye (now Zhukovka) and Barvikha are villages on the banks of the
    Moscow River, west of the city.

2   Plutarch, a native of Boeotia in Greece, author of the Lives of
    distinguished Greeks and Romans.

3   In 1760, during the Seven Years' War.

4   The many place names here refer to different districts of Moscow.
    Sadovniki and Tolmachi are districts of central Moscow, while Kuskovo
    and Kuzminki were outlying noble estates.

5   Anton Antonovich Antonsky-Prokopovich taught at Moscow
    University's feeder school, the preparatory School for Noble Youth, and
    was later Rector of the University itself. Jean Lamiral was a French actor
    and ballet teacher at the Bolshoy Theatre, Sila Sandunov an actor and
    director. The names mentioned in the following paragraphs are those of
    actual scholars, professors and others connected with Moscow University
    from its foundation in 1755.

6   An inscribed eleventh-century monument, rediscovered in Crimea
    in 1792. The stone and its inscription aroused great interest among
    nineteenth-century historians and palaeographers.

7   A Masonic circle with mystical and philanthropic interests. Although
    Freemasonry was outlawed in Russia in 1794 by Catherine the Great,
    many important political and literary figures continued to practise it more
    or less secretly. The New Cyropaedia (1728) was a widely studied treatise
    on the ideal monarch by the Scottish-born Mason Andrew Ramsay,
    banned in Russia.

8   The Petrovsky Theatre, an opera theatre opened on Petrovka Street in
    Moscow by the British entrepreneur Michael Maddox in 1781. It was
    famous for its vast, mirrored masquerade rotunda. The Petrovsky burnt
    down in 1805; in 1825 its successor, the modern Bolshoy Theatre, opened
    on the same site.

9   The celebrated Russian dancer and choreographer Yevgeniya Ivanovna
    Kolosova (1780–1869).

10 From the 1600s onwards, Augsburg was famous for its production of
    complex clockwork devices, including human and animal automata.

11 One of Moscow's major thoroughfares, leading north from Theatre
    Square to the Petrovsky Boulevard.

12 Until the mid-nineteenth century the Kamer-Kollezhsky Wall, guarded
    by sentries, acted as Moscow's administrative and defensive boundary.
    Marino Grove was a wooded region just north of the Wall.

13 An important commercial district in the city centre.

14 In Greek mythology, a princess who is ravished by Zeus in the form of a shower of gold.

15 A powerful demon associated with the deadly sin of lust; he has also been described as the overseer of demonic gambling dens.

16 A Cabbalistic system using numerology to interpret the hidden meanings of words and numbers.

17 Located in the city centre (and now renamed Prechistenka) near the Mogiltsy (literally, Tombs) district.

18 One of Catherine the Great's leading generals, victorious in many campaigns.

19 A town approximately sixty miles east of Moscow.

20 Elizabeth I (Peter the Great's daughter) ruled Russia from 1741 to 1762; her court was noted for merriment and frivolity.

21 August von Kotzebue (1761–1819), a German dramatist and diplomat who spent much of his life in Russia; Nikolay Karamzin (1766–1826), Russia's first major prose writer and historian, whose Letters of a Russian Traveller (1791–92) describes a tour through continental Europe and Britain; Gavrila Derzhavin (1743–1816), the first great Russian poet.

22 In 1812, when Napoleon's troops occupied the city.

23 The monument on Red Square to Kuzma Minin and Count Dmitry Pozharsky, who led the defence of Moscow against an invading Polish-Lithuanian army in 1612, was formally unveiled in 1818.

Aleksandr Chayanov: The Venetian Mirror

1 The author's second wife, whom he married in 1921.

2 The pond under the walls of the ancient Simonov Monastery where 'poor Liza', the peasant heroine of the famous 1792 story thus titled by Nikolay Karamzin, drowns herself after her lover betrays her. It was a popular site for sentimental literary pilgrimages.

Mikhail Bulgakov: A Seance

1 Glavkhim was the Soviet department responsible for the administration of factories producing chemical products; similarly, Zheleskom supplied timber for railway construction.

Sigizmund Krzhizhanovsky: The Phantom

1 The narrator is using the word 'phantom' in its medical sense. The Oxford English Dictionary defines a 'phantom' as (among other things) 'a model of the body or of a body part or organ, esp. one used to demonstrate the progression of the fetus through the birth canal'. However, the narrator also intends the word to keep its generally

accepted meaning: a ghost or illusion (the Russian language offers the same ambiguity). While in obstetrics the term 'phantom' refers to the mannequin of a pregnant woman, the narrator primarily – and incorrectly – uses the word to mean the artificial infant, in this story a mummified fetus, that is 'born' from the phantom. Here the narrator draws a distinction between the phantom and its 'appurtenances' – i.e. the artificial fetus – which he will subsequently overlook.

2   The second half of this medical student's unusual name may refer to N.V. Sklifosovsky (1836–1904), a distinguished Russian surgeon and clinician.

3   Jean-Baptiste Duhamel (1624–1706), a French natural philosopher; Hans Vaihinger (1852–1933), a German Kantian philosopher whose theory of 'fictionalism', which argues that reality is a fictional construct, is an obvious precursor of Krzhizhanovsky's 'phantomism'; the inevitable Soviet edition of the Young Hegelian philosopher Ludwig Feuerbach (1804–72); Charles Richet (1850–1935), a Nobel-Prize-winning French neurochemist and physiologist with an interest in spiritualism.

4   Immanuel Kant's 'Kingdom of Ends', discussed in his 1785 treatise Groundwork of the Metaphysics of Morals, is an imaginary society governed by universal principles of rationality and ethics, whose members will treat each other benevolently as ends in themselves rather than exploitatively as means to an end.

5   Here Fifka conflates the miracles of Christ and the vaunted feats of Baron von Münchhausen, who claimed to have pulled himself out of a swamp by his own hair.

6   The flag of tsarist Russia from 1896; it remained in use under the Provisional Government.

Aleksandr Grin: The Grey Motor Car

1   An early type of Belgian motor car, manufactured between 1904 and 1932. It had a highly efficient engine and often triumphed in Grands Prix.

2   Jacques Callot (1592–1635), renowned for his etchings of grotesques and outcasts.